As Devious as the Devil.

K.W Traynor

This Book is dedicated to all my family and friends and thank you to them for being so patient and supportive during the writing of this book.

I would also like to give a special mention to my Editor Calley Worden for helping me make this possible and for all her help and guidance.

GW00499150

PROLOGUE

Sitting relaxing on the balcony of the penthouse suite in the luxurious five-star Belvador Hotel in Rhodes, he was amazed by the splendour of the place. The hotel was an absolute dream; colourful yet refined, with understated luxury that was apparent in every detail. It sat in glorious surroundings overlooking the bustling historic harbour of the Old Town, which glowed in the fading evening sunshine. His suite, with gleaming white walls that blended seamlessly into exquisite marble floor tiles, was large enough to house a whole family. He had just enjoyed an extremely luxurious and relaxing shower.

The searing August heat and the flight over from Birmingham had compounded the exhaustion he felt following the recent events in his life, but no amount of tired could crush his excitement about what lay ahead.

He tried to imagine how the Colossus of Rhodes, one of the Seven Wonders of the World, must have looked as it stood in the entrance to the harbour all those years ago.

The beautiful scenic port now hosted numerous small fishing boats, large expensive yachts and an ocean liner, almost swamping the busy waters.

Taking in the grandeur of his magnificent surroundings and savouring the high life, he thought, *Detective Chief Inspector Thomas Anthony Sharkey, you've made it.*

Just for a moment, triggered by the harbour, his mind wandered back to his early days as a young boy sitting in the bedroom window of his Aunt Bet's boarding house on the Parade in Donaghadee, County Down. The house had overlooked the small fishing harbour there, and he reflected on the stark difference between his past and present.

In the Donaghadee harbour there had stood the old lighthouse, the lifeboat and a few fishing boats, but that was where the similarities ended. It was a world away from his current environment and, although cosy in its familiarity, was considerably less appealing.

He thought about the day his mother had taken him there from the old run-down house in Fawney, six miles from Londonderry, to stay with his Aunt in the quiet fishing town.

His dear father had been killed in action while serving with the military in France, leaving his mother to bring up the young family on her own.

The Second World War had brought poverty to their home, as it had done to so many others. They'd had very little money, food or clothing, and the limited rationing coupons had not been much help. He recalled the vision of his mother's sad face with tears streaming down her cheeks as she left him with his Aunt, trying to explain. 'It's all for the best, son.' Even then, at just six years old, he knew in his heart it was the only way; she could not cope with all of the family on her own.

A sudden knock on the door of the suite brought him back to the present; room service had arrived with the evening meal he had ordered earlier.

The waiter carried the lavish feast of lamb kleftiko, a bottle of his favourite brandy and, of course, a bottle of the hotel's best champagne.

Why not? This was a big day in his life, after all, and he was not paying a single penny for anything.

Chapter 1

Christened Thomas Anthony Sharkey but known to everyone as just Tom. His first real memories began around Christmas morning 1945, in Fawney. He recalled being disturbed by his elder sister, Tilly, who had got out of bed early to see what presents Father Christmas had brought.

Tom had just endured another cramped, cold night in the old hard bed he shared with his two younger brothers, Peter and Paul. He slept at the head of the bed, and they slept at the foot. The three of them fought each night for the bedding in a desperate attempt to keep warm in the draughty old bungalow where condensation ran down the windows and the peeling green distempered walls. He had been kicked and shoved every time one of his brothers had turned over, making it another bloody miserable night. And now he was awake at some unearthly hour. To say the very least, he was pissed off.

The isolated bungalow, with its thatched roof and whitewashed walls, was situated on farmland, about half a mile from the nearest neighbour and six miles from the nearest city, Londonderry. The lonely abode was surrounded by fields that played host to grazing cattle, or crops of potatoes, swede and corn. There were two bedrooms and a scullery-cum-living room.

Tilly and baby Kathleen slept in the big room with their mother. *The 'big' room, ha! What a joke,* he thought. It wasn't that much bigger than his own. With the bed pushed up tight against one wall there was barely enough space to squeeze past on the other side. There were no wardrobes; you just dropped your clothes on the floor. The local farmer who owned the house rented it to them for six pence a week, and you could believe that was all it was worth.

'Tom, Santa's been, come on, get up,' Tilly whispered. Tilly was a lovely young girl, always pleasant and smiling, with long red hair that hung in ringlets over her shoulders. The boys tumbled out of bed, and shivered as they followed Tilly across the freezing stone floor into the living room to see what delights Santa had left for them.

Hanging by nails on the stone fireplace were socks for each of them, filled identically with an apple, an orange, a bar of chocolate and a small toy.

They also had one main present each; Tom's was a wooden rifle, painted red and black.

Tom knew that the rifle had been made by a carpenter who lived not far away – he had seen him making it a few weeks earlier in his garden shed. Even in those early days Tom had been crafty and missed very little. He even knew where his mother had hidden the toy, but he never let on. *Why spoil the dream?* he thought.

The two lads and Tilly were mumbling, 'Thank you Father Christmas for our presents.' Tom smiled at their delighted innocence and, knowing how hard his mother had worked to create the magic, resolved to thank her properly one day for all her efforts.

Then his mother shouted, 'Tom, light the fire, son, so I can get up with the baby.' Tom groaned. He hated this cold and dirty job.

First, he had to clean out the previous day's ashes from the old black enamelled stove, then fetch the wood and coal from the coalhouse in the back garden, and finally get the fire going before they could get any warmth.

Ashes cleared, Tom braced himself for the cold and eased open the back door. He was met with a wall of snow three feet deep. To avoid the need to go out in the cold twice, he first battled across to use the lavatory in the yard. He didn't linger as he usually did to gaze at the pictures of film stars and footballers on the strips of newspaper that hung on the wire hook – it was too bloody cold. By the time he'd scraped snow from the coalhouse door and returned to the house with an armful of fuel his hands were red, and raw with cold.

Still shivering, he managed to get the fire going and the rest of the family gathered round it while his mother made them all tea and toast for breakfast, and he and Tilly looked after the baby. Tom adored Kathleen and loved looking after her. She had received a doll for Christmas, which was much bigger than her and was sitting at the head of his mother's bed. He played a game of peek-a-boo with the doll's arms, at which Kathleen cooed and giggled in delight.

On other mornings they would normally have made themselves something to eat – Tom would have made himself bread with jam or syrup – but Christmas was his mother's treat, and she wanted to spoil them all.

They were a devoted Catholic family and Tom's mother, a lovely, gentle lady, good looking, with big blue eyes and wavy black hair, led them all in Christmas prayers before she began to cook the dinner.

Sitting down with the family for their annual roast chicken dinner around the old scrubbed wooden table was the best part of Christmas for Tom. It was followed by his mother's homemade Christmas pudding, which would take her days to prepare and was rolled up in a bed sheet and boiled in a big black pot.

Chicken was a real treat; dinner was normally rissoles, mincemeat or sausages, bulked out with loads and loads of potatoes. The festive bird was always a gift from their landlord farmer, who was perhaps seeking to ease his conscience for the state in which he let them live.

Food was scarce, so it was never left or wasted; when they had finished eating, the plates were all but licked clean. Bellies full, the family would then sit round the fire telling stories and singing Christmas carols, and his mother would let them listen to the wireless for a short while as a festive treat. The wireless was a big contraption in a wooden frame which had a dry battery, and a wet battery that crackled like mad when it was turned on, but it entertained them.

'Thank you, Ma, that was lovely. I'm feeling full now,' Tom would say. He realised how hard his mother had worked. She'd put her arm round him and give him a hug. Every Christmas she would sing her favourite song, 'Danny Boy', to them, which Tom found quite sad.

The day would never pass without his mother telling stories of their father and what a good man he had been.

'He was an honest, hardworking man and I hope you grow up to be just like him one day, Tom,' she would say. *And look where it got him*, Tom would think, his heart heavy. *And us.* No one could have foreseen the struggles the war would bring to their lives, but if he'd learned one thing from his father it was that life was unpredictable, and if you weren't prepared, you suffered. His mother would end up crying, swiftly followed by the rest of the family, with Tom acting as the father figure trying to console them all.

'We'll be all right Ma, you know we won't forget our Da, he'll always be close to us,' Tom would whisper as he held her tight and kissed her on the forehead. His only memories of his father were of the colossal man in uniform who would come to the house at intervals, pick him up, cuddle and talk to him. He never really got to know him properly. 'We just have to keep going, Ma. That's all we can do.' And even as the words spilled from his lips he knew they weren't true. There *was* more to be done. He just didn't understand what, yet.

Chapter 2

Life in Fawney for the Sharkey family could be tough. But the countryside offered its own rewards, and Tom enjoyed great freedom, roaming the fields, and playing all kinds of games.

Often, he would climb over the high fence into the farmer's orchard and help himself to the many varieties of apples and plums growing there. His mother would say, 'Tom, it's a sin to steal, you shouldn't take those apples! I hope you confess your sins when you go to chapel, and in your prayers tonight.' His mother insisted that all the family say their prayers before going to sleep. As far as Tom was concerned the farmer usually enjoyed a plentiful harvest, and seemed unconcerned by windfall crops that he left to rot on the ground. Tom was preventing wastage, nothing more.

When harvest time came he would gather potatoes for the farmer who would pay him three pence a week, until once when the farmer ran out of money. Once, the labourers had all finished for the day, and were lining up to be paid. Tom was at the end of the line, and when the farmer reached him he offered a curt 'Sorry, Tom,' and that was it. Tom was livid. He had worked for nothing, and to top it off when he got home that night he could hardly straighten his back from the pain of bending down all day.

'You won't believe this, Ma, but I didn't get paid today,' Tom moaned to his mother.

'Why not?' she asked, angrily.

'He ran out of money,' replied Tom.

'I have a good mind to go and talk to him. That isn't fair,' she said.

'No, leave it Ma.' He didn't want to complain too loudly; the farmer's generous lunchtime servings to his workers of thick crusty sandwiches washed down with jam jars of hot tea were too precious to jeopardise.

Many days, Tom would sit in one of the fields and peel the skin from a swede with his teeth and eat it raw; it helped fill him up. At harvest time, he enjoyed helping the farmer bring in the corn by leading the horse and cart. The farmer had two shire horses but Tom only had time for the one called Bob, and treated it like the pet his family could never afford.

Times were very hard for the family and Tom had begun to get envious of some of the other children at his school who, although far from well off, had more money than he did.

He hated going to school in the hand-me-down trousers his mother altered to fit him and an old pair of brown boots, although he did like the lovely pullovers she knitted. The old boots had holes in the soles so he cut shapes of cardboard to fit inside to help keep his feet dry.

Some of the other children at school would make fun of him in his ill-matched clothes of various colours and sizes, and he despised them for their spitefulness.

One sadistic bully, a big lad called Hugh, would shout, 'Look at his baggy trousers and big brown boots, doesn't he look a right wanker!' Tom thought, *What a big mouthed shit,* and hoped one day he would find out what it was like being very poor. When his anger brewed strong he imagined shoving his fist right down Hugh's throat.

At lunchtimes several of the children would go to the corner shop and buy chewing gum or marshmallows, while all Tom could do was watch with envy.

Regular indulgences were simply beyond reach for Tom's family, but as an occasional treat his mother would let him go with Tilly to the Minor's Club at the ABC Rialto cinema in Derry where he could watch his favourite heroes such as Hopalong Cassidy and Tarzan on the big screen.

Every Sunday the family had to walk three miles each way to worship at Ardmore chapel, whatever the weather.

Tom was not the greatest believer, and getting cold and wet for no good reason pissed him off.

Even at this early stage Tom often found life lonely and boring. Some of his few pleasures of living in Fawney were when the breadman or the coalman called, which helped relieve the boredom and offered a glimpse into another world.

The breadman would come on his horse, which pulled a carriage with massive drawers in the back filled with loaves of bread and various cakes. When these were opened, the smell of fresh baked goods was mouth-watering. While the breadman was distracted talking to his mother, Tom would often sneak a cream cake from the rear of the carriage, even though he would receive one later anyway. *What's one cake?* he thought.

When the coalman called he would take Tom for a ride in his lorry while he delivered to some of his other customers in the area, dropping him off when he had finished to walk back home through the fields. Tom loved these trips and wanted to learn to drive. On one trip while the driver was busy with a customer, Tom decided to try his hand at driving and managed to start the engine. But as his legs were too short to reach the pedals he couldn't engage the gears.

'What the hell do you think you're doing,' raged the driver upon his return.

'Sorry, just wanted to have a go,' Tom replied.

'Don't try that again, do you understand? It's stupid and dangerous,' continued the driver.

In the winter, the days were short and the nights were far too long.

On many evenings Tom would sit alone in the dark on top of a small hill not far from home, watching the lights from the RAF warplanes taking off and landing at Eglinton Airfield in the distance and wondering where they might be going to bomb. In the autumn evenings he liked to watch the splendour of the Northern Lights. There were no lights for miles and Tom had to use torchlight to move about. It got very lonely at times.

Chapter 3

The winter brought no joy at all for Tom, who one day slipped and fell over on the ice and landed on a hawthorn bush. He didn't think anything of it at the time, he was just left nursing a bruised ego and an irritating small thorn in his left hand.

As the days passed, though, he began to lose the use of his left arm. It eventually got so bad that he was having great difficulty moving his arm at all.

'My left arm is so painful and I can hardly move it,' he complained to his mother. After examining it she took him to see the family doctor, who decided Tom had probably sprained his arm, and simply put it in a sling.

But the sprain didn't heal. The days passed slowly now, and after a week or so Tom was having trouble even moving his body. Concerned, his mother took him to the City Hospital in Derry for a second opinion but, despite numerous x-rays, the cause of Tom's problem remained elusive and he was sent home, still in pain.

When Tom's condition didn't improve, something snapped in his mother. She whisked him back to the hospital. 'I'm not leaving here until something is sorted out. The boy is in pain, you need to find out what's wrong,' she demanded, refusing to leave until they received a proper diagnosis. Finally under specialist care, Tom had further x-rays that revealed a broken collar bone, and blood poisoning caused by the thorn in his hand going septic.

His mother's persistence had saved Tom's life. He was

immediately admitted to the hospital and given penicillin injections every four hours, day and night, to counteract his life-threatening condition. His arms, backside and thighs felt like pin cushions. It was three weeks before he could be discharged; the scar on his finger would remain with him for life.

The days darkened further as the depths of winter brought more tragedy to Tom's home; his baby sister, Kathleen, developed tuberculosis. For weeks the family nursed her, sat round the bed wrapped up in blankets. One morning, as Tom held her in his arms, she gave one big sigh, then died quietly.

Tom, his mother and the family cried inconsolably while the priest gave the last rites. The last days of Kathleen's young life had not been a pleasant sight; it had been a devastating experience.

His mother sobbed. 'Oh god, Tom, what have we done to deserve this, please god help us.'

Struggling to contain his own tears, he said, 'Ma, don't cry, we just couldn't watch her suffer like that any more now could we,' and continued, 'you know that she'll be better off where she's gone.' They comforted each other, tears running down their cheeks. In that moment it felt to Tom that the entire world was against them.

The day of his baby sister's funeral came, and although the winter sun was shining there was a nip in the air and everyone was wrapped up to keep the heat in. There was a tremendous turnout at the graveside; neighbours and friends came to pay their last respects to the young baby. Standing among the gravestones everyone looked very sad, and many were crying. Even the funeral flowers looked droopy and forlorn.

Tom's mother clung to his arm for support, and he knew that he would never forget the small white coffin and its tiny little grave. As he placed the large doll atop the coffin, a great sadness fell over him and he reflected on the great waste of a life that had barely begun.

His father had never even seen the baby; he had been killed before she was born. Tom then made a vow to himself that he would try to live life to the full for the both of them.

During the months that followed, Tom watched his mother struggle to overcome the deaths of his father and the baby. Still a good-looking woman, she now had to be strong and full of determination in order to survive, and it showed – her black hair turned quite grey and the strain began to show on her face. Yet she still continued to wash and iron, cook and clean, and do all the other tasks to keep the family going. Day to day life was hard, as even simple tasks like washing the laundry involved monumental effort.

She would boil the washing in the same big pot she made the Christmas pudding in, and then bash it around in the Belfast sink with a piece of wood to get it clean. Then she would take it out to the back garden and put it through the large, heavy mangle before hanging it out on the line to dry.

Their home had no electricity or running water, and all the children were expected to help their mother with the mundane chores that were necessary to keep the household running. As the older boy, Tom shouldered much responsibility, the daily half-mile round trip to collect water from the well was one of his least favourite jobs. His hands were raw from carrying the heavy tin bucket, and he had to stop every few yards to change hands. Rainwater was also collected in a barrel at the rear of the house. This was used mainly for washing and bathing. A big metal bath was filled once a week so that they each could have a bath. And every week Tom's legs were further exercised in a mile-long trudge across the fields to procure paraffin oil and candles from the local store. As 'carrier-in-chief' Tom was also expected to collect a pail of milk from the farm every few days. These lonely journeys gave him plenty of time to reflect on his lot. *There has to be more to life than this,* he thought.

Every so often, on a Saturday afternoon, his mother would say, 'Tom, we're going over to the free state to get some shopping.' He knew what she meant; they would take the Lough Swilly bus from Derry towards Buncrana, but as soon as the bus crossed over the border into the southern county of Donegal they would get off.

They would cross the road to the little grocery shop on the other side, where his mother would purchase things like sugar and butter, items they could not get in the North. The shop was no more than a wooden hut built for the benefit of a few locals, but acted more so for the benefit of people from the North.

Tom and his mother would conceal the goods under their clothes, cross over the road again and catch the next bus back to Derry. The customs officers at the border knew what was going on, but they just turned a blind eye and let them pass.

Any home-grown produce eased the daily struggle to feed the family, and Tom enjoyed working with his mother to create a vegetable patch on the piece of land at the rear of the house. They planted potatoes and cabbages and grew rhubarb, blackcurrant and gooseberry bushes. His mother also nurtured a lovely flower garden. Tom was not into flowers and preferred growing vegetables, but he enjoyed the pleasure the colourful blooms brought to his mother. 'I love the smell of these lovely flowers Tom, and they are so beautiful. They really brighten up my days,' his mother would say, looking satisfied.

'I know you do Ma,' Tom would reply. *It's so good to see her happy,* he thought.

Sometimes, to earn some money, Tom would go around the area collecting glass jars and bottles and take them to the local store where he got paid a few pence for them. At the end of summer, he would also collect blackberries in a bucket and take them to the shop to sell.

Entertainment was scarce in Fawney, so they made their own. Tom loved listening to music on his sister's old His Masters Voice gramophone, with its big horn. They would play old, scratched 78 rpm records and Tilly would try to get him to dance with her, but he would have none of it.

Now and then Tom's mother would arrange with a man from Derry to come to their house and cut the three boys' hair. He would arrive with his blunt scissors and a comb, and would cut or more often pull their hair out. Tom didn't like the man or the mess he left his hair in so sometimes, when he knew he was coming, he would go off into the fields and hide. Once he knew that the man had left, he

19

would reappear. 'Tom the barber has been and cut the boys' hair, where did you disappear to?' his mother would ask, furious with him.

'That man makes a mess of my hair. And it's painful. I don't want him touching me again,' Tom would reply, quite determined.

Young Tilly had a pet pigeon which she kept at the top of the garden in a small wooden loft that Tom had made out of old timber. The pigeon had flopped, injured, into their garden one day and was unable to fly. Tilly had put it in a cardboard box which she lined with an old jumper, and fed and watered it. She'd named it Kay. When it had fully recovered, the pigeon didn't want to leave again, so it was then that Tom had built the loft.

At school one day a friend told Tilly that she also had two pigeons, which she and her father had caught in a farmer's barn where several nested during the night. Her friend explained that this farm was quite a distance away and the owner was unfriendly. It was believed that he patrolled his land with a shotgun and would threaten any trespassers. But Tilly wanted Tom to take her there, to get a companion for her pigeon. 'Please, Tom, would you take me? An extra bird would be great company for Kay,' she said.

'I've heard about that farmer. He's a right old villain. It could be dangerous,' said Tom.

'Please, please, Tom,' Tilly begged.

Tom relented. 'Okay, we'll go over and take a look one night, but don't tell Ma,' he said.

On the following Saturday night after dark they set off over the fields, armed with a torch and a sack. They had to be extremely careful and quiet not to be caught by the farmer. Eventually they found the barn they were looking for, and sneaked in. Once inside they got a terrible shock when they heard a man's voice. Tom thought immediately that it was the farmer, and froze. 'Help me, please,' the voice said. Tom shone his torch in the direction of the sound and was horror-struck when he saw a man lying in the straw. 'Please help me,' the man said again.

Tom was reluctant to go near him, but plucked up the courage. 'Who are you? What are you doing here?' he asked.

'I'm a pilot from Eglinton, I think I've broken my leg. I had to parachute out of my plane just before it crashed. There'll be a search party out looking for me, but I'm in terrible pain, please find help.' he begged.

Tom assured him that they would go and find help, but he was reluctant to go looking for the farmer. 'God, what shall we do, Tom? The poor man needs help badly. Where shall we go,' Tilly said.

'It's about two miles to the airfield, but we'll have to go there. He's in a right state,' Tom said.

They sneaked off the farm and headed for Eglinton. The road was very dark, but fortunately there was no traffic. When they eventually reached the airfield they were confronted at the entrance by an armed guard. He listened to their story and called for assistance. Very soon they were travelling in a military ambulance, accompanied by a doctor, with Tom directing them to the barn.

When the pilot was attended to, the doctor insisted on taking

Tom and Tilly home.

He was so grateful for what they had done. The pilot's plane had been shot at and damaged on returning from a mission on the continent, and he was lucky to have almost reached the airfield before having to bail out.

When they arrived home, the doctor met their mother and said, 'These two young children of yours have saved the life of one of our pilots tonight. You should be very proud of them both for what they've done.' Tom's mother was extremely angry with the pair of them, but at the same time extremely proud of their actions. *All that, and we didn't even get the pigeon we went looking for; maybe another day,* Tom thought.

Chapter 4

The war had come to an end and Winston Churchill was being claimed a hero, but life in the Sharkey house was as hard as ever. It was then that his mother decided to take Tom to Donaghadee to live with his Aunt Bet and Uncle Harry for a spell, to ease the burden on the family and at the same time give Tom a better start in life.

Donaghadee was a quiet little seaside town, with nothing like the bustle of Derry but very much bigger than Fawney. The people seemed friendlier and would take the time to talk to you. The Parade, where they lived, overlooked the seafront and harbour, and the waves at times reached across the sleepy street and slammed into the front of their house.

Aunt Bet was his father's older sister; they also had a brother called Robert who had emigrated to America many years earlier, but had been neither seen nor heard from since he left. Tom's aunt told him stories of how she and his father has grown in up in Fawney in similar conditions to his own, before she had married and moved to Donaghadee.

On leaving Fawney, life started to improve for Tom; his aunt and uncle had no children of their own and were able to give Tom more money and attention than he had received at home, which he really enjoyed. There were the added bonuses of electricity and running water. Life was good. His new school was more organised and challenging, and he discovered that he was quite clever, good at arithmetic and geography, and, although English was not his favourite subject he could get by in that too.

His Uncle Harry was a fisherman and would often take Tom out in his small boat.
He had rosy red cheeks and a big grey beard and always appeared to be grinning.

Some days he would drop Tom off on the nearby Copeland Islands and leave him there to wander around on his own. There were a few run-down houses still on the islands but no one lived there now. It was there that he learned to snare rabbits, which he would take back to Donaghadee and sell to the local butcher for a few pence.

They had a large greenhouse in their rear garden and Tom would also spend time sitting there, savouring the beautiful aroma of home-grown tomatoes. It was a smell that would stay with him all his life, grounding him back in Donaghadee whenever he encountered it.

Tom soon made friends with a lot of the local lads, and with the money he made from selling the rabbits he bought an air pistol from one of them. He smuggled it over to the islands where he hid it from his uncle, who would not have approved. By practising shooting at tin cans and bottles at every opportunity Tom soon became quite a good marksman.

Like everywhere else, Donaghadee had its local bully, but this one pushed Tom too far. He was not going to stand for bullying any more, and one day lured the lad to a quiet spot by the sea. The bully didn't have the brains to see what was happening and still tried to niggle Tom, as he followed behind him.

They walked along the sand with only the sound of the waves and the odd seagull. The tide was high, and great waves rolled in from the rugged sea.

'Is everyone from Derry as thick as you?' the bully sneered.

Tom was furious now but didn't react. He just continued walking.

The bully picked up a piece of wood that had drifted ashore and kept prodding Tom in the back. When they reached a secluded area of the beach, Tom stopped and turned to face him.

'I've had enough of you,' he said. A detached calm settled over Tom.

'What you going to do about it then?' the bully sneered.

Tom caught hold of him by the throat, forced him to the ground and sat on top of him. Looking him in the eye, he said, 'This is the last time you're going to bully anyone. I'm going to kill you and dump your body in the sea.'

'You can't do this to me.'

The bully struggled to get away, but Tom held him firmly, and leaned his forearm across the lad's throat, watching as his eyes began to pop. 'Can't I?' he replied.

'Please don't! I'm sorry, I'm sorry, please let me up,' the lad pleaded.

Tom continued to sit on top of him until he was satisfied that he had got the message. When he eventually let him up the bully ran off crying. Tom felt sure that he had taught him a lesson, and drew a quiet satisfaction from the knowledge that he would never let anyone bully him again.

Chapter 5

Now eleven years of age but a lot wiser, Tom returned to live in the new corporation-owned house on the Creggan Estate in Derry that his mother had been allocated; they had escaped from Fawney at last.

There were electric lights, a bathroom and running water; his mother even had her lovely flower garden at the front of the house. The Creggan Estate was built on a hill that overlooked the city, and its properties stretched over a wide area. The houses were allocated to the poorer classes, and certain areas became quite rough.

Although Tom missed the freedom of Donaghadee it was good to be back with his family again and living in the city, away from Fawney. The other significant change was that Tom's mother had invited an Englishman named Oliver Black from Coventry to move in and live with her.

Oliver had served in the Royal Navy during the war, and had met Tom's mother when his ship had docked in Derry harbour. The new man in his mother's life was about five feet seven inches tall, slightly overweight and had brown teeth from too much smoking. He had served in the navy many years and had seen the greater part of the world on his travels. Tom enjoyed hearing some of his stories and wished that he could see the world himself one day.

His mother sat Tom down and explained: 'He's a good man and looks after us, but he will never replace your da, always remember that, Tom. I still love and miss your da.'

Tom listened to his mother's explanation and accepted Oliver, who was working at Pennyburn Engineering as a welder. Everything seemed cosy and the family were much better off with Oliver's money coming in. His mother had also taken a job, in the Star shirt factory, and she and Oliver appeared to be getting along well. It was so good to see her happy again.

These were much happier times for the family and some summer days Tom would say to Tilly and his brothers, 'Who fancies coming for a swim, then?'

Tilly, who was always full of enthusiasm, would shout, 'Yes, please!' He would then take them across the railway tracks to the River Foyle, where they would bathe and try to swim in the icy water. Treacherous currents and deep holes posed a danger to the unsuspecting and weak swimmers, but Tom was undeterred. Many afternoons of fun splashing about saw Tom's water moves evolve to doggy paddle, and he was soon a reasonably strong swimmer with a more refined stroke.

At other times, he would fish in the same spot of the river while one of his brothers kept a lookout for the water bailiff, as Tom had no fishing permit. He caught the odd salmon, and many trout, which came in handy in feeding the family.

Unfortunately, one day Tom went fishing on his own without his brothers to keep a lookout, and sure enough the inevitable happened.

'Can I see your permit, son?' the bailiff asked.

Tom had to do some quick thinking. 'I haven't got it with me, sir, I left it at home. Do you want me to fetch it?' he asked.

'Just give me your name and address. I'll call and see your parents later,' said the bailiff.

Of course, Tom was crafty enough to give him a false name and address, but it meant an end to his fishing.

***

The days seemed to fly by now for Tom; maybe it was because he was so much happier.

This was eventually to change, though. Oliver had begun to drink heavily, often returning home drunk late at night, hours after work had finished. Unknown to the family, Oliver's drinking habits were nothing new, and had emerged during his years travelling around the world. Arguments between Oliver and Tom's mother became frequent.

Many nights Tom was disturbed from his sleep by them shouting at each other and he could hear his mother crying late into the night. He didn't like what was going on and began to detest Oliver.

Despite these quarrels, his mother and Oliver always made up by the next day and carried on as if nothing had happened the previous night. Tom would be much older before he learned that this was quite a common practice between couples. He wasn't happy, but accepted it for his mother's sake and never made any mention of it to her.

By now Tom had started at the technical college, and was doing very well in his studies. The headmaster informed his mother that he had great potential but that he spent too much of his time

29

daydreaming. Tom knew this to be true: he was always dreaming of becoming rich and powerful one day. It was his one ambition in life.

One of his classmates at the tech was a lad called Jimmy Dunne who was an extremely good footballer. During sports periods the class would walk to a local park where they would practise athletics and football. Tom was quite a good footballer himself, but Jimmy Dunne was something special. He was the star of the team.

Jimmy would scribble his signature all over Tom's books, asserting that one day he would be famous, and that Tom would be the first to have his autograph. This turned out to be true; Jimmy was eventually signed to play for Derry City and very soon moved on to play for an Italian club and to represent Northern Ireland in the national team. With Jimmy's new-found fame he and Tom soon drifted apart, but it was great to follow his success in the media.

Tom loved going with his brothers to Brandywell to watch Derry City play. They were doing very well thanks to their latest signing, Jimmy Delaney, who was an excellent international footballer.

Unemployment in Derry was very high and finding a job was an almost impossible task. The town was full of shirt and collar factories, which meant plenty of work for women but little for men. Most men were leaving for England and Scotland to find employment. So, when he reached sixteen and was offered a job as an apprentice motor mechanic at a garage on the outskirts of the city, Tom had no hesitation in leaving the college. His mother tried in vain to persuade him to stop on.

'You're doing so well at college, son, why don't you take your exams and try to make something better of your life,' she said.

But he had made up his mind – he was taking this job and would wait to see how things went.

Chapter 6

Tom started in his new role and thoroughly enjoyed learning to do little jobs on the various models of car which had come in for repair, and having the chance to drive them around the workshop.

For the first time in his life he began to earn steady money and he liked the feeling of independence it gave him. Although he didn't earn much, he always insisted on giving his mother some money towards his keep.

In the light of his success he went out and treated himself to a new Hercules bicycle, which he managed to get on the knock, paying it off at six pence a week. This was the first nice thing he had ever owned and so he cleaned and polished it at every opportunity.

Tom loved his job at the garage and the people he worked with, but he couldn't bring himself to like the owner's son, whom he thought was a right stuck-up prat. The young man would cruise around in his Jaguar in his leather driving gloves, never speaking to anyone other than the manager and acting like he was above the rest of the staff.

Tom could see he had little substance, and relied on his father for everything. Tom loathed the idiot, prancing about the garage in his pinstripe suit and expensive shoes. *Maybe I'm just jealous*, thought Tom. The obnoxious git had everything he dreamed of for himself, after all.

There was great excitement at the garage one day, when everyone abandoned their tasks and gathered round the wireless.

'What's going on?' Tom asked one of the mechanics.

'It's Jim Laker, he's fantastic,' came the reply. Tom soon realised that they were all listening to the test cricket match being broadcast from Old Trafford. England were beating Australia in the Ashes, and Jim Laker had just taken his nineteenth wicket. Everyone was overjoyed, but Tom was not a great cricket fan and preferred soccer.

As time went by, Tom fell in with a gang of youths of his own age from the neighbourhood and became much tougher and more streetwise. He had now grown to over six feet tall and wasn't the skinny kid he used to be. People began to take notice of him and he liked the feeling of power it gave him. His real hero now was James Dean, and he imagined himself in the role Dean played in the film *Rebel Without a Cause. What a dreamer,* he thought.

One day he found the old black suit his father had got married in, tucked in the bottom of a wardrobe where it had been for years. He asked his mother if he could have it. 'What do you want that old thing for? I've been keeping it as a memory of your da, but you may as well have it,' she said.

'I'll show you when I'm done with it,' he told her.

The first thing he did was to stitch up the inside of the trouser legs and turn them into drainpipes. His mother shook her head in vigorous disapproval at the way he dressed in his drainpipe trousers, long jacket, thick soled shoes and string tie, with his long hair combed into a DA at the back.

The only colour of socks he wore were shocking pink, lime

green or white. His mother would rage, 'Tom you look like a Teddy boy, and I don't want to see you ending up in trouble.' Tom was quite proud of being referred to as a Teddy boy, and of being a member of one of the toughest gangs in the neighbourhood.

His best mate was Dave Parkhill. Like Tom, Dave had a bit about him and this drew them together. Although Dave was only five feet seven inches tall and very slim, he was tough and could hold his own in any fight. He had sandy wavy hair which he grew down to his shoulders, and of which many a woman would have been proud.

Often on a Saturday evening before going out on the town, Tom would go along with some of his mates to a neighbour's house to watch *Six-Five Special.* The neighbour owned the only television in the street, a small black and white set. Tom liked watching Cliff Richard, and enjoyed his music.

On Sunday evenings, all the gangs and all the girls would meet in Carlisle Road in the city centre. They would walk up and down the street for hours showing off their wares in mannequin-like parades.

In the summer of 1957, at 18 years of age, Tom was to get his first taste of alcohol; he and his mates would sneak bottles of Guinness to behind the Brandywell football ground, and all get tipsy, talk about girls and dream of becoming famous one day.

Over the months that followed Tom realised that he had a very stubborn streak and was always prepared to fight for what he believed in. He still resented the years he had spent being poor, but most of all he despised the people who had bullied him when he was younger. He was devious and ruthless and, with his fighting ambition to succeed, he soon became the leader of the gang. He was the boss now. Nobody tried to push him around, and he was respected by his followers. He felt that he never wanted to be second best ever again and fought hard to overcome any obstacles that got in his way.

His four best mates were Roy Best, Jack Ramsey, Victor Beard and, of course Dave Parkhill, and they were inseparable. Jack was a giant of a lad, about six feet four inches tall and eighteen stone. He was not the brightest person in the world but a really nice guy. Victor, a Protestant, was the odd one out, but was accepted as one of the boys. How he had become involved with a bunch of Catholics like them was a mystery, but he had, and Tom admired him for it. They never discussed religion with him.

Many evenings they would all assemble in Tom's bedroom where they would play their 45 rpm singles on an old record player and dance to the likes of Bill Haley and Little Richard.

In the summer of that year they all went on their first holiday, heading off to Portrush for a week. It was a popular seaside resort in the north that had lovely beaches, and amusement arcades. They stopped in a boarding house not far from the sea and spent most of their days on the beach and their nights in Barry's Amusements arcade or in one of the bars.

Roy was a real comedian, a bit like Frank Carson, and kept them all entertained, while Dave was a good singer and earned them all the occasional free drinks in the bars. In a bar one evening a man who'd had too much to drink accused Tom of trying to chat-up his girlfriend. The man approached Tom and said, 'Keep your eyes off my bird, mate.' Tom, who was not interested in his girlfriend, had to bite his lip. The man wouldn't let it rest and poked a finger into Tom's chest.

'You poke me again, mate, and I'll lay you out,' Tom hissed.

Dave could see Tom's shoulders were hunched and his fists clenched into white balls of skin and bone, so he stepped in to calm the situation and save the man. 'Listen, mate, you don't know who you're talking to. He's a right hard bastard, and if I were you I'd piss off before he hammers you,' Dave told the man, who got the message, grabbed his girlfriend and dragged her out of the bar.

As the days went by they met a few Belfast girls and would take them onto the sand dunes at the back of the golf course. They had a great time, and when the week was up Tom promised his new girlfriend, Rita, that he would keep in touch with her. Of course, he never did.

The night before going back home to Derry Tom decided to steal a car to use as their transport. 'Can you really do that, Tom?' Victor asked. Tom picked out a car and told his mates to keep watch while he got into it and got it started. He knew how to do this from working in the garage. They all jumped in and Tom drove it back to Derry, even though he didn't have a licence. Tom had done this as an ego trip, and to show off, but the gang now admired him even more; he was the boss.

In Derry there were regular gang fights, usually about religion or where you could or could not go in the city; the boundaries were marked out and they had to be policed. If you wandered beyond them, you had to be prepared to defend yourself. Tom was ruthless in his enforcement of these boundaries, an approach that gained him a fearsome reputation as a hard man, with a tough gang.

The city was becoming extremely violent, with Protestants and Catholics fighting daily, although Tom often wondered why they were fighting over religion at all when both sides believed in the same God.

A tricky situation arose when a young lass of seventeen, called Una McBride, made a false allegation of rape against Dave. She was known as the local bike on the estate because everyone was shagging her.

When she became pregnant she blamed Dave because he was the one she fancied. It was widely accepted that anyone could have been the father, and when Dave rejected her she didn't like it and went to the police to report that he had raped her. Dave was arrested and interviewed but denied rape and went on the offensive, telling the police of Una's dubious reputation.

All the gang, including Tom, were interviewed and made statements. Dave was never charged, but the incident made Tom realise just how easy it was to create trouble for someone by making an allegation against them.

Tom's young brother Peter was now working as a packer in one of the shirt factories and had started to date one of the machinists. Unfortunately, they had to meet secretly because she was a

Protestant. Peter was warned many times by members of her family to stop seeing her. The Sharkey stubborn streak prevailed, though, because he refused to give her up.

Upon getting home from work one evening, Tom discovered that Peter had been beaten up by the so-called friends of the girlfriend. He had a black eye and several cuts and bruises to his face. 'Do you know who did this to you? I'll bloody kill them,' Tom said, enraged.

'Three lads were waiting for me when I came out of work,' Peter said.

'Who?' asked Tom.

'You know them, Tom, the chap called Ben with the red hair and his two mates from the Irish Street estate.' Peter wanted him to leave it, but Tom had made up his mind. He made enquiries to find out where the group were hanging out, and discovered they used the Central bar in the Waterside area of the city.

With his gang, Tom went along to the bar on the following Saturday night and, through the window, saw the three men inside, drinking. It was decided to wait until they came out of the bar. About forty minutes later they emerged, but went straight in to the fish and chip shop next door. 'Okay, I'll go in with Victor; we won't start anything, but I'll warn them that we'll be waiting outside for them,' Tom said.

Declarations made, Tom and the gang waited outside for almost an hour, but the three men remained in the chip shop.

Just then, a woman came out. 'Are you Tom Sharkey?' she asked, and continued, 'I want to lock up but those three chaps in there won't leave, they're afraid of you.' Tom and the boys went back inside and dragged the group into the street, giving them a battering in the process.

'We're sorry, Tom, it won't happen again,' the one called Ben muttered.

'I know it won't or I'll kill you,' Tom warned them. At that he let them go, they were not worth the bother he decided. The three stumbled off, licking their wounds.

The next move was for Peter to leap over the fence and become a Protestant. Then he had to run the gauntlet with his so-called Catholic friends. Love blossomed despite the religious friction, and Peter and his girlfriend got married six months later at the Church of Ireland church in the Waterside area of the city. It was a very quiet affair and although his mother and Tom both thought Peter was too young to be getting married, he had made up his mind and they decided the important thing was that Peter was happy.

Chapter 7

It was during this period that the gang seemed to get involved in many more fights and handed out several beatings, but Tom always believed the persons involved deserved what they got.

When a stranger came into your pub they were asked the question, 'What religion are you?' If he was in the wrong pub he soon left. Of course, the same happened to Tom and his mates if they wandered into a Protestant pub. The whole situation was to really show face.

One day, Tom got offered for sale a revolver and ammunition by a man in his local pub. This was the sort of situation that was developing in Derry; if you were anyone, you needed a gun. He eventually decided to buy it. He wrapped it up in plastic sheeting, placed it in a small metal box and buried it in a safe hiding place in the local park. Afterwards he honestly didn't know why he had bought it, but it had seemed the right thing to do at that time.

Tom was also approached about joining the IRA, who at that time were actively engaged in a campaign designed to agitate relations with the British and ultimately deliver a united Ireland, but Tom wasn't interested.

At work, Tom had befriended a man named George Smith who worked at the garage as the cleaner and handyman. He was an ex-army soldier who had fought in the Korean War, during which he had been taken prisoner. His family had been informed at the time that he was missing in action, but when the war ended he had been discovered in a prison camp. During his time as a prisoner he had been made to walk for miles in the ice and snow and had suffered from frostbite, along with other injuries.

These afflictions had left him with a severe limp. At lunch breaks Tom would listen to his many stories and it became clear that the horrific torture George had suffered had left invisible scars, too.

One evening when Tom and his mates went to a Chinese restaurant for a meal they were confronted by a disturbance. They saw George, struggling with two members of the staff like he had gone crazy. Tom stepped in to help the staff calm him down.

It transpired that George had been enjoying a meal when the Chinese music, the decorations, and bells ringing had triggered a long-buried trauma. The atmosphere had made him imagine that he was back in the prison camp and, unable to cope with the emotions this unleashed, he had gone completely wild. Tom had a long chat with him and then explained to the staff what had caused the outburst. They were very understanding, and the restaurant was happy when George apologised.

As Tom matured he met his first serious girlfriend; her name was Nina, and she worked in the local fish and chip shop for her uncle. They would meet in the evenings and go to the cinema or walk in the local park together.

She was much smaller than Tom, only five feet two inches tall, with a slim figure, brown eyes and long auburn hair, which hung down loosely over her shoulders. He honestly thought she was the most beautiful woman in the world.

They had become an item; at least, that was what the carvings said. 'Tom loves Nina' was carved out on the bark of the trees and chalked on every available surface in the locality.

Nina had been born in Greece, and would tell Tom stories of her early days there before moving to live in Ireland with her aunt and uncle. They'd had a very similar upbringing and could relate intimately to each other's family life.

Tom remembered vividly the special summer night that they lay in the park kissing and caressing each other, when he confessed to Nina that he loved her and wanted to be with her always.

He slid his hand up her jumper and felt the softness of her olive coloured skin as he searched for her breasts beneath her bra. Her breasts were small but firm. He caressed them slowly, running his finger and thumb over her hardening nipples, and she began to breathe heavily and started to groan.

Tom felt the rising between his legs and her hand fumbling with the front of his trousers. She grabbed his hardness, edged it out of his trousers and began to stroke it gently. At the same time, he was pulling down her tiny pants, almost ripping them from her.

She pleaded, 'Tom, I'm afraid, you're so big, please don't hurt me.' It was too late, he was thrusting hard between her legs trying to enter her. He was inside her at last, her worries swept away. She started to pant and move with him as he thrust himself in and out.

He came quickly in a sudden burst, shouting out, 'Oh, Christ, that's fantastic!'

As she felt him come inside her she, too, shouted, 'Tom, Tom, I love you, I really do!' After the passion was spent they lay in each other's arms and he looked at her; she was his possession, his love and the only one he had ever really wanted.

They made love every time they met and would confess their undying love for each other. Nina would say, 'Tas, I will never love anyone else but you.' Tas short for Thomas Anthony Sharkey, and was her nickname for him.

Then one day Nina disappeared, to Tom's great confusion and bitter disappointment. He was extremely concerned, and began to make enquiries to find out what had happened to her. It was many months later that Tom found out that she was pregnant, but he never saw her again; her aunt and uncle had sent her back home to Greece.

Her two brothers came looking for him seeking revenge; the Greeks were close and didn't like intrusion into their families. One dark night in an alley Tom pleaded with them that he still loved her, but it didn't prevent him from getting a kicking for what he had done. He didn't fight back at the time; he knew that, in their eyes, he was in the wrong.

He later thought about seeking revenge himself, but decided he probably deserved what he'd got. If someone had done the same to Tilly he would probably have wanted to kill them. Her absence made him realise just how much he loved and missed Nina, and he carried her photo with him all the time.

***

To add to Tom's woes, the situation at home had deteriorated;

Oliver's drinking had got much worse, and he was losing a lot of his money gambling.

Tom could tell that his mother was now having second thoughts about having Oliver in the house. She had very little money again for the family because she was subsidising Oliver, and was also having to put up with nasty behaviour that surfaced when he was drunk.

One evening when Tom got home from work his mother confessed, 'I can't stand him much longer, he's wrecking our lives completely with his goings on.' Tom offered to talk to him and see if he could make him see some sense or, alternatively, suggested he could kick his stupid head in. His mother reluctantly agreed to his first plan, but Tom would have preferred to execute the latter.

Three days later, arriving home about eight o'clock at night, Tom heard his mother screaming from her bedroom. He rushed up the stairs and into the room just in time to see Oliver punch her in the face.

She fell over the bed with her mouth bleeding, begging for Tom to help her. Oliver turned to him and ranted, 'What do you want, you big cunt. Come to save the old bag, eh?'

Anger flared inside Tom as the remnants of pain inflicted by bullies from his past ignited in his gut. He lunged at Oliver, missed him completely and landed on the floor. He got up and dived at him again.

This time he caught him and carried him straight out of the bedroom and onto the landing. Tom was now mad enough to kill him as they stood wrestling with each other in the small space.

Tom pushed him hard, and he fell backwards, head first down the stairs. Rushing down after him, Tom found him lying motionless in the hallway. He immediately ran to a phone box and called an ambulance, and Oliver was taken to the Altnagelvin Hospital. He died a week later from a brain haemorrhage.

Tom and his mother told the police, and later gave evidence at the Coroner's Court, that Oliver had been very drunk on the night in question and had fallen down the stairs; in the absence of any other evidence to the contrary their account was believed. This was supported by statements from neighbours attesting to the fact that they had seen Oliver in a drunken state on many occasions before that night. The recorded verdict was accidental death.

Tom and his mother were closer now than ever, if that were possible, and he knew their secret would be safe forever. He also realised that, for him at least, trust was one of the most important things in life.

The strange thing was that he held no regret for what he had done; he honestly felt that Oliver had deserved what he got. Oliver's brother, Adam, came over from Coventry for the funeral. He was very much like Oliver, and seemed to be a bit of a rough diamond who also liked his beer.

Tom didn't particularly hit it off with him and had the feeling that he didn't completely believe the story of what had happened to his brother. Tom didn't really care. After a few days, Adam returned home, still not completely satisfied with their explanation but with no means to challenge it.

Another great tragedy hit Tom's world when it was discovered that Jack Ramsey's two elder sisters, both in their twenties, had been diagnosed with cancer. The worst thing about the whole situation was that they were in two different hospitals and, when visited, each asked about the other. Why had they not visited? The family had not informed either sister of the other's situation, in an effort to limit their stress. Tom could see that it was breaking Jack's heart. Sadly, both sisters died within days of each other. It was a desperately sad and distressing time for Jack and his family, and the gang offered as much support as they could. Painful memories of his lost da and baby sister were stirred deep within Tom, making him appreciate his remaining family all the more.

One day, Tom took Dave to Fawney to show him where he had been born and raised for much of his young life. The old house was now in ruins, the roof had collapsed and shrubbery was growing out of the windows. 'Christ, Tom, how did you survive in this lot,' Dave exclaimed. 'Now I know why you're such a tough bastard.'

Chapter 8

A new episode now began in Tom's life when a woman called Mary Murphy, one of the customers at the garage where he worked and the wife of a wealthy accountant, took a shine to him. Every time she called at the garage she would flirt with him.

She was in her late thirties and quite attractive, with short auburn hair, blue eyes and a slim figure. He thought she was a bit too old for him and definitely a bit above his class. She obviously had other ideas, however, and had set her sights on Tom. One day, she persuaded the manager of the garage to get Tom to deliver her Jaguar to her at the City Hotel.

On arriving at the City Hotel, Tom went to the reception. 'I'm looking for a Mrs Murphy. I've brought her car round for her, can you tell me where she is please?' he asked.

'Yes, sir, Mrs Murphy is expecting you and has asked that you take the keys of her car up to her room, number sixty-four; the lift is over there,' the receptionist replied. The City Hotel was something else, and Tom had never seen luxury like it. Deep-pile carpets everywhere, chandeliers, and large mirrors and paintings adorning the walls.

The lift confronted him. He had not used one before, but entered and took his chances. He got out on the first floor and knocked on the door of room sixty-four.

Mary Murphy opened it wearing a dressing gown, and invited him in. The bedroom and bathroom were absolutely beautiful, he had only ever seen such opulence in films.

He had never been in a position like this before, and felt quite embarrassed by the situation. 'Tom, it's great to see you, come right in. Would you like a drink?' Mrs Murphy asked. He wasn't sure what to do.

'Can I have a beer, please,' he muttered.

'You can have what you like,' she said, and poured him a bottle of beer.

'Now come and sit down,' she said, gesturing to the bed.

Tom realised she had been drinking and was quite tipsy. 'What do you think of me, Tom, do you like me?' she asked.

'Yes, I think you're a very nice lady,' he mumbled.

It was only a matter of time before the inevitable happened, and they ended up making love for over an hour in the sumptuous bed.

Mary Murphy was a very rich but very bored housewife, and this was to be the start of a long-term affair. Tom was not going to complain; he was learning all there was to learn about the art of lovemaking and Mary was also extremely generous. They visited many places together and she took him to her home in the heart of the country when her husband was away on business trips. The house was like a mansion, with five bedrooms and three bathrooms.

Mary was never worried about being caught out by her husband. Many summer evenings when they could not go to her house they would sit in the back of her Jaguar sipping wine; it really was a very enjoyable period in his life.

'Tom, you know what I would like to do? said Mary, one

evening. 'I have thought about it many times. I would like to go into a field of corn, make love and have champagne and strawberries. What do think?' she asked. Tom just smiled. A few days later they found a cornfield in a very quiet area and had their champagne and strawberries.

In the meantime, while he was working at the garage several people had approached Tom on the quiet and asked if he was able to acquire spare parts for their cars. So began another new era in his life.

At the start, he was reluctant to do anything about it, but as time went by he began to take little parts from stock, such as spark plugs and points. With access to the stores he was able to get practically anything he wanted, and very soon was running a lucrative little business on the side. It was so easy to get away with what he was doing, there was just no security. He started to get greedy.

The other mechanics were also taking little bits and pieces, but nothing on the same scale as Tom's pilfering. He knew he had to be careful, and was crafty and well organised.

Tom discovered that the store foreman was also on the fiddle, and so he went out of his way to catch him at it. It didn't take long before he got him bang to rights. But he kept his mouth shut. Tom's real intention was to team up with the foreman, and to possibly use his knowledge of the other man's stealing as insurance in case the wheels should come off his own little enterprise.

He knew the foreman would be the first to hear of any management suspicions. Although everyone took it for granted that they were all on the fiddle taking little bits and pieces, nobody at the garage really knew just how much Tom was taking. He was extremely cunning.

His thieving became so chronic he decided he needed someone he could trust to assist him in distributing the parts, and decided to recruit his best mate, Dave, to help. Dave had an old banger of a car which would help keep him beneath suspicion.

Tom arranged to meet Dave one night in the pub, and asked, 'How would you like to make a few quid on the side moving some car parts about for me?'

'What does it involve?' asked Dave.

'I get the parts and leave them for you somewhere safe to pick up. You pass them on to the buyers and collect the money,' Tom explained.

Dave, who was now singing several nights a week with a local showband, was in an excellent position to work during the day shifting the parts about.

'I'll give it a go, mate,' Dave replied. 'You are as devious as the devil, Tom Sharkey.' And so their little business began. Tom managed the financial side of things, and looked after Dave for his side of the operation.

**

It was around this time that Tom's sister, Tilly, met a chap called Eddy Grey from Drumahoe, who had his own newsagent business.

They had decided to get married. Tom gave his big sister away, standing proudly by her side at the altar. The wedding was held at the local chapel and all the family and friends joined the happy couple in a local hotel for the reception.

After the meal and the speeches Tom had arranged for Dave and his band to provide the entertainment. Dave made sure they played for only a small fee. Tom's mother thoroughly enjoyed herself and thanked Tom and Dave profusely. Tom loved his sister very much and honestly hoped everything would work out well for her.

When Tilly moved out of the house, Tom continued to support his mother in raising his younger brother Paul.

Tom often thought of lovely young Nina and his baby boy or girl. Were they both well and living in Greece? He thought then that he would probably never find out, and the thought made him sad.

Tom had accumulated quite a bit of money now from his fiddle at the garage, and from Mary Murphy's generosity. He decided it was time for his bicycle to be replaced and upgraded to a car. A local bus driver in the town ran a second-hand car business from his home, and Tom had noticed a few of the cars he had for sale. He went along and looked at some. He selected a cool two-tone maroon and black Ford Consul, which even had a heated rear windscreen. He paid the man in cash. The local girls loved it, and although Tom realised that he was a bit of a show off, he didn't care – he was enjoying myself.

Now with his own car, Tom started doing quite a bit of smuggling of cigarettes and alcohol from over the border in Buncrana, Lifford and Muff where these goods were much cheaper.

He had recruited many customers for his services and made huge amounts of money. The customs officers at the border crossings took very little notice of him, but he was taking a significant risk. If he had been caught he faced heavy fines and a prison sentence.

Tom told Dave all about his missions into Donegal. 'You're crazy, Tom, if you get caught they'll string up. Is it really worth all the risk?' asked Dave.

'I get a kick out of it, and I like the dosh I make,' Tom replied, so he continued doing it.

Tom was now twenty-one years old, and he was getting restless. He was a fully qualified motor mechanic and still had some money left after buying the car, but felt his real ambitions were not being fulfilled. He felt that he was getting too big for Derry.

He had seen for himself that wealth brought power, and that was what he intended to have. He also realised that, sooner or later, even with the store foreman's shrewd organisational abilities a rigorous stocktake at the garage would almost certainly lead to his fiddle being exposed. Arrest and potentially doing time didn't appeal. He thought hard about what to do and decided it was time to get out, time to escape, move on and try to better himself.

He rationalised that maybe most people were thieves in some way, just that some were bigger than others; the secret was not to get caught. He was ambitious for himself and for his dead sister, he needed to do better.

When he told Dave of his decision his mate expressed disappointment at the idea of losing his best friend and the extra revenue his presence delivered, but said he fully understood Tom's decision.

When he told Mary Murphy she tried hard to persuade him to stay, but his mind was made up. His mother was his biggest hurdle, and she did everything to make him change his mind. 'Faraway fields look greener, son,' she said.

Before leaving, he sold his car to one of the local dealers for less than its true value, and gave the money to his mother. He also paid a visit to his young sister's grave and laid flowers.

It was a very painful experience leaving his mother standing crying on the Belfast docks as he caught the night ferry to Heysham.

Once ashore, he caught the train on to Birmingham, and a fresh start.

Chapter 9

Eleven forty-five on a damp, dreary miserable morning arriving at New Street station, and his first stop was the left luggage office where he deposited his heavy suitcase.

The scrap of paper he had clutched in his cold hand told him to catch the bus to Hall Green and ask the conductor to let him off by the Mermaid pub in Sparkhill.

Leaving the station, Tom took in the wide, congested streets, seething with traffic and swarms of people moving in a rush of noise. There were dozens of cream and blue buses everywhere. Large grey buildings towered above the bustle. He realised just how big and busy Birmingham was and it gave him quite a shock standing there on his own. He took deep breaths, then coughed. Not the clean fresh air of the Irish countryside.

How was he going to find the bus to Sparkhill? Then he saw the queue of black cabs. He knew he couldn't really afford a taxi but approached one for directions.

He was taken aback at first by the driver's thick Brummie accent, but got directions to the bus stop. He had to be careful what he spent, he had left most of his money with his mother to keep her going until he sorted himself out.

He eventually caught the right bus but then encountered verbal abuse from the Asian bus conductor who accused him of trying to pass off foreign money. Tom quickly caught on that he had given the man an Irish two-shilling piece, and, extremely embarrassed by the incident, hurriedly exchanged it.

Arriving in Stratford Road, Sparkhill, he got off by the Mermaid pub and set out walking to find the first of the few addresses he had been given.

God, it's just like being at home; a little Ireland right in the middle of Birmingham, he thought. Almost everyone he asked for directions was Irish. It seemed all the Irish were over here looking for work, but that didn't surprise him as there was very little at home.

What did surprise him were notices in several boarding houses stating, 'No blacks or Irish.' He'd heard these tales but hadn't believed them.

The door of an old Victorian house in a back street of Sparkhill was answered immediately by an attractive woman in her late thirties with a southern-Irish accent.

'Yes, can I help you?' she asked.

'I've been given this address by a friend of mine in Ireland. I'm looking for lodgings,' Tom said.

'Well hello. I'm the landlady, Kay Doyle. You're lucky, I do have a vacancy if you would like to have a look at the room,' she said.

'Yes, please,' he replied.

She showed him up a poorly lit flight of stairs to a large room on the second floor.

A smell of damp mingled with the distinctive aroma of sweaty feet. A Brylcreem jar sat in the middle of the floor filled with cigarette ends and the lino around it was covered with burn marks. The wallpaper was peeling and it reminded Tom of the old house in Fawney. Five single beds were made up around the large room.

She turned to him. 'If you want the bed and your meals, it will be two pounds ten shillings a week, with two weeks in advance,' she said.

Tom didn't particularly like the thought of sharing a room with four other people, especially complete strangers, but in the circumstances he had very little choice. 'I'll take it, thank you,' he said, and handed her the five pounds in exchange for a front door key.

When she enquired if he had a job, he replied, 'Yes, I'm very busy at the moment, overworked,' giving her a wink and a big smile.

He'd lied, just in case she refused to let him stay. Then he returned to New Street station to collect his suitcase. On returning to the lodgings he met three of his roommates; two were from Ballymena and the other was from Galway. They appeared to be friendly, hardworking lads who told him they were all employed at the Lucas factory in Shaftsmoor Lane.

Liam, the Galway man, said, 'What do you think of our Kay?' and gave a big grin.

'She's a bit of all right, isn't she,' Tom replied.

Kay was plump but well proportioned, with large breasts and voluptuous hips. Her long red hair matched the freckles that covered her pleasant face with its wide mouth and full lips, and when she smiled he noticed her eyes seemed to sparkle.

'Who sleeps in the other bed?' asked Tom.

They informed him that it was a lad called Big Pat, from Tipperary, who never came home until the early hours of the morning. and that they really only spoke to him at weekends.

The next morning Tom got up early for breakfast with the others. The breakfasts had been cooked much earlier and placed in the oven where they had all dried up. Still, it was hot food. He ate and left at the same time as all the others. He went straight to the Labour Exchange to find a job.

After the usual questions and answers he was given the names and addresses of two firms who had vacancies. The first one was for a mechanic in a paint manufacturing company. He went to the premises, didn't like the look or smell of it, and never went in.

The second job seemed perfect; they required a motor mechanic to work on their fleet of vehicles and on the manager's car. Tom decided to try for the job and after a short interview he was accepted and required to start work in nine days' time.

He was worried with the delay in starting the job because he would have to work a week in hand, and that meant he would have no pay for nearly three weeks. To pass away the time until five o'clock he walked around the town, up and down New Street and Corporation Street and around the Bull Ring market. Then he dirtied his hands and face and headed back to the digs for his evening meal.

Tom carried out this routine for several days, walking for miles to kill time, just to make believe he was employed. On the sixth day he was getting desperate. He was feeling so hungry now during the day that when watching people throwing bread to the ducks he had to refrain from grabbing it.

Finally, he caved in and went to the National Assistance office and queued with all the tramps and dropouts who, like him, were begging for a hand out. Before the office would give Tom any money he had to provide them with his address and answer numerous questions. Eventually, they gave him two pounds.

Had leaving home been the right thing to do? Tom was no longer sure.

When he arrived back at the digs two nights later Kay was waiting for him, 'I've had the welfare people in today checking if you lived here. They said you were at their office and they wanted to give you some assistance. What's going on, Tom?' she asked.

Tom thought he would be thrown out immediately when he told her the truth, but in fact her response was quite the opposite and she offered to lend him some money until he got paid. *What a darling,* he thought.

While walking around the city killing time until he was due to start his job at the factory he noticed a sign in the window of the Old Talbot pub that indicated they were seeking a part-time barman. He decided to have a look inside. The bar was quite full with working men mostly drinking pints and playing cards or darts. He had never been behind a bar in his life, let alone an English one, but thought the job was probably much the same as he'd seen done back home. He also realised that he had never pulled a pint because most of the beer drank at home was from bottles.

After observing for a while he asked the barmaid where the gaffer was, and she informed him that he was upstairs having his lunch and would be down in about ten minutes.

Presently, a tall man who looked to be around twenty stone and spoke with a southern Irish accent appeared behind the bar. After a few words with the barmaid he came over to Tom.

'Are you looking for me?' he asked.

'Are you still looking for a barman, because I might be interested,' Tom replied.

'I am. What experience have you got?' Tom lied, and told him he had worked in a bar back home in Ireland but had never pulled a pint and wouldn't know the prices.

'I'm Ted Burke, don't worry I'll soon show you the ropes. You can have the job but I could do with you starting tonight,' the gaffer said.

'Yes, that's fine, what time?' Tom replied.

Tom's first night behind the bar was an unfamiliar nightmare of new experiences, but he survived. After closing time, the staff piled up the chairs on the tables, swept up, and mopped the floors. Then they all sat down and had a staff drink.

Over the nights that he worked Tom got to know Ted well and became involved in some of his little fiddles. He helped top up the spirit bottles with water, and watered down the soft drinks bottles. A percentage of the brewery profit went in his pocket and the stocks remained right.

The pub entertained a lot of after-hours drinking, but during this time they only served the gaffer's own bottles of spirits, which he got from the warehouse; they never used the brewery stock. This meant that, again, all the takings went directly into the gaffer's pocket. He was very well organised in his fiddles; he and Tom had a lot in common. Ted introduced Tom to his wife, Sandra, who very seldom came down to the bar. He soon realised that Sandra was a heavy drinker who was fond of her vodka.

One night in the bar an Irishman began to sing 'Danny Boy' and it made Tom feel incredibly sad, and brought tears to his eyes. His mind wandered to his mother, and life back home.

After a few weeks he informed Ted that he had started his full-time job as a mechanic and could only work at weekends. Ted was quite happy with this arrangement, but said he would miss Tom during the week.

***

Whenever he had the opportunity Tom would go and watch Manchester United play against all the local clubs. He loved to watch his hero George Best play, and longed to maybe meet him one day.

Back at the digs, as the days passed, Tom realised that Kay had a soft spot for him. One Saturday afternoon she asked him if he was working or going out anywhere. When he told her that he had a night off and might go down to the Mermaid for a pint, she said 'Wish I could come along with you.'

'Why don't you?' he asked.

'I have to go to the dance at the Harp Club every Saturday night with Jim,' she said.

Tom knew she was married with two children and lived with her family in the house next door, but had thought he would ask anyway.

Later, when Tom went to the Mermaid with a few of the lads from the digs, he realised what a rough dive it was. He asked where he could find the Harp Club. It was only in the next street, so he decided to go and have a look. The club was a typical Irish dance hall with an Irish showband playing, and it was packed to the gills.

He fought his way to the bar and eventually got served with a pint of beer, which his mate Dave would have described as being, 'as flat as a witch's tit'. He was stood drinking by the stage and listening to the band when he felt a tap on his shoulder.

'What are you up to?' Kay asked.

'Just come to have a look,' he said, feeling slightly awkward.

'Are you going to give me a dance then?' she asked.

'Where's your old man?' he enquired.

She shrugged. 'Out there somewhere in the crowd.' They began to dance to a slow waltz and he realised that she had been drinking. She pushed her body up close and he could feel her large breasts heaving against him.

She clung tightly to him and their thighs rubbed rhythmically together as they moved very slowly around the floor. Tom could feel himself getting worked up and thought she must be able to feel his hard pushing against her, but she said nothing. The dance ended, she kissed him on the lips and drifted off to find her husband. Tom thought the prospects there were looking good.

Another night, while sitting alone and bored in the bedroom he shared with the other lodgers, Tom was pissed off with having to put so many pennies into the gas fire to keep it burning, so he decided to dismantle it. This gave him access to the payment mechanism, and enabled him to put in a penny and collect it again from the other side.

For about half an hour he kept feeding the same penny through the meter, and when he thought that he had enough credit to last for several weeks he put the fire back together again. He didn't tell his room-mates, but they must have wondered who was putting all the money in. They didn't complain.

Tom eventually met the other room-mate, Big Pat, for the first time. He was a giant of a man, six feet four inches tall with not an ounce of fat, leathery and brown with hands like shovels, and all muscle.

He spoke so quietly it was hard to hear what he was trying to say. Tom found him to be one of the shyest men he had ever met, a real gentle giant. Pat was dressed in a new suit, shirt and shoes. As a matter of fact, everything he wore was always brand new, and Tom only later found out why.

Pat was working on building the new motorway, ten hours every day, and when he finished work he would go straight to the pub until closing time. After this he would carry on to a local Irish club, drink a few more pints of Guinness into the early hours, and eventually get back to the digs for a few hours' sleep.

Tom learned that Pat had no change of clothing. Every weekend he would buy a complete new outfit, wear it over the weekend, and then continue to wear it to work all week before binning and replacing it the following Saturday. He was earning excellent money but never seemed to save a penny, blowing it all on food and piss and, of course, on new clothes every weekend.

But Tom soon discovered that Pat was not as reckless with his money as it appeared. He was a married man with two young kids who were still back in Ireland, and sent a lot of his money back to his family every week.

'I'd like to bring them all over to Birmingham but I don't think this is a place to bring the kids up,' Pat explained.

He and Tom became close friends, going out for a drink together now and then, when they would discuss their families back in Ireland.

Chapter 10

Tom's work at the factory was not hard.

His job was to maintain the company fleet of eight vehicles, and the manager's private car, which left him plenty of time on his hands. His colleagues were welcoming, and Tom would join them for lunch some days in the work canteen. One man, who looked to Tom to be about his own age, sat by him one day eating something Tom had not seen before.

'What's that you're eating mate?' he asked.

'It's bread and dripping, want to try some?' the man replied.

Tom thought, *Bloody bread and lard! What sort of people eat lard?* But they were a friendly bunch, and the eleven pounds a week pay was not bad for what he had to do. Tom was happy enough, but he couldn't help wanting more from life.

He had been working there for just a few weeks when some of the staff approached him and asked if he would be prepared to work on their private cars in his own time. It was a good way of making extra cash, and soon he was making as much money working on foreigners at lunchtime and weekends as he was working for the company.

The management appeared to turn a blind eye to what he was doing, perhaps viewing it as a company perk. Tom had landed on his feet again.

It was time to pack in his bar job, he didn't need it any more. He went along to the Old Talbot to inform Ted of his intention to leave.

At the pub he was met by a very anxious Ted who confided that he was extremely worried about Sandra. He told Tom that she had been getting drunk and wandering off. She had been found a few times sleeping in the streets and had been brought home by the police. 'I might have to give the pub up if I can't sort her out,' Ted explained.

'I'm sorry to hear that, Ted, but I really hope you can sort things out with her. I'll keep in touch,' Tom promised, before leaving.

Inspired by the confidence that others had in his skills, Tom soon began to find other ways of capitalising on his abilities. He started to buy cheap second-hand cars and do them up, turning back the mileometers whenever necessary, and made an excellent tax-free profit selling them on.

He opened his very first bank account and soon saw his money start to grow. *This was more like what I had in mind,* he thought.

With his new-found wealth Tom began to dress more smartly, in tailor-made suits from Burton. He had two suits made to measure in different colours, and felt like a millionaire wearing them. He started to visit the nightclubs in the city centre, and drive around the area in his tuned-up Mini Cooper; he was having fun, and dared to believe that things were coming right for him at last.

While doing the rounds of the pubs and clubs Tom met and dated several attractive young women, but none of his relationships were to last long. Sex was really his only motive, and many of the girls obliged.

Tom knew he would not fall in love again easily after Nina, and he certainly would never tell anyone else that he loved them; it would feel like a betrayal. During this period he never went to bed with an ugly woman, he thought, but he sure to hell did wake up with several. Still, it was good fun.

Despite being busy, Tom never forgot to send his mother some money every month, and would occasionally telephone her at a neighbour's house, who would go and fetch her to the phone for a long chat.

He would also ring his mate Dave, and get an update of what was happening in Derry. One of the questions he always asked was 'Have you seen Nina?' but the answer was always negative.

While sitting alone in the digs daydreaming one evening Tom began to analyse his life and try to establish in what direction his future was heading. He felt he was not bad-looking, with a good physique, and was quite intelligent with a good personality.

He was still very ambitious and aware of just how devious, cunning, and ruthless he could be when it came to making money. Pondering over these qualities he believed he possessed, he decided he now needed a change of direction in his life in order to fulfil more of his ambitions.

The question, then, was what was he going to do?

The very next night he had a stroke of luck. He had arranged to take Ann Payne, the manager's secretary from work, out for a night on the town. Little did he know then how that night was to change his life forever.

Ann was in her early twenties, tall and slim, with blonde hair cut short with a fringe at the front. She had a thin face with high cheekbones, beautiful green eyes and perfect teeth. Tom found her very intelligent and quite humorous, which is really what first attracted him to her.

After picking Ann up he took her to one of the best clubs in town. She was dressed in a dark green catsuit, and looked staggeringly attractive. They sat on two high stools at the bar, she sipping a gin and tonic, and he drinking a brandy and Coke.

She put her hand on his knee, gave him a kiss on the cheek and whispered, 'Thanks for a nice evening.'

'It's not over yet,' he of course replied, and kissed her on the lips.

Just at that moment Tom felt a hand on his shoulder and heard a gruff voice say, 'That's enough of that.' He jumped up from the stool expecting trouble, but found a man about his own height standing there with a big grin on his face.

It was Ann who spoke first. 'Oh, Tom, this is my big brother, Ken.'

Tom shook his hand. 'Pleased to meet you,' he said. 'Would you like a drink?'

'No, thanks, I'm with my mate up in the corner talking to the gaffer. I'll get both of you one,' he replied. Ken returned to his friends, and a few seconds later the barman placed two drinks in front of Tom and Ann.

'That was nice of him, wasn't it?' Tom said.

'He didn't pay for it, he gets all his drinks free in here,' Ann said.

'What do you mean, "all free"?'

Ann explained to him that her brother was a detective sergeant in the Criminal Investigation Department, or CID, of the local police, and that he never paid for anything in the clubs and pubs.

Ken had told her that the gaffers always insisted on paying, adding that, 'They scratch our backs, and we scratch theirs.' Tom was very impressed; there they were all dressed up, sitting in a club drinking free beer all night while supposedly working. *This is just the type of job I want,* Tom thought.

Upon leaving the club he took Ann back to her parents' house, and she invited him in for a coffee. He didn't really want a coffee, but was interested in getting into her knickers and so joined her inside. They sat on the settee and he began to kiss her, gently at first, and then it became quite passionate.

She got up and said, 'Wait a minute,' and went off up the stairs. She came back a few minutes later in a red dressing gown. 'Just checking if my mum and dad are asleep,' she said.

She sat down and they picked up where they had left off. Tom was pleased to discover that she had taken off her bra. Her breasts were pointed and hard, with large nipples that grew as he caressed them. He took one in his mouth and began to run his tongue around it. She slid down her black pants and he could see the triangle of light hair between her legs.

He ran his hand down over her flat tummy and felt the wet silk opening between her thighs. She opened her legs and he placed his fingers between her moist lips. She gave a sigh, lifted her bottom off the settee and began to pant and heave her crotch against his hand. 'I want you, Tom, please give it to me, please.' Quickly removing his trousers, his prick now standing like a flagpole, he lifted her onto the carpet.

He lay on top of her and she wrapped her legs around him as he entered her. She matched his every thrust with a rhythmical movement of her hips, screaming, 'Give it to me, fuck me, fuck me!' He had to put his hand over her mouth, in case she woke up her parents.

They came together, she shouting, 'I love your prick, Tom, I love it!' and almost heaving him off as she jerked her bottom up and down violently. He eventually kissed her goodnight, or more like good morning, and headed back to his digs.

His night with Ann had been great, but Tom had other reasons for wanting to meet up with Detective Sergeant Ken Payne again as soon as possible. Tom was really keen on the idea of joining the police force, and particularly interested in becoming a detective.

When he eventually met up with him again, Ken explained. 'It takes time to become a detective, Tom, you have to serve about four years before you can transfer to the CID. Even then it's not certain you'll make it out of uniform.'

But Tom had made up his mind; he was going to join the police even though it meant a large cut in wages. He rang and told his mother of his decision, but she had mixed feelings about it. He explained to her that it was nothing like the Royal Ulster Constabulary (RUC) back home in Northern Ireland.

The police were not armed in England, and did not have the IRA shooting at them.

Chapter 11

Tom applied a week later to join the Birmingham City Police and was eventually invited to go for the entrance examination and his medical assessment at the police headquarters.

He passed both with flying colours. Three months later he was informed that he had been accepted. He was relieved that nothing detrimental had come back from Derry regarding his character, which might have prevented his admission to the force. When he told Kay he was leaving the digs she became quite emotional.

On the day he left she threw her arms around him and kissed him hard on the lips. She made him promise that he would go back see her again. She pushed her soft mature body hard against his and ran her tongue around the inside his mouth. Tom was very much aroused and knew that he would have to go back soon.

Tom spent his first week of enrolment attending an induction course at Tally Ho, the local training centre, and then being fitted out with his constable's uniform at the police stores in Duke Street. He loved wearing his helmet, it made him feel proud.

The following Sunday evening he reported to the Number 4 district police training centre at Ryton-on-Dunsmore, where he met his new colleagues, the people who were to be his companions for the next thirteen weeks.

There were officers from all over the country, both male and female. On the Monday morning the college commandant, a chief superintendent seconded from Staffordshire Constabulary, welcomed them all to the course and pointed out to them how very lucky they all were to have the privilege of becoming police officers.

The training began, with many hours of spit and polish, square-bashing, and intense classroom study. The men were given short back and sides haircuts by the visiting barber, and were expected to keep the toecaps of their boots like mirrors, and the creases in the uniform like razor blades. Tom found it very difficult getting used to the front and back collar studs of their shirts.

The trainees were taught about the importance of crime scenes, and how to read and manage them. Control of and methods for handling traffic were also taught on model streets set up in the training centre. Mock trials were created in make-believe courts to provide training and experience in giving evidence properly. Skills in first aid, self-defence, swimming and life-saving were also taught.

Tom found many of the class subjects – such as the Larceny Act, the Offences Against the Person Act and the Criminal Damage Act – thrilling, as he tried to imagine himself as a detective, locking up crooks for the kinds of criminal offences covered by these laws.

The Road Traffic Act and the Road Vehicles (Construction and Use) Regulations, however, he found extremely boring, who wanted to get involved with motorists anyway? He knew he was not interested in that side of the work.

The men's and women's quarters were segregated, and it was a dismissal offence to cross the line. Tom found it very frustrating not being able to get to grips with the policewomen. He quite fancied a little blonde from the Nottingham force, but discovered that she was married to a senior officer from that force. *Pity – what a waste,* he thought.

At the weekends, most of the recruits went home leaving only a few of them at the centre. Those who were left behind went out on a Saturday night to the local pub for a few drinks, and maybe had fish and chips on the way back. *Only so they can finally get to spend some time with the policewomen,* he thought.

The enforced self-restraint and intense workload were killing him, and he wondered at times if he had made the right decision in joining. Two of his classmates decided to leave after a few weeks as they couldn't handle the pressure, but Tom decided to stick with it. *It's all for a purpose*, he thought, remembering the enviable lifestyle of detective Ken Payne.

It was on the sixth weekend that he got friendly with Anita, one of the catering staff in the canteen. After breakfast on the Saturday morning he managed to find a bit of privacy and asked her if she fancied a night out. She was a little reluctant at first but, after a some persuasion, agreed.

He met her outside the local pub, but she seemed very nervous. 'Can we go some place else for a drink, I'd like to get away from here,' she said.

'Yes, any suggestions where?' Tom asked.

'I know a pub outside Coventry, it won't take long to get there. You see, I don't want any of the other staff to see us together, it might cause problems,' she replied.

Tom could understand that she didn't want any of the other staff to see her out with a recruit, so they set off for nearby Coventry.

Tom didn't know his way around, so she directed him to an old half-timbered pub on the outskirts of the city. It was a lovely quaint old building with low wooden beams, and horse brasses, shovels, scythes and other antiques dotted around the walls inside. It had a medieval feel. The atmosphere was laid back and Tom immediately relaxed into the evening.

He learned that Anita was Austrian; her mother and father had come to England at the end of the war when she was a young child. She was a plain-looking girl, with hair tied up in a bun and a small gap in her two front upper teeth. Quiet and well spoken, she had received a good education at an upper-class catering college.

She wasn't the type of girl that he would normally be attracted to, but six weeks without female company had made Tom very grateful for anything he could get. *What a selfish bastard I've become,* he reflected, the sudden flushing in his cheeks nothing to do with the warmth of the room.

At the end of the night they returned to the car park of the training centre. Anita lived in a block at the rear of the centre, and so Tom tried to persuade her to let him go back there with her, but to no avail. He was very persistent, and she eventually took him by the hand and led him out of the car park.

They walked to a quiet block where she opened the door and led him inside. He soon realised that it was the laundry room: sheets and pillowcases were stacked high on the floor. They sat down on a pile of clean sheets and he put his arm around her and kissed her. She didn't respond to his approaches. 'Tom, I like you, but I don't want to do anything,' she said.

He was feeling incredibly randy. 'Just let me touch you then.' She let him touch her breasts over her clothing, but that was as far as she was prepared to go. They parted company, and Tom was walking back towards his block when he heard someone shout, 'What are you doing?' He realised that it was one of the training staff on security patrol, and took off, running, followed by the member of staff.

He saw a low privet hedge and tried to jump over it, but unfortunately for him it had barbed wire threaded through it, which caught and ripped the arse out of his trousers. Despite this, Tom managed to beat his follower to the block. He ran in, jumped into bed fully clothed, pulled the bedclothes over his head and lay quite still. It seemed that his pursuer must have lost sight of him, because Tom wasn't followed into the room.

A very close call, he thought, *and all for nothing.*

Training progressed, and Tom was regularly placed in the top three in his class in the periodic examinations they had to take to track their progress. This pleased his class instructor, who advised him to keep studying when he left the centre as, once experienced, he had the ability to gain promotion should he choose to. But all Tom really wanted was to become a detective. The reports on him included remarks such as 'Qualities of leadership', and 'He has an intelligent and constructive mind'.

Around eight weeks into his training, Tom attended a dance in the gym to celebrate the final examinations of the course cohort who were about to leave the training centre. Prior to going to the dance, he had been out to the local pub with a few mates and, to say the least, they were all quite merry.

When he saw Anita standing there, all dressed up in her party clothes and with her hair let down over her shoulders, he made a beeline for her. He asked her to dance but she told him it was a bit awkward, and that he should ask someone else.

Tom couldn't understand what was going on but, as the night went by, he became aware of someone else paying her a lot of attention. It was one of the instructors, Inspector David Hamilton, who was spending a lot of time with her. Tom guessed, then, that the old pub in Coventry that Anita had taken him to had been identified first by Hamilton, as a place where no one would be likely to see him or catch him out.

He thought Anita and Hamilton were probably having an affair. That was why she didn't want to be seen by any of the staff the night she and Tom were out together.

A few days later he got the opportunity to speak to Anita on her own, and asked her outright. 'Are you having an affair with that pompous prat of an inspector?' Tom didn't like him; he was a Special Course man and an ex-army officer who talked with a plum in his mouth, had a boyish face and looked down his nose at everyone else. Tom thought he walked like he had a drumstick stuck up his arse.

Anita denied it at first. 'I can't talk now, can we meet in the car park at eight o'clock?' she whispered.

'Okay, I'll be in the car waiting,' he said.

At that, she left him.

They met in the car park, and he drove to the safe pub in Coventry.

'I'm a fool, Tom,' she said. 'I've got involved with him, and he's a married man. He won't let me go, he watches me like a hawk.'

'Do you love him?'

'I thought I did at first, then I found out he was married.

He told me he was going to leave his wife, but now nine months later I know he has no intention of doing that,' she said.

'What are you going to do about it?' he asked.

She told him that she wanted to end it, but Hamilton would not agree, telling her that she could lose her job if she was not careful. Tom knew that the crafty bastard was emotionally blackmailing her; she was extremely frightened of him and what he might say or do.

Tom thought hard about what he could do to help her. Confront him? Possibly not. He could inform the commandant, or another member of staff, but then realised they probably all knew already and were turning a blind eye.

The solution came to him as he lay in bed one night. Hamilton was a career man; he wouldn't like any bad publicity that would ruin his reputation. Yes, blackmail; do to him what he was doing to Anita.

It worked.

Soon, Hamilton had asked to go back to his force for domestic reasons, and of course the commandant obliged. Anita asked Tom what he had done. Shrugging his shoulders, he told her that Hamilton must have had a pang of conscience. She knew he'd had something to do with it, but she never would have guessed the deviousness involved. She was simply grateful for his intervention, and rewarded him with several memorable nights in her bed for his efforts.

At the end of the thirteen weeks, Tom passed out with flying colours, sailing through all the examinations with outstanding results. Back at his force he was instructed to move immediately into single men's quarters at Bloomsbury Street police station on the D Division. There, he met some of the single men he was going to work and party with in the coming months.

Chapter 12

Tom was a very proud probationary constable reporting to the chief superintendent at nine fifteen on the Monday morning at Victoria Road police station.

The old building looked depressing, grey and dismal. It was situated in the middle of Aston and the smells from Ansells brewery, and the HP Sauce factory situated next door gave the area a sickly atmosphere.

Marched into an office by the administration inspector, Tom came to attention and saluted. The chief sat before him at a long, polished desk in a high-backed leather chair. 'Probationary Constable Sharkey, sir,' the inspector said.

The chief was overweight, and looked about fifty. He stood to shake Tom's hand, welcoming him to the division, his solid frame just shy of six feet tall by Tom's estimation. His new boss spoke with a strong Welsh accent, and congratulated him on his achievements at the training centre.

'Welcome to the division, Sharkey. I see you did extremely well in your training at Ryton and I hope you continue in this vein,' said the chief. Then he continued. 'Work hard and pass the promotion exams, young man, and you should do well in the job.' Clearly enjoying the sound of his own voice, he went on. 'There are three things you must be very, very careful of dealing with as a police officer, Sharkey: they are property, prostitutes, and policewomen: the three Ps. They can mean big trouble if not handled properly.

Remember that and you shouldn't go far wrong.'

'Thank you, sir, I will do my very best,' Tom said, then saluted his superior and left his office.

'Well done, son,' the admin inspector said, then added, 'There's a fourth "P" the chief didn't mention – prisoners,' and made it clear to Tom that several police officers over the years had found themselves in trouble after careless handling of one of these four. Both the inspector and the chief were giving him a warning, of which Tom took grateful note.

He learned that he would be working three shifts: mornings – 6.00 am to 2.00 pm, evenings – 2.00 pm to 10.00 pm, and nights – 10.00 pm to 6.00 am, and would have to parade fifteen minutes before each shift. Tom knew the money was terrible for working these hours, but recognised he would have to put up with it if he wanted to become a detective.

He was very excited as he went on parade at nine forty-five that first Tuesday night. He stood in line with the other officers as the sergeant ordered them to produce their appointments. He wasn't prepared for this, and stood there motionless.

The sergeant roared, 'Sharkey, don't you want to join us? Produce your appointments.' Tom hadn't a clue what he was on about but, looking along the line at his colleagues, he realised that the sergeant meant him to produce his truncheon, torch, pocketbook, and first aid kit for inspection. These were his appointments it would appear, although no one had bothered to tell him this.

Then the sergeant said, sarcastically, 'Thank you, Sharkey.' He was then given a wad of pink slips, to be used to write down any relevant information such as wanted persons or recently stolen cars, or anything else of interest on his patch.

He was posted to work with PC Dave Evans until 1.00 am, and then to canteen duties.

'What are canteen duties?' he asked Dave, when they got off parade.

'You have to open up the canteen, cook for the shift and wash up afterwards,' explained Dave, in a strong Welsh accent.

'I'm not really able to cook, I can't do that,' Tom protested, but was assured by Dave that it only involved frying sausages, eggs and chips, and making tea. Before the night was over, Tom had learned how to make an omelette, not to burn sausages, make tons of chips, prepare numerous sandwiches and make gallons of tea.

When everyone had finished eating he washed up, and then mopped out the canteen. He thought, *What the hell?* He hadn't joined the police to do this. Over the weeks that followed he learned that all the probationary constables took it in turns to do canteen duty, and then it didn't seem quite so bad.

Other tasks he didn't like doing were stoking the old boiler in the cellar and making endless cups of tea for the sergeants, but the reward for these was to be let off duty an hour early in the morning, which eased the pain considerably.

Very soon Tom discovered what it really meant to be a police officer on the street. Prior to joining, he could walk round a corner and no matter what he saw happening he could ignore it, walk away and no one would take any notice of him.

Now when he walked round the same corner and saw something wrong happening he had to do something about it. Everyone looked to the police for help and expected they should know what to do in any situation.

Tom felt very conspicuous. Conversely, the uniform did give him a great sense of power and he found that almost everyone acknowledged him, a theme that extended inside the station too; one of the things that amused Tom, was that when you wished to leave the station and go out on the streets you had to say to the sergeant, 'Carry on please, sergeant' or to the inspector, 'Carry on please, sir' and salute them.

He had not been working at the station long when he saw some of the perks the inspector and sergeants enjoyed. They played snooker at every opportunity, and the lucky senior constables were occasionally asked to make up a foursome. Unfortunately, he hadn't reached that stage yet.

The more senior officers also took it in turns to go off duty a few hours early when on late shifts and on nights. The inspector and the sergeants were like Gods; whatever they said was gospel. The sergeants licked up to the inspector, and Tom thought they would lick his arse if he asked them to. But when any ranking officer said jump, the officer lower down the food chain did just that.

One of the sergeants, Jock Green, an ex-sergeant major in the Guards, reminded Tom very much of a bear with a crew cut and a permanent sore head. He was a nasty bastard who followed everyone around on his Velocette motorcycle, giving out bollockings at the drop of a hat, and usually for very trivial matters.

Tom learned that most of the inspectors and sergeants were ex-service personnel who had joined the force after the war. They tried to administer military discipline but the police force was meant to be about self-discipline, rendering their methods counter-productive, and universally despised among the rank and file.

For the first three months Tom was always doubled up with a senior constable and plodded the beat in all kinds of weather. Every two hours they had to make a point at a designated telephone box where any outstanding messages were passed to them.

It was explained very early to Tom what the expression 'he will do off at two' meant: if you arrested anyone early when on nights you were allowed off duty at 2.00 am in order to be fresh for court next morning. Officers enjoyed taking advantage of this little perk, making the night shift arrest rate very healthy indeed.

After completing his introductory stint of doubling up, Tom was posted to working a beat on his own. During daylight he found it quite interesting, but he thought that walking around on his own at night was the most unsociable thing he had ever encountered since living in Fawney.

On nights when it was raining he would enter the unoccupied factories and houses to search for anyone stealing the copper pipes or sleeping rough, but mainly to keep himself dry. One night he found a young man about his own age sleeping rough. 'Where do you come from?' he asked him.

'I've come over from Belfast, sir, but I'm thinking of going home. Don't like it here, can't wait to get home,' he replied.

Feeling sorry for him, and having been in a similar situation himself, Tom asked, 'Have you got any money?'

'Got a few bob,' he replied.

Tom gave him ten pounds, and said, 'Now get off and don't let me see you around here again.' Helping someone made him feel good.

On night duty the lads would wear lady's tights or long johns to keep out the cold. Tom thought it must have been a woman who designed the long johns because wearing them made it nearly impossible to have a pee.

Tom had one good tea spot on nights, at one of the engineering factories, when he called in to see the security guard there. He, too, was an Irishman and they had long chats, especially about back home. Tom could sit and drink tea, keep warm and would sometimes accompany the guard while he did his rounds through the factory.

'Do you enjoy being a policeman, Tom?' the guard asked one night.

'I don't like *this* very much, I get bored just walking around. I want to be a detective,' Tom explained.

In all honesty, though, Tom was now beginning to hate working shifts altogether and could see a long hard road ahead to get into the CID. He felt down, and wondered if the police really offered all that he wanted out of life. His reality seemed a long way from the detective drinking free beer in the night clubs.

Lying in bed one morning, off duty for the day, he decided to go back to his old lodgings to see Kay and try to cheer himself up. First, he went to a garage on the patch and traded in his Mini. In its place he bought a red Ford Cortina GT with a black mat bonnet, a car he'd had his eye on for weeks. It had chrome sports wheels with wide tyres, and a wooden dashboard and he felt like a million dollars driving it.

Arriving outside the digs at about eleven thirty, he parked up and went to knock on the door, but there was no reply. He knocked again, heavily this time just in case she was upstairs and hadn't heard him. At that moment, an upstairs window of the house next door opened, and he saw Kay leaning out.

'Who is that?' she shouted down.

Tom stood back from the door to where she could see him, but before he could speak she shouted, 'Tom! Come round.' He went next door to her private house and the door was opened a few seconds later. She stood there in a dressing gown, her hand holding the top up close to her chin.

'Great to see you, I was just getting out of the bath and thought I heard someone. Come in,' she said.

She took him into the front room and he sat on the long vinyl sofa and she asked him if he would like a cup of tea. He thought, *This is a lot more comfortable and warmer than what we had to live in next door*, but accepted a cuppa with good grace.

She came back from the kitchen carrying two mugs of tea. 'Tell me what you've been up to, Tom. We have a lot of catching up to do. I honestly thought you wouldn't come back to see me,' she said.

They reminisced about old times and he told her of his exploits – well, some of them, anyway. She looked radiant sitting there in her pink dressing gown, her hair still damp, and he could see her large breasts fighting to get out as she leaned over to place the mug on the low coffee table. Her gown fell open as she crossed her legs and he could practically see up to her crotch. Tom knew he had to make a move.

'You look terrific, Kay,' he said, and placed his hand on her shoulder. She edged towards him and he sensed that she wanted to be held. He took a chance and put his arm around her, pulling her close. She raised her lips towards his and he began to kiss her.

Very soon her dressing gown was open, and she shivered as he kissed and caressed her breasts; they were the most enormous he had ever held. Her nipples were like walnuts. He tried to guide her down onto the sofa, but she stopped him. Then she stood up, took him by the hand and led him towards the stairs. He was thinking, *Is this it?*

In the large cosy bedroom she dropped her dressing gown. She stood there, her beautiful body that of a woman in her prime, covered in freckles right down to the mound of red hair between her legs. She got into bed and very soon he was beside her, wearing nothing but a smile.

They touched each other gently. He was ready for her, but she slowed him down and directed his head towards her thighs, spreading her legs in encouragement. He ran his tongue along her wide-open juicy lips and could taste her moistness as she writhed

86

and groaned beneath him. He pushed his tongue inside her and ran it up towards her hard little peak, and she groaned, 'Don't stop, don't stop, it's lovely.' He continued to lick and kiss her outer lips.

'I'm coming, I'm coming, and its fucking great, don't stop Tom, don't stop,' she pleaded, as she jerked her body up and down so violently that he had trouble keeping his head in place.

Then he crawled up on top of her and she held him tightly in her arms and whispered, 'That was great love, I needed that.' Tom was almost bursting now as he got between her legs and slipped into her wet parting. She was ready to go again and wrapped her thighs around him. They thrust away at each other and very soon came together.

Tom now lay back, exhausted, but she came at him again, her mouth searching for his limp prick. She very soon got it to stand again as she stroked and sucked it, practically swallowing him up.

'I want you from behind, love,' she said, and turned over onto her hands and knees. He entered her doggy fashion, and played with her breasts as they hung down practically touching the mattress beneath her.

When he eventually kissed her goodbye he was tired, but well satisfied.

'Keep in touch, won't you, Tom,' she shouted after him.

He smiled, and thought, *Well, that really lifted the gloom. By god she knows what it's for!*

Tom decided on his way back to the nick to call in to the Old Talbot and see his friend Ted. He got a great surprise at the state of the inside of the pub – it had been badly neglected. 'How is Sandra getting on?' Tom asked.

'Have a look for yourself,' Ted said, pointing to one of the bench seats in the corner of the bar.

Tom went and had a look under the seat, and got a shock when he saw Sandra curled up asleep.

'How long has she been there?' he asked.

'More or less all the time, I just can't keep her off the vodka. She nicks the bottle when I'm not looking. I can't do anything with her, she'll drink anything.'

'Have you tried to get help for her?'

'I've decided to give up the pub and move. I've made up my mind, should be out of here within the week,' Ted replied.

Tom told Ted that he was now in the police and gave him his phone number. 'If I can be of any help, Ted, just give me a ring and I'll do what I can,' Tom assured him as he left, feeling anxious and upset for his friend.

Chapter 13

Back on duty one evening making a point at the phone box, Tom was directed to the Aston Cross pub, where a fight was supposedly taking place. He got there at the same time as Sergeant Mooney and Constable Smith to find that the troublemakers had already left the premises. When the landlady offered them all a pint, Tom was not sure what to say: it was an offence to drink on duty. But then the sergeant pitched in and ordered three pints. It was Tom's first drink on duty, his first free pint. *Maybe the job isn't so bad after all,* he thought.

Tom got many bollockings from his supervisors while he was still on probation. One evening, due to finish at ten o'clock, he strolled into the station at two minutes to ten to be met by the inspector, who pointed to the large station clock, and snarled, 'Where are you going, Sharkey, you don't finish till ten. Go out and come back in then.' Tom seethed, bit his tongue, walked out the door and turned around, and walked straight back in again.

How bloody petty, he thought.

His next run-in with the inspector was one morning upon returning to the station for breakfast, when he met up with one of the other probationers and they walked in together. They were met at the station door by Sergeant Mooney, who informed them that the inspector wanted to see them both in his office immediately.

'When are you two getting married, then?' the inspector snarled.

'What do you mean, sir?' Tom asked.

'I saw you walking in together, I'm surprised you weren't holding hands. Don't do it again. I don't want to see you together, understand?'

God, so we must ignore each other and walk in one behind the other like bloody sheep, thought Tom. *How pathetic.*

About three o'clock one morning Tom was walking his beat when he was directed to take over at Bloomsbury Street station and run the front office until going off duty. At around four o'clock the telephone rang. He answered, and a voice told him to 'stand by'. He held on for several minutes, but as there was no further response he thought it was some crank and so he hung up.

At about five o'clock, Sergeant Green called into the station and asked what the force broadcast had had to say. Tom just looked at him blankly. *What the hell is he talking about?* he thought.

Very soon he learned that the phone call he had hung up on was the force broadcast. The system was that the force control room would ring round all the stations and, when they were all connected, they would give the force-wide broadcast.

This would consist of details of recently stolen vehicles, persons wanted, and serious crimes that had recently been committed. Tom should have made a note of all this information for the officers calling into the station.

'Have you got a bloody brain, Sharkey?' the sergeant raged.

'No one told me anything about it, I'm not a mind reader,' Tom replied, feeling angry and frustrated.

'Well, now you know, you prat,' the sergeant said as he left.

Tom felt aggrieved that no one had bothered to explain the system to him.

***

It was 1966 and the football World Cup was being staged in England. The Group 2 matches were being played at Villa Park, not too far from Tom's station. Everyone was very excited for Alf Ramsey, Bobby Moore and the rest of the England team, maybe this could be their year.

Tom got posted to perform traffic duties at Aston Cross during the three games. He enjoyed this post because he had been given the key to the traffic lights and had complete control over all the drivers. Being able to control them gave him great satisfaction. His post brought him into contact with supporters from West Germany, Spain and Argentina and he found it very exciting. People were approaching him for directions to the ground and speaking all sorts of languages. At times it was difficult to understand what they were saying but the majority were extremely friendly. Tom watched the Wembley final between England and West Germany on the television in the Aston Cross pub with several of his mates. Some of them were in uniform, some in half-uniform, nobody cared. Geoff Hurst and the England team were their heroes when they lifted the World Cup.

For Tom, this kind of privilege was the good side of the job, where the uniform allowed him to take advantage of a situation and nobody questioned it. It made him forget the bad times; it made sense of the work he was putting in to reach the CID.

But there were the downsides, too. Tom felt very sorry for young Constable Jock McDonald, one of the new recruits that had recently arrived from his training. Jock was baby-faced and quiet, and didn't have much confidence; he was bullied mercilessly by the inspector and the sergeants. They took the piss out of him at every opportunity. Tom tried to help him, but he was really not in a position to do much about it.

The senior officers would often post Jock to police one single street for his eight-hour shift, which was enough to drive anyone mad.

After several weeks of bullying Jock resigned and returned home to Aberdeen. Tom tried in vain to talk him in to staying, but he had made up his mind he was going back home. Tom reflected on the kind of personality that was needed to thrive in the police. He knew it was thanks to his own determination and upbringing that he was able to withstand the environment he worked in.

The job kept Tom busy, but dealing with motor accidents was something he didn't like. It meant completing an accident book and mountains of paperwork, mostly just for statistical purposes. There was one thing about accidents that did pique his interest, though.

He noticed that every time he attended an accident where one of the cars involved was not drivable and needed a front-wheel lift, from out of nowhere a traffic patrol car would turn up. The traffic officer would remain at the scene until the breakdown lorry came and removed the damaged car. Then the officer would leave, and let

Tom deal with all the paperwork with the usual saying 'leave it with you, son'.

Tom made discreet enquiries, and discovered that there was always a bung from the callout garage to the officer dealing with the incident, which was around five pounds. He now realised why everyone was in such a hurry to get to such an accident first, and from that day on made sure he got the bung when he dealt with one.

During this period of his service Tom also enjoyed some humorous moments, such as the time he was caught with a bag of chips under his helmet, or the time one of his prisoners, a young lad, chinned the inspector for poking his nose in where it wasn't needed.

Under normal circumstances the prisoner would have got a smack, but this was such a delicate young kid. 'Can we keep this our little secret?' the inspector asked Tom. It was the first time the inspector had been pleasant towards him, he was so embarrassed by the incident.

There was also the time Tom doctored the petrol flow to the sergeant's motorcycle, so that it would travel about a mile and then stop. The sergeant would have to walk back to the station pushing the machine, cursing his head off. Tom did this several times and thoroughly enjoyed the state of the sergeant on his return to the station, exhausted.

The thick bugger couldn't figure it out.

***

Life in the police force was getting slightly better now for Tom. He enjoyed the challenge of going to work each day not knowing what to expect. Although he still didn't like working shifts, he still had his sights set on becoming a detective.

Sundays were generally quiet, but on one occasion as Tom strolled along Hunton Hill enjoying the sunshine, he found his peace interrupted. He could hear children laughing and shouting but could not figure out where the sound was coming from. Then he realised they were playing under the railway bridge by the tracks. He immediately went to investigate and saw three children aged around eight or nine playing on the track. 'Get away from there now. Come here to me,' Tom shouted.

In a panic, they ran off along the track with Tom in close pursuit. He was terrified: he had frightened them and he was now worried for their safety. They were more scared of him than of the trains. He was so relieved when he eventually caught up with them before any trains came along. He led them away from the track, but the frightened look on their faces upset him. The three of them lived locally and he escorted them to their individual homes and had strong words with their parents, who hadn't noticed that they had left their gardens.

Tom was thinking how the situation could so easily have been a tragedy. And he was concerned about how the children were afraid of a police officer who was trying to help them. He resolved to make more of an effort to engage with the youngsters he came across when on duty, and try to change their view.

Next day, while escorting children over the road on his school crossing duties, Tom was joking with a few of the kids when an attractive young girl, about twenty years old, walked passed and acknowledged him with a big smile. This was the kind of attention Tom didn't mind when in uniform. The very next day he was doing the same crossing duty and the same girl walked passed and again acknowledged him. Much to his frustration, the responsibility for the safety of the schoolchildren prevented him making a move.

A few days later, he'd just finished helping the children across the road when, to his surprise, the same girl approached him. 'Excuse me, officer, but could you help me please. I can't get into my house, I've locked myself out,' she explained.

'Where do you live?' he asked, and she pointed to a place just along the road.

It was a beautiful large detached house set in its own gardens, with a long winding drive to the front. *There's some money there,* thought Tom. He accompanied her to the front, where she indicated to a small open window in the kitchen.

'If you could help me up, I think with a bit of a struggle I could get through that window,' she said.

He put his arms around her waist and managed to lift her so that she could stand on the window ledge. She was dressed in a tight skirt, which she had to pull up to her thighs while she tried to scramble through the small window. To assist, Tom pushed her up by the bottom. She didn't complain, and from where he stood he could see her tiny black pants and the top of her stockings. *What a lovely arse,* he thought.

Once inside, she opened the front door and let him in.

'Thank you very much, officer, don't know what I'd have done without your help. Would you like a coffee?' Tom accepted, and she disappeared off to the kitchen, returning swiftly with two steaming mugs.

He was taken with her short black hair, pale blue eyes, and her taut nipples that poked through her tight blouse like organ stops, and decided he would like to get to know her better. He began to chat her up. She appeared to be interested, so he invited her out for a drink at the weekend.

'I have a steady boyfriend but I could still meet you in the Queens at about eight on Saturday night if that would be alright? My boyfriend's away in London for the weekend,' she said. Tom quickly agreed, finished his coffee and was about to leave.

'My name's Tom, by the way. What's yours?' he asked.

'I'm Julie. Julie Wallace.'

'See you Saturday,' he said, and left happy with himself.

On the Saturday night they met as arranged in the Queens and had several drinks. 'What do you do for a living, Julie?' he asked.

'I'm training as a nurse at the Good Hope Hospital.

Where do you come from, Tom? I know you're Irish, but which part?'

'I come from the North, a town called Londonderry,' he replied.

'Oh, yes, I've heard it on the news, quite a bit of trouble there, isn't there.

I've never been to Ireland but I hear it's a lovely place,' she said.

As they were leaving the pub to go for a Chinese meal at a restaurant in the high street, Julie said, 'Tom, I've been going out with my boyfriend for about six months. He's just gone to visit some family in London.' After the meal, he drove her home, ever hopeful, but she told him that she couldn't invite him in because her mum knew she was going out with someone else.

'Can I at least have a goodnight kiss, then,' he asked, and put his arms around her and kissed her. Her lips were so soft and willing, and it soon became very passionate. She laced her arms around his neck and continued to kiss him. He responded, and soon they were deeply engrossed in a heavy petting session.

'Can we go someplace quieter,' she whispered. He drove up the back of some houses to where some garages were situated, and found a dark spot. She had climbed into the back seat of the car by now, and when Tom looked round she had stripped down to her bra and pants.

He immediately climbed over beside her, removing his trousers as he negotiated the front seats. She pulled down his underpants and took out his prick, which was now erect in her hands, and began to play with it.

'Lie back,' she said, and took him in her mouth.

He felt like he would explode if she didn't stop, so he pulled it out and sat up as she began to remove her bra and pants. He could feel and see the mass of black curls between her legs; it was by far the longest pubic hair he had ever seen. She lay back and spread her legs wide apart over the back of the two front seats. Tom thought,

This is not the first time she's done this. He entered her, straight up to the hilt as she wrapped her legs tightly around him, jerking her hips up and down.

She never spoke a word, and when he came with thudding thrusts, all she did was groan and moan. They lay breathlessly beside each other, he with sweat running down his back. 'I want you again,' she whispered.

This time she got on top and worked herself up and down, writhing and shuddering. She had a wonderfully fit body, and he took her breasts in his hands and began to suck her nipples until she came with a sudden shriek. Tom dropped her back home but there was no mention, from either of them, of another date.

Chapter 14

The police force was now going through a period of great change, with personal radios and panda cars being introduced. Sub-divisions were being further divided into beats, with dedicated beat officers and panda cars allocated to each. The new Theft Act came into being to replace the old Larceny Act, and there were new breathalyser laws. Adapting to the new structure and procedures was very challenging for the service.

On his first tour in his shiny new panda car Tom was posted to cover an area in Erdington. The evening sun was still shining, and he sat parked up in George Road reading the *Evening Mail*. The late sun cast a warm glow through his window and Tom reflected on what a treat this was from walking the beat.

His evening was soon disturbed, though, when he was directed by radio to go to Highcroft Hospital, where a man was drunk and causing a nuisance.

When Tom arrived, he was confronted by a burly man who stood about six feet four inches tall and was shouting abuse at everyone who passed by. He reminded Tom of Desperate Dan, the comic character. When Tom tried to calm him down he became quite aggressive. Fortunately for Tom, he was not alone – other officers had been directed to the scene to assist.

The man had taken hold of the iron railings that ran alongside the road in front of the hospital, and was refusing to let go. Tom and his colleagues wrestled him loose and manhandled him onto the ground, face down. There were five officers now, all trying to hold him still while Tom attempted to handcuff him. The man was so strong Tom had to put a knee on his elbow, and use both hands to try and bend his powerful arm up behind his back. The next problem was getting the handcuffs to go around the man's thick wrists.

When the man was handcuffed at last, the officers began to push him into the back of the panda car. Thinking that he was being clever, Tom went round to the door on the other side and tried to pull the man into the car while the others pushed. But the man wasn't daft, he let them all push, launching himself straight over Tom and out the other side of the car, where he tried to run off. Tom was in pain as he jumped on top of him, using all his weight to try and subdue the man. He managed to hold on to a leg until the others recovered.

Unable to get him into the car, the officers decided to put the man into the rear of the dog van and, with the German Shepherd breathing down his neck, there wasn't any more trouble from him. Tom thought that they must have looked like the Keystone Cops to all the members of the public looking on.

***

Making extra cash continued to be Tom's main hobby, and he always volunteered to work overtime at the Saturday afternoon football matches at St Andrew's, because he knew it was such a cushy number.

Still a probationer, he was always posted to what the gaffers called one of the 'horrible jobs' – preventing cars parking in Green Lane, before, during and after the match. But to Tom, this was the perfect assignment; he had got to know the gaffer at one of the Irish pubs in Green Lane, and the guy would always leave him a pint inside the unlocked side fire door.

Tom would patrol the street for a few minutes, then stand with his back to the door and, when no one was looking, push it open and slide inside. There was always a pint waiting and, as the match went on, a sandwich was also left on the little table by the soft chair. He very rarely ever saw the gaffer, but the pints kept coming all afternoon.

Tom knew the real reason for the gaffer's generosity – the pub was full of illegal after hours drinkers – but Tom didn't care; he was being looked after. The sergeant or inspector never paid him a visit, as they were too busy in the ground watching the match. *What a doddle, and still getting paid overtime as well*, Tom thought.

Back on night duty again, and very bored because nothing was happening, Tom was directed to a burglar alarm ringing at the distillery store on his patch. He went along and checked the premises, and found that they had not been burgled.

When the keyholder eventually arrived to open up, they both searched the premises to make completely sure everything was in order. This was the policy. The good part, was that as the keyholder was leaving he slipped Tom a bottle of whiskey and thanked him for his assistance. *What a nice little perk of the job,* thought Tom. Every six or so weeks or so after that, he would go to the rear door of the premises after dark and kick it to set off the alarm. It never failed, always a bottle.

During the two years of his probationary period Tom had made numerous excellent arrests for crime, which he hoped would benefit him in the future when he sought promotion or a transfer into the CID. He still desperately wanted to become a detective.

Some of Tom's favourite arrests were for offences of Loitering with Intent. The law stated that once a potential offender had tried three car doors you could arrest him. Tom never bothered waiting until a thief had tried three; he short-circuited the system. Once they had tried one door and Tom believed they were at it, he would arrest them. They would always have some type of key or screwdriver in their possession.

Well, he figured, they were definitely at it, and it saved a lot of time. His evidence would show they tried three cars and in court it was his word the magistrates believed; he always won the cases. The gaffers thought very highly of him and praised his hard work. Maybe they knew what he was doing but they never said anything.

Tom needed this reputation to get into the CID. He received several chief superintendent's commendations, which he hoped would also help to advance his career.

At the end of his two-year probation, Tom was recommended for appointment and that night went out with some of his mates for a celebration drink. In the Shareholders Arms the gaffer had got a strip show running upstairs and invited him and the lads up for the fun. The two policewomen in their group had to be coaxed into joining them.

The one called Sue had legs like a Victorian chair, and couldn't stop a pig in an alley. As the night went on she became more attractive to Tom and, *Shit, the legs are the first thing you throw out of the way,* he thought. They ended up on the dance floor having a smooch. He must have got very drunk because the next thing he knew was waking up with a terrible headache in bed with Sue.

'Where am I?' he asked, through a thumping head.

'You're in my room in single quarters,' she replied, with a grin.

'Oh, God no. What time is it?'

'Twenty past eleven,' she said.

Christ, how the bloody hell am I going to get out of here without being seen by one of the gaffers? He waited his chance, managed to sneak down the back stairs into the rear car park without being spotted, and escaped.

Later, he reflected on the chief superintendent's advice: remember the three Ps. *Phew, that was too close for comfort*, he thought.

One type of prisoner Tom didn't like dealing with was shoplifters; hardly a day passed when he didn't have to arrest at least one from the Erdington High Street stores. He noticed how many of them had plenty of money, but for one reason or another seemed to enjoy taking a gamble on not getting caught.

One wealthy man he arrested was a local dentist who would go to the food counter, get served with sandwiches or sausage rolls and would then eat them as he walked around the store. When he came to

103

leave the store he wouldn't pay for them at the checkout, and one day he was spotted by a store detective and arrested for theft. Tom thought, *What a stupid bastard for only a few pence,* but it was another prisoner to add to his numbers.

***

During the next year, and with the help of a correspondence course, Tom studied hard and passed the promotion exam for sergeant. But he knew this was only the first hurdle to progressing in the force. He had to continue to arrest as many prisoners as he possibly could for committing crime, and to carry on and make a name for himself, too.

On several occasions when Tom stopped motorists he found had been drinking, if it was at all possible he would take their keys from them and make sure they got home safely. He appreciated that driving under the influence of drink was a very serious offence, with many drivers caused serious injuries or death to themselves or other road users. Using strong language, he would point out the error of their ways. Many stupid drivers lost their jobs and their livelihood this way.

What annoyed him was when several of his colleagues would boast of how many drink drivers they could catch. It was viewed as an easy arrest. When a driver had clearly had more than one or two drinks he would arrest them and take them into custody, but he disliked having to spend hours in the station while the lengthy breathalyser procedures were carried out. He wanted to be on the streets arresting prisoners for other offences and protecting the public.

If the taxpayers knew their money was being spent with officers deliberately taking all this time off the streets, they would squirm, he thought.

One dark, cold and rainy night as Tom stood in the shadows of a shop doorway attempting to keep dry, a silver-coloured Jaguar car approached at speed, braked suddenly and mounted the pavement just feet from where he stood. He approached the driver just as he was getting out. The man, who was about fifty years old, over six feet tall and well built, hadn't seen him in the shadows.

'In a hurry, sir?' Tom asked.

The man, dressed in a pinstripe suit, was visibly shaken by Tom's presence and said, 'I'm late, officer, have to meet a colleague in the club.' Tom could smell from his breath that the man had been drinking.

'Have you been drinking, sir?' he asked, knowing quite well that he had.

The man stuttered, 'God, officer, I'm a businessman, I can't afford to lose my licence. Please let's be sensible about this.' At that, he took a roll of money out of his jacket and pushed it into Tom's breast pocket.

'Surely we can be friends, officer. Have a drink on me, eh?' He then said, 'I don't want to upset you, but we're both men of the world, just let's forget you ever saw me,' and before Tom could utter a word, he walked off.

Tom's first reaction was to run after him, the cheeky bastard, but, realising no one was around, he stepped back into the doorway.

He counted the money later in an alleyway; there was thirty pounds, about what he earned in a month.

The world is a venal place, he thought, *and greed is just a basic drive; nothing much wrong with it, it just needs to be organised, regulated and directed properly. Anyway, there's not a lot of glory in arresting the man for having a drink.* The police force was definitely nothing like *Dixon of Dock Green,* he now realised.

The chance meeting with the man in the Jaguar was to be a big turning point in Tom's life, although he didn't know it at the time.

Tom was instructed one afternoon to go and see the superintendent. 'You're getting some excellent arrests, Sharkey, but being an ex-traffic man myself I would like to see you getting more summonses for traffic offences. You'll have to broaden your outlook if you wish to advance in this job,' the super said.

Tom thought, *What a plonker, but he'll have traffic offences if he wants them.*

He was not a happy chap as he sat in his panda car and watched as traffic began to back up on the Outer Circle route. He went to investigate the cause, and discovered it was a number eleven bus travelling at about ten miles per hour that was causing the long tailback. He was not happy, and followed the bus to Six Ways where it pulled in at the bus stop. He approached the bus driver. 'What do you think you're playing at? I've a good mind to book you for obstruction,' snapped Tom.

'I was early, officer, so I was killing time,' the driver replied.

'In future when you're early just wait at the stop, then,' Tom said, calming down a little. But following the super's bollocking, he booked him; normally he would have just cautioned him.

***

As time went on, Tom learned that having the black on people paid excellent dividends, whatever your position. It had worked well for him with the garage store manager, the inspector at the training school, and now his own inspector at the station. His latest intelligence had been gained while on night duty, when he had come across the inspector with a young lady in the supervision car, parked up in a dark side street. Tom kept the car under observation, and waited until they were in a compromising situation before he approached them.

He shone his torch into the car and, startled by the light, they tried to cover up their embarrassment. But Tom just walked away without saying a word. He now had the inspector where he wanted him, right in the net.

Sergeant Jock Green also got a surprise on one of his nights off duty, because Tom had received a little bit of information on the bastard. Green was working on the side as a security guard, which was against regulations. Tom didn't much care; he probably needed the money.

It was the look on his face as he approached him, and said sarcastically, 'Hello sarge, doing a bit on the side, eh?' that brought Tom a sense of deep satisfaction.

The sergeant was dumbfounded, and took a while to answer. 'Tom, mate, how are you? I'm just helping a pal out. You won't say anything will you?'

'As if I would. I was just passing and thought it was you I saw.' Tom knew a lot of officers were doing something on the side to earn extra cash. He just wanted to have something on him.

Tom never again mentioned the incidents to the individuals involved, but they must have appreciated his discreetness, because they started to show him much more respect. Whether it was through fear or admiration, Tom didn't care. The balance of power had shifted, and that felt good.

On one round of night duty Tom and another constable were assigned to guarding a prisoner in the General Hospital who was being treated for injuries he had sustained during a burglary. The prisoner had been breaking into a factory when he had fallen through the roof and injured his back.

The only thing that broke the boredom was when one of the nursing staff brought a portable television into the ward. They were all glued to the screen as they watched the first men landing on the moon. It was a pleasure to observe an event that was wholly positive, because as a police officer Tom often had to witness scenes that were anything but.

One foggy evening, while chatting up a girl in the paper shop in Slade Road, Tom was directed by control to go to a house in Erdington where it was reported a woman was being hysterical. Arriving at the house he found the front door ajar and a woman screaming from inside.

He entered, cautiously, and saw her standing at the top of the stairs waving her arms about. Climbing the stairs, he tried to calm her down but she continued to scream, pointing into a bedroom. He went into the room but could see nothing suspicious.

The woman then pointed to under the bed, but looking underneath all Tom could see was a blanket. She continued to scream and point, so he leaned in and pulled the blanket out.

To his horror, the head of a young child rolled out of the blanket along the floor. He recoiled and stumbled away from the bed. He was nauseated and fearful of what else he was going to find. A terrible scene awaited him in the bathroom, where he found the remainder of the body. The woman, in a frenzy of temper, had chopped the head off her three-year-old son with a meat cleaver.

Struggling with his words Tom tried to calm her down, told her he was arresting her and then called for assistance. He felt desperately sorry for the woman, she must have been very distressed to have killed her own child. She obviously needed some kind of help that she wasn't getting.

Back at the station Tom was told by the inspector to return to the house and accompany the boy's body to the central mortuary to prove continuity. Tom was not looking forward to going back to the house, and was shocked at just how quickly a life had become nothing more than an object in a criminal case.

At the mortuary, still in a state of shock, he identified the body for the pathologist. It was the first time that he'd had to attend a post-mortem and he found it very emotional and daunting. He had tears in his eyes as he watched the procedure.

Three stainless steel tables stood in the room, each with gutters running along the edges and drain holes in the corners. There was a smell of death and industrial strength disinfectant, and he had to wear a gown and boots. He wondered how people could work with dead bodies all the time, but he knew he must get used to periodic exposure to it, as the experience would be invaluable to him in the CID.

***

Tom missed his nights on the town while working shifts, and it pissed him off a bit seeing everyone enjoying themselves. Working the evening 2.00 pm to 10.00 pm shift one Friday, bored to death with nothing happening, he stood watching the people coming and going at the Elbow Room club, and wished he could join them. He saw two detectives going into the club and envied them. *That's what I want, the lucky buggers,* he thought.

Then he spotted a man acting suspiciously. He watched him come from the back of some shops close to the club carrying a sack, and go to a Transit van and place the sack in the back. As soon as he got into the van and started it Tom stepped into the road and stopped him. The guilty look on the driver's face said it all.

'What have you just put into the back of the van?' Tom asked.

'Only my tools from work, officer,' the man replied.

'Let me have a look then.' In the rear of the van Tom found the sack full of new electrical appliances.

He arrested the man for breaking into the electrical shop, and then thought about the terrible state the van was in. It only had one headlight; the brake lights and the rear number plate light didn't work either. There were two bald tyres, and the man didn't have a driving licence or insurance. *An arrest for theft, and multiple offences under the Road Traffic Act and the Construction and Use Regulations. That should help satisfy the super,* he thought.

Several weeks later, Tom was given the job of Acting Sergeant. He wore the two stripes on his arm with great pride, and had much more freedom to move around the sub-division and do what he wanted. He relished the power it gave him.

Accepted more now by the inspector and sergeants, he was even invited to join them in a game of snooker. It did seem a little strange at first, being in a position to order his colleagues on the shift around, but they seemed to respect his position and never questioned his authority.

Chapter 15

Several months now passed, and because he was qualified for promotion Tom was given a twelve-month attachment to the Divisional Plain Clothes Department (DPCD). The system was that anyone waiting for promotion was given as many attachments to various departments as possible, to widen their experience before being promoted. Tom wanted the CID, but knew he would have to be patient.

He immediately went to work with Sergeant Tony Brown, and two other constables at the DPCD. Tony Brown was very pale, overweight and almost bald. He had a genial, avuncular way about him and had a great sense of humour. A married man with three children, he liked to get home and see them at every possible opportunity. Born in Yorkshire, Tony had come to Birmingham ten years earlier to take up a career in the force. He seemed to have very little ambition and was happy doing what he was doing.

'Welcome to the department, Tom. I don't stand any bullshit, just call me Tony. We're like a close family here,' Sergeant Brown said. He and Tom soon hit it off, and became close friends both on and off duty.

The duties of the DPCD included enforcing the licensing and gaming laws, controlling prostitution, and the investigation of offences involving indecency. These areas of policing held far more interest for Tom, and to get out of uniform was a real bonus.

There was another perk for Tom, too. One of their duties was to parade at Villa Park on the days Aston Villa were playing their home games. They were deployed in the crowd to keep observations for troublemakers. But Tom was able to enjoy the matches, especially so when they were playing the best teams.

The sub-divisional superintendent, Matthew Blake, summoned the team to his office one day. 'We have had several complaints from the local residents regarding men using the toilets in the high street as a meeting place for homosexual practices,' he said.

'I want your department to keep observations there, and arrest the persons responsible. I want it stopped, do you understand, stopped.'

'Yes, sir, we'll start on it at the weekend,' Tony replied.

That afternoon, Tom went along with Tony to examine the toilets, and they discovered four men talking inside. Two of the men were in cubicles talking to each other and the other two were using the urinals. When the two men using the urinals saw Tom and Tony they shut up and quickly moved out.

There was a third, unused, cubicle which Tom entered. He sat on the seat, and saw that a hole had been knocked in the adjoining wall. After a few seconds, a hand came through holding a note.

It read, 'You want some fun?' Tom stood on the toilet seat, looked into the next cubicle, and saw the man masturbating. The startled occupant quickly rose and hurriedly left the toilets, followed by the second man from the other cubicle.

On examining the cubicles Tom and Tony found that large holes had been knocked in the adjoining walls between all the cubicles.

'We need to start our observations as soon as possible, Tony,' Tom said.

'You're right. When do you think?' asked Tony.

'Let's start Friday night,' Tom replied, feeling assertive and enjoying the fact that his opinion was being sought by a sergeant, with whom he shared rank in all but name. They agreed to begin their observations in earnest on the Friday night.

When Friday night came, Tony decided to go into the toilets and see what was happening. Several minutes passed and Tom saw a man come out and stand by the door, followed by Tony. The sergeant made a signal to Tom and walked away. They both then watched the man go back inside again.

Tony grunted. 'That cheeky bastard is at it, Tom, he was smiling at me and playing with himself. I'm going back in and if he propositions me I'll nick him for importuning.' Tom waited several more minutes before Tony re-emerged from the toilets. This time he held the man by the arm, and said, 'I've arrested him for importuning for immoral purposes. Put him in the car.' Back at the nick they charged and processed him.

The following day they returned to the toilets, only to find the cubicles completely empty, and they soon discovered why. Corporation workmen had been in and put metal plates over the holes. Tom thought the superintendent had likely been on to the council to complain, and had cocked up their operation in the process. 'Only one thing for it, Tom, I'll bring my hand drill tonight and make a peephole between the cubicles, so we can see what's going on,' Tony said.

In the early hours of Sunday morning they returned and locked themselves in two of the cubicles. Tony began to drill, and as soon as the tip came through Tom blew down the hole to clear it out. A scream came from Tony in the other cubicle.

'You've blinded me!' He had just put his eye to the hole as Tom blew and had got an eyeful of plaster. Tom couldn't stop laughing, but Tony didn't see the funny side of it.

Modifications complete, they left the toilets, planning to return later. Apart from Tony's bad eye, it had been a successful operation. At about seven o'clock that evening they returned to the toilets, and this time found one man in the middle cubicle. They entered the empty cubicles either side and waited.

Within minutes a note came over the partition to Tom. It read: 'Come round here if you fancy some fun.' After Tom made no reaction, a second note came over: 'If you would rather go to my car, follow me out, it's only down the street.' Tom looked through the peephole, and saw a middle-aged, well-dressed man masturbating.

Tom stood on the seat and looked over. The man said, 'Do you want this?' indicating his erect penis.

At that moment Tony's head appeared above the other cubicle, and he said, 'We're police officers, please come outside.'

It was some time before the man reluctantly emerged from the cubicle, and said, 'Show me some identification.' He was shown the two police warrant cards, and said, 'I have friends in high places, you'll regret this.'

Tom thought, *Why do they all say that?*

As they were escorting the man outside, he began to shout. 'Kidnap! They're kidnapping me, help!' Unfortunately for Tom and Tony, running past at that particular moment was a local rugby team out training. They naturally took the man's side and bundled on top of them. It was some time before Tom and Tony could persuade them that they really were police officers making an arrest.

The man turned out to be a local estate agent, married with two children and living in what was doubtless a massive house in the well-to-do area of Four Oaks. The man was charged and bailed to appear at Birmingham Magistrates' Court the following morning.

Later, when Tom related the story of the rugby team to his colleagues back at the station they all fell about laughing. Tony wanted to get off home to his wife and kids, so Tom gave the man a lift to verify his address. On the way, the man quizzed him as to what would happen at court the next day.

Tom explained. 'As you've not been in trouble before, it won't take long if you plead guilty. I'll give the brief facts to the court and you will most likely be fined, as simple as that.'

'Will there be any press there?' the man asked.

'I'll look after you, make sure it's done as quietly and as quickly as possible,' Tom said.

'Do you have to tell my wife what this is all about? If you could avoid it, I'll owe you one, officer, I promise,' the man pleaded.

Tom didn't like what the man had done, and would have liked to expose him for it, but then thought he might just need a favour in the near future, so agreed to help him. He was thinking seriously of buying a flat, and who better now to help him find one at a sensible price than a friendly estate agent. Tom stayed in the car and watched the man enter the house by use of his key; he was satisfied he lived there and saw no need to talk to the man's wife.

Next morning the case went as Tom had explained and the man was fined. Many weeks later, Tom went to the estate agent's office, and left having agreed to purchase his first property at an exceptionally affordable price. The man had looked after him as promised.

Tom had bought a two-bedroom flat in a quiet cul-de-sac in a fashionable area of Erdington, where most of the neighbours were elderly men or women living on their own, their partners having passed away. The flat was badly run-down and he had to do a lot of work to it to get it up to scratch, but when he had finished it was worth a great deal more than he had paid for it.

***

During his time on the plain-clothes squad he found dealing with prostitutes quite humorous at times; most of them were friendly, plain, working-class women who liked a laugh, but for various reasons ended up working on the streets.

The situation he didn't appreciate, was where the pimps bullied them into doing it, and then lounged around in bed until lunchtime while living on their earnings. The pimps were often harsh in their treatment of the girls, dishing out brutal beatings for no reason and depriving them of any personal cash.

Tom met one such girl in the Last Chance cafe in Lichfield Road one lunchtime, when he had called in to see the owner to discuss the licence for the one-arm bandit. The girl approached him. 'You're one of the coppers who chase us around, aren't you?' she asked.

He saw that she had a black eye, and her bottom lip was split. 'What if I am? Anyway, what have you been doing to your face?' he asked.

'Look, no bullshit, are you a copper or not?'

He indicated that he was, and she whispered, 'Buy me a cuppa and bring it over to the corner; I want to talk to you.' Sitting in the quiet corner, she said, 'I'm Rita and I'm worried sick. My pimp is knocking me about. But I'm really terrified for my two young children.' She told Tom that she was prepared to set her pimp up, and do whatever was necessary to have him locked away.

Tom learned that she worked from home, where she lived with her two children, and Leroy, her pimp. She had to work every evening and give her earnings to Leroy, who would then go out to the clubs for most of the night.

'When he does get home he wakes me up and gives me a beating, I've had enough. I'm scared he'll kill me, I need your help,' she pleaded.

Tom found his anger rising, clenching his fists as he listened to her story. 'I'll do what I can to help but it will take time to organise. I'll contact you later.' he said. He left her knowing that he had a lot of research to do, but he would help her, there was no question of that. Tom knew his own morals were questionable at times, but there were lines that he believed should never be crossed, and beating up women was definitely one.

Tom checked out Leroy and discovered he had previous convictions for living on immoral earnings. He owned a new Ford Capri motor car which he had bought for cash even though he was apparently jobless and collecting the dole – all good evidence to count towards a conviction.

An observation point was set up in the upstairs window of a house opposite Rita's. Tony, Tom and the other two DPCD constables, Brian and Sam, took it in turns to keep watch on Rita while she worked for two evenings.

Registration numbers of clients' cars were taken; their times of arrival and departure, and their descriptions, were all recorded as evidence. At one point, Leroy was seen through an upstairs window to catch Rita by the hair while smacking her round the head. He left the room making angry gestures, and clearly still shouting at her.

You nasty bastard, Tom thought.

On the morning of the day they intended to strike, a warrant was sworn out before the magistrates, and Tony briefed a team of uniform officers on what their duties would be once inside the house. Rita worked hard that night; in two hours she entertained eight clients in her home, while Leroy rested.

God, she must be sore, Tom thought.

When the order was given to go in, Rita was caught with a customer who had his trousers around his ankles, and Leroy was arrested in the next room where he had been watching television. Having been told by Tony the nature of the intrusion, Leroy protested that, 'I don't know what she gets up to.'

The most disturbing moment for Tom was finding the two young children still fully clothed and asleep in each other's arms, standing upright against an armchair. They were taken away by a policewoman to a place of safety and to be examined by a police surgeon. Tom reflected on how, by assisting Rita, he may have helped change their world for the better, too. It felt good.

Next afternoon, Rita went to the police station to make a comprehensive statement regarding her relationship with Leroy. Sitting in the small, cramped office warmed by the sun, the stench from her prompted Tom to try and open the window even wider than it was. 'Doesn't my fanny stink,' Rita remarked, as the young policewoman present turned away in embarrassment.

When they were done with the statement, Rita asked Tom what his name was. 'I have a bit of information, Tom, that you might be interested in,' she said.

'What is that?' he asked.

'There is a young girl, about seventeen, who lives next door to me. She tells me everything. Anyway, two or three times a week an old guy with plenty of dosh pulls up in his Rolls Royce and she gets in. She gets her tits out and gives him a blow job.' She continued. 'He never shags her, but gives her thirty quid a time. If you want the number of his car I can get it for you.' Tom told her to find it out for him.

He wasn't really that interested, but decided he would like to know who the rich old man was. Leroy was later charged with living on the immoral earnings of Rita, still protesting his innocence. At his trial at Birmingham Crown Court he pleaded guilty and was sentenced to three years in prison. Tom was happy to have helped Rita and hoped that her situation would now improve.

About a week after the trial, Brian and Tom were on patrol in Albert Road when they spotted a young woman touting for business. She was in her mid-thirties, good-looking with an excellent figure, and dressed in an expensive two-piece suit. Most people would have taken her for a successful businesswoman. They had not seen her before and Tom thought she looked like a lamb going to the slaughter.

Brian sat in the front seat of the Austin A40 they were using as cover for their red-light operation, while Tom lay under a coat in the rear. The woman approached the driver's window. 'Looking for company?' she asked.

'Jump in,' Brian said, throwing open the passenger door.

Once she was seated, Tom put his hand on her shoulder. 'You're under arrest for soliciting,' he said.

She almost jumped out of her skin. 'So that's what you do down here in Birmingham.'

Tom thought this an odd thing to say, because this same method was used by vice-squad officers the country over, and very few pros fell for it. He decided she was definitely new to the game.

They took her to the police station and she was shaking as they led her to an interview room. Tom could see that she was terrified. He checked her out for previous convictions: there were none. He then completed the standard antecedent form on her, using it as a starting point to find out more about her.

At that moment Sam, the other constable of the team, walked in wearing a doctor's white coat, which he must have found in the medical examination room.

'I'm Doctor Rose, I need to examine you, please strip off,' he said.

Before either of them could stop and explain that it was joke, the woman stood up and pulled her jumper over head, revealing a pair of beautifully shaped breasts. Tom was not happy and felt embarrassed for the woman. He was now convinced she was out of place on the streets, she was too naïve. He was intrigued, and decided he would have to find out more about her.

After officially cautioning her for the offence, Tom explained to her that he would have to escort her home to establish her address. Once in the car, she began to sob. 'I'm a fool, what am I going to do?' she asked.

'What do you mean?' said Tom.

He was curious and, against regulations, decided to take her for a drink while she explained how she had arrived in Birmingham a week earlier and ended up as a prostitute.

Her name was Pauline McClurg, a company secretary who had quarrelled with her husband and run away from home.

'What do you mean? Have you just left your old man?' he

asked.

She told him that her husband was a very rich and successful businessman in Manchester. The problem was that he was also a very jealous and violent man who beat her up on a regular basis.

'I couldn't stand it anymore. I was dreading him coming home and having a go at me,' she explained.

'So, he was beating you up for no apparent reason?'

'He has a terrible temper. I'm so scared of him. I made the decision to get away,' she said, with tears in her eyes.

'Where are you staying now?'

'I've booked into a small hotel in Handsworth Wood, but I've come away with very little money. It was a spur of the moment thing. I was desperate, that's why I tried this stupid thing tonight. God, will anyone find out?' she sobbed.

'So you haven't had any customers tonight,' Tom said.

'No, I'm stupid, a real stupid fool. I'm no prostitute,' she said.

Tom took her to the hotel and settled her into her room, and said, 'Ring me on this number tomorrow and I'll see what I can do to help.' Tom was curious. *What an unusual woman to be soliciting in the street,* he thought.

Early next morning he was woken when she called, and he arranged to meet her for a drink. He gave her directions to a local pub. They met at one o'clock in the White Swan, and she looked the picture of elegance, her hair done up on top, her face made up to perfection, and he thought, *This can't be the same person who was soliciting last night.*

They had a soft drink and discussed her current situation. Taking pity on her, Tom invited her to move into his flat until she could find a job and a place of her own. Her situation reminded him very much of his mother and Oliver back home, and he wanted to help.

Then he thought, *Christ, the second P… or was it really?* Next day she moved into his spare room, but because of the unusual way they had met, and Pauline's situation, there was no intimate relationship involved.

Within days she got employment as a store assistant with Rackhams, and she and Tom rarely saw each other, except at the breakfast table on the odd morning. A week later, around midnight while he lay in bed, he heard the door of the flat close, and then Pauline's voice: 'Are you asleep, Tom?' She came into his bedroom, sat on the edge of the bed, and said, 'Tom, I must thank you. You've been so good to me.'

Realising that she was quite intoxicated, he said, 'You would have done the same for me in the same situation. I know you would.'

'You just don't know what you've saved me from. If he ever finds me, he'll kill me, I know he will,' she whispered.

Tom took her in his arms and drew her close, kissing her on the forehead. She cuddled up to him, fully clothed, and they must have dropped off to sleep together because next morning that's how they woke up. They had a close relationship but still there was no sexual involvement. Tom viewed her more as a sister, and wanted to care for her.

At the nick next day Tom rang one of his opposite numbers in the Manchester vice squad and related the story to him, asking him to check out Pauline's old man.

'Did you say Harry McClurg?' he asked.

'Yes, supposed to be a big businessman up there,' Tom said.

'Jesus, mate, don't get involved, he's a real villain, into everything; he is the local backer up here for drugs, armed robberies and anything else you can think of, his business is just a front.'

Tom thanked him, and thought, *That's all I need.* Tom knew that it would not take her husband long to track Pauline down through the social services or any police contacts he might have in Manchester.

Pauline didn't appear to be aware of the nature of McClurg's business dealings. She just thought that he was a bad-tempered old bugger at times and took his moods out on her. She told Tom she had loved McClurg very much when they first met and got married, but she was not sure any more; she was always frightened of what mood he might be in when he came home.

Again, the relationship between Pauline and her husband made Tom think of his mother and Oliver, and he sat down and wrote his mother a long letter. He told her how he was getting along, and all about the antics he got up to, but he never mentioned Pauline. He also told her that he was thinking of coming home for a holiday. Maybe this was a twang of conscience.

Chapter 16

A new police station had now been built in Queens Road to replace the old Victoria Road station, and the DPCD had been given instructions to transfer over anything that was needed. The new station was installed with modern equipment and was a much more pleasant place to work.

A week later, Tom received a letter from his mother. She had received several threats from a paramilitary group, stating, 'We believe your son is serving as a British copper, we will be watching for him,' and was keen to let Tom know that, in her opinion, it wouldn't be safe for him to go home at that time.

Tom didn't like that. *Nobody is going to stop me going home to see my mother,* he thought, and immediately began to plan what he was going to do about it. He was not going to be bullied by anyone.

He decided to leave it for a few weeks and tell no one except Tony Brown, not even his mother. He would catch the ferry to Belfast, and then the train down to Derry. That way there was little chance of anyone finding out about his visit. He told Pauline he had to go away for a few days, and asked her to look after the place.

He purchased a little ornament for his mother from Lewis's – she loved that kind of thing – packed only a small holdall, and headed off to Heysham. It was Autumn and term-time, so the ferry to Belfast was very quiet and no one took any special notice of him in his anorak and jeans.

Arriving in Derry late afternoon, he caught a taxi to the Creggan, explaining to the driver that he was a merchant sailor home on leave. It was dark as he walked the last half-mile home, with his hood practically covering his face.

He approached the back door of the house quietly, hoping his mother was in, and tapped gently so as not to attract the attention of the neighbours. He knew he could trust the immediate locals, but Tom didn't intend to let anyone know of his arrival, just in case the wrong people found out.

His mother opened the door, and stood completely shocked at the sight of him. She threw her arms around him in a fierce hug. He had to push her gently backwards into the kitchen before anyone saw them.

Tears ran down her cheeks as she tried desperately to articulate the mass of questions clearly crowding her head. Her first words were, 'You've lost weight, aren't they feeding you over there?' followed by, 'God, it's great to see you, son.'

'Ma, I'm well, how are you?' he asked.

'Much better for seeing you, son.' She hugged him again.

They had a lot of catching up to do; how were his brothers, how was Tilly getting on, and what about Aunt Bet and Uncle Harry in Donaghadee?

In her homely kitchen she soon brought him up to date with all the gossip, as she bustled about preparing food and drink for him. He could see the fear in his mother's eyes as she told him it was not safe for him to be home.

'There are riots nearly every single day, Tom. Many people are being injured daily. It's out of control,' she said.

'I'll be all right, Ma. No one knows I'm here and I'll be very careful,' he replied.

Next day, Tom didn't leave the house, but watched all the neighbours coming and going. How things had changed in his absence. That evening, against his better judgement, he took a big chance and went to the outskirts of the city for a drink with his two brothers and Dave Parkhill. The pub was well away from their neighbourhood, and in an area where they believed no one would know him. They all assured him that he would be safe there with them. His mother reluctantly accepted the idea, after trying hard to talk him out of going. He could tell she was worried to death for his safety.

In the dark and dingy pub nobody took any notice of him, and he thought, *You don't have to be away long before you're forgotten,* but at that moment in time he knew it was for the best.

The only time he felt any fear was when he went to the toilet and two men followed him in. He could feel the goose pimples rise on his body, and his hands were cold and clammy as he shook his prick. Safely back in the lounge, he felt very relieved that nothing had happened.

Tom could feel the tension in the neighbourhood; everyone was on their guard, and his mother kept nagging him about not taking risks by going out. He decided after three days to only stay until he had seen Tilly, and promised his mother he would then return to England.

Early next morning, Tilly called at the house to see him. *She's a younger version of our mother,* he thought, as he hugged her tightly. They talked for hours, reminiscing about the old days when they were young children, and agreeing on how lucky they both were now. Tom asked her if she had heard anything of Nina, but there was nothing known of her whereabouts. He also wanted to visit his young sister's grave before he left, but his mother insisted it was too risky. Tom felt annoyed but, reluctantly, didn't go anywhere near the graveyard.

That evening, after Tilly had gone, he gave his mother some money to spend and enough to have a telephone installed. He kissed her goodbye under a dark sky, shook hands with his brothers, and headed off to catch the train to Belfast. His mother sobbed uncontrollably as he left, and he told her he would send her a ticket to come and stop with him for a while.

At the station in the Waterside two men approached him, and his heart missed a beat as he thought the worst.

'Where are you going?' one of them enquired, as they both stood close to him.

He thought, *Should I make a run for it, or front them out?* Then decided to stay put. 'Who wants to know?' he asked.

'Detective Constable Green, RUC,' one of them replied. Tom sighed with relief, told them who he was and explained his fears. The officers wished him a good journey back to Birmingham.

When he got back to his flat he found a note from Tony Brown telling him to report to the nick at seven o'clock the following morning. Miners were picketing the gasworks in Saltley as part of a national strike, and he was to report in uniform. He had to find his uniform and iron it, as it had been dumped in the bottom of his wardrobe for several months.

Early next morning, he reported with his colleagues to Nechells Green police station and the officer in charge of manning the strike. They were then formed into a unit, and all taken in a coach to Saltley gasworks where the strike was in full flow. At times it was a frightening and dangerous experience, with so few officers trying to hold back so many miners.

A few times they were nearly pushed under the wheels of the lorries as the drivers tried to get in and out of the gasworks gates. It was a struggle to hear anything above the angry noise of the jostling mob, and their violent outbursts when a lorry arrived. The battle continued for a week, but between the bouts of pushing and shoving there was quite a bit of friendly banter between some of the miners and the police.

Occasionally, the miners offered the officers a drink of tea from their flasks. Tom and his colleagues were ferried to a local school where they would be fed and watered, before returning to the strike. Food was plentiful, and Tom would bring a few sandwiches back and offer them to some of the miners. He could sympathise with them, having heard some of their stories. They would tell him of how they would have to travel up to four or so miles of tunnel underground, just to get to work. Often, they were forced to strip naked and wade up to their waists in water, carrying their grub in plastic bags which they then had to hide up high, away from the rats. It was a terrible, shitty job, but Tom knew the police had to do their duty. He was happy when the strike ended and he could get back to normal duties again.

A few days later, Pauline told him that she was leaving to go and live with her workmate, Avril. Tom got the impression that she really didn't want to leave but, although he didn't show it, he was relieved.

Upon leaving, she said, 'I'll keep in touch, Tom, thanks for all you've done. I'll miss you; you're a real friend,' and kissed him. Tom knew he would miss her company; she was an intelligent and glamorous woman, with a marvellous personality.

Back at work, Tom was met by an anxious Tony Brown. 'Trouble, Tom. Some smart arsehole has written to the chief constable about Charlie's shebeen.' The blues party was run every Saturday night in Albert Road, with the unofficial approval of Tony. It kept all the noisy, drinking revellers together in one building. Less trouble, Tony would say, and Charlie kept them informed of what went on.

The parties were, of course, unlawful; prostitutes and their pimps would go there partying all night. Cans of lager, and glasses of whiskey and rum were sold without a licence, and Charlie made an excellent living.

Tony, Tom, and the rest of the lads from the DPCD would go there, have free drinks all night and tuck into a good goat curry at the end of it all. Well, that was what the others thought, but Tom had in fact got much closer to Charlie. For covering his back, and making sure there was no police interference, he was paid a good backhander every week.

'We'll have to go and visit the complainant, see what we can do,' Tony said.

The following lunchtime they went along and saw the elderly man who lived three doors from the party. He had become fed up with the regular late-night noise, and the comings and goings at all hours.

'I wrote to the chief constable because I could get no satisfaction from the local police,' he said, meaning the local uniform lads.

Tom thought, *We know why.*

They painstakingly took details of the incident and promised the gentleman they would do everything in their power to stop the parties. Next stop was to see Charlie, and tell him that he could not hold a party that Saturday night. 'Just give it up for a few weeks and everything should be all right,' Tom said. The party was stopped, for that Saturday night at least.

Tom and Tony returned on the Monday morning to see the complainant. He was very pleased, thanked them for their assistance, and informed them that he would write again to the chief, this time to thank him. 'I'll give him your names, you've done a marvellous job, officers, thank you both,' he said.

Tom liked that. The chief might just remember him in the future, although he doubted it. Returning to the station, Tony completed a report and forwarded it to the chief superintendent, marked: 'For the attention of the chief constable'. Another happy customer, the chief should be pleased with them.

The duo then went to inform Charlie that he could start up again with the parties in two weeks' time, but that he must find new premises in the very near future. Charlie was happy again; he would continue to supply information and, of course, Tom was happy that his money would keep coming.

Tom's good mood only lasted until he got home at about midnight, however, when the phone rang. He answered, and a female voice said, 'Is that Tom Sharkey?' He replied, and she said, 'Tom, this is Avril, Pauline's flatmate, you remember Pauline?'

'Of course I do, what's happened?' he asked.

'Two men came to the flat this evening and dragged her away, said they were friends of her husband and everything would be all right. Pauline wasn't happy, and nor am I, but what should we do, Tom?' she asked.

Tom calmed Avril down and told her to leave it to him, he would find out what had happened to Pauline and keep her informed. Next morning, Tom contacted the police in Manchester and asked them to discreetly check if Pauline was all right. They came back to him later that afternoon to report that they had seen her, she seemed content with the situation and didn't wish to complain.

Tom knew that her husband had got to her, but there was very little he could do about it without her making an official complaint. She would have to make the next move. He wondered if that was the last he would hear from Pauline McClurg? He rang Avril, and explained everything to her.

Tom's attachment to the DPCD was about to come to an end, and he wasn't looking forward to going back on shifts in uniform. He was hoping that his CID attachment might come through sooner rather than later.

Chapter 17

Nine o'clock one morning a week later, and Tom sitting in the DPCD office, half asleep, with a hangover from the previous night and thinking he would have to pack the booze up. The door opened and in walked Detective Inspector Tommy Burns, his trousers held up with bright red braces and his half-moon spectacles perched on the point of his nose.

'Sharkey,' he said, 'do you still want to come attached to the CID?'

Tom jumped up. 'I certainly do, sir,' he exclaimed.

'Right, you start on Monday week, report to me in my office at nine o'clock sharp,' he said, and left.

Tom felt quite dazed. His wish had come sooner than expected, and he was delighted; this was the first step towards fulfilling his ambition of becoming a detective constable. His hard work had paid off.

On the appropriate Monday morning, Tom reported as instructed to the detective inspector in his office. The inspector explained to him what he expected from him over the six months of his attachment: plenty of prisoners, but most of all he would have to prove he could cope with all the paperwork involved. Cases could be lost on poor paperwork.

'You can be the best detective in the world, but it counts for nothing if you can't document things properly,' he said.

Tom knew there was more than paperwork involved; he would

have to be accepted by the office and to get this acceptance he would have to be susceptible to their education, otherwise he would be rejected.

This education would cover many things, from bending the rules where necessary while still surviving, to being very discreet and loyal to his colleagues in all types of situations. It would also involve how to become a good detective, which could only be learned from more experienced colleagues.

Tom was introduced to Detective Sergeant Raymond Mason, better known as Ray to his friends and his senior officers. Tom would not yet have that privilege, and would have to call him sergeant.

DS Mason was in his mid forties, proportionally built, and good-looking with well-groomed silver hair. He was educated, well spoken, full of confidence, and dressed immaculately. Tom quite envied him.

'Sit down. Tom, isn't it?' he said.

'Yes, sergeant,' he replied.

The DS continued. 'Well, Tom you will work on my team with Detective Constables Danny Black and Peter Kirby. You've come to us with a good recommendation, so it's up to you to prove your worth.' Then he took him into the general CID office and introduced him to all the staff who were present.

'This is Tom Sharkey, our new attached man,' he said.

Tom had met most of the others before on his travels around the division, but there were still handshakes all round. Danny Black took him firmly by the hand and slapped him on the back. 'Welcome to the mad house, Tom,' he said, laughing.

Danny was a real Brummie and had a heart of gold, but his dress sense left a lot to be desired. He was about six feet two inches tall, going bald on top, had a broken nose and was built like a tank. He had a Pancho moustache and his stomach hung out over his trousers where his shirt buttons were undone. *This is the kind of man you need behind you if you ever get in trouble,* Tom thought.

Peter, on the other hand, was a much smaller man who was very thin, pale-faced and wore glasses. He was extremely confident, and Tom could tell he was the brains behind Danny. He later found out that Peter was an engineering graduate and was destined for the higher ranks of the service.

The CID office was long and narrow with desks placed along each wall, each workspace with its own telephone. Papers were strewn about on most of the desks, with some stacked in precarious piles, and one of the officers was typing with two fingers trying to complete a report on an old typewriter.

'Tom, I'm going to a burglary, just been reported this morning, come with me,' Danny said. They went along to the reported burglary at a semi-detached house in a good area of Erdington. The occupier of the house, a white man in his late forties, invited them in and pointed to a broken pane of glass in the rear door.

'They broke the glass and put their hand through and opened the door,' he said.

'Anything stolen?' asked Danny.

'Just the new television,' the man replied.

Tom examined the broken window. 'Are you insured?' he asked.

The occupier told him that he was insured, and while Danny wrote down all the details Tom went out into the rear garden to look for clues. He had made up his mind that this job was faked by the occupier to claim the insurance.

Tom walked to the end of the garden, and looking through the window of the shed he could see a large object covered with a sheet. It looked very much like a television. He returned to the house. 'I don't think you're telling us the whole truth, sir, are you. Come with me please,' he said, and escorted the man down the garden and made him open up the shed.

It was a lucky start for Tom when he discovered the television and arrested the man. This was an old trick used by many people to claim the insurance money and they were rarely caught, but like many before him this man hadn't the brains to think it through properly.

Back at the office the DS said, 'Excellent work, Tom, a good start.' Tom had noticed that the glass had obviously been broken from the inside and thought the man was a fool, but his bungled fake burglary had given Tom the start he wanted, and he wasn't about to draw attention to the ease which he'd been able to effect his first arrest.

'Thank you, sarge,' he simply said.

The DCI told Tom to come to his office one Friday afternoon a couple of weeks later. 'Go over to the off licence and get a bottle of scotch and a dozen cans of beer and bring them to me,' he said, handing Tom a wad of cash. Tom returned to the office with the gear to discover the DI, the DSs and a few of the DCs gathered there. Glasses were waiting to be filled and Tom discovered that this was a regular Friday afternoon event, and this was his first invite. It was a sort of unofficial meeting where all sort of topics were discussed, and anything went.

During his six-month attachment Tom made many good arrests, fitted in well with the rest of the team, which was very important, and his paperwork appeared to pass all the tests because there were no complaints from the gaffers.

A week before he was due to finish, he had another stroke of good luck. Peter was to be promoted to uniform sergeant, which would leave a vacancy in the CID office. It was a case of being in the right place at the right time. The detective inspector summoned Tom to his office.

'Sharkey, you've had an outstanding attachment to the department. The DCI and I have discussed the matter and want you to fill the vacancy being left by Peter Kirby,' he said.

Tom felt like jumping up in the air and shouting with excitement, but just said, 'Thank you, sir, I could think of nothing better.' The detective superintendent would have the final word on the transfer, but would usually go along with the recommendation of the DI and DCI. Which he did.

As Tom sat in the pub that night with Danny, Peter and some of the others from the office celebrating Peter's and his own success, he thought, *I've arrived, thank you, God. Detective Constable Sharkey, you are on your way.*

The CID office was made up of three detective sergeants who each had three detective constables and an attached man. Tom knew most of the staff and found them a friendly bunch of people. He was really looking forward to working with them.

A few days later, and Tom was settling in well. The front office constable came into the office, and said, 'Tom, a young lady left these for you,' and handed him a carton of fresh-cream cakes.

He continued, 'Said she was from the Nat West Bank on the high street and you would know who she was. Oh, yes, and she said congratulations.' It was a cashier Tom had chatted up the last day he was at the bank. The one with the big brown eyes, whose father was one of the local licensees.

She had invited him to her twenty-first birthday party at the pub. Word that his face was now a permanent fixture on the team had obviously spread; the licensees were keen to protect their extra-curricular activities and made it their business to know who the local officers were, and keep them happy.

Tom went along to the party and took Danny. He introduced Danny to Sally, the birthday girl, who said, 'Thanks for coming, Tom.' Tom had really gone along to see one of the barmaids, named June, whom he had got to know and fancied more than Sally.

June was in her mid twenties, about five feet six inches tall, fair hair that hung in ringlets, and an impish face which seemed to say, 'You've got no chance, pal.' Tom saw her as a bit of a challenge.

Danny, realising that Tom was interested in June, said, 'Tom, you've got no chance, the local beat bobby is knocking her off.'

'Not that fat slob, Smith? Surely she doesn't fancy him, does she?' he asked.

But it was true.

What a waste, he thought.

Then Sally came to him. 'Can I have my birthday kiss, then?' she asked.

Tom gave her a kiss, and she whispered, 'Meet me outside.' She was obviously keen, so Tom decided that as he couldn't have June he might as well go with the flow with Sally. Outside, she stood in the car park in her party dress, a small black number with silver sequins dotted all over it. He took her to his car and did his best to seduce her.

He was doing quite well until someone opened the passenger door and began to drag her out. 'Come inside, and you leave her alone,' her father shouted. Her father was not impressed with him, and Tom could have said something but decided to keep quiet. She was old enough to make up her own mind, so he figured maybe he would have his chance with her another day.

Tom liked working with DS Mason and Danny; both were very experienced, professional detectives and he was learning a lot from them. He also knew that investigation was about instinct, imagination, sometimes guesswork and most times just plain good luck.

But you had to make your own luck, at times. Informants were vital; a detective was only as good as his sources, but you had to be in charge and have tight control over them.

Tom loved the thrill of the chase, the camaraderie among fellow officers.

While working in the department he sat and passed the promotion examinations for the rank of inspector, and was congratulated by the chief superintendent for gaining such a high pass mark.

Danny had taken a few days leave and Tom had to team up with DS Mason on the late shift, working two till ten. At seven o'clock, the DS said, 'Tom, get the car, were going out.'

He got the car and collected the DS, who directed him to drive to the local cinema. Tom parked the car in the car park and they went inside where he was introduced to the manager.

The DS led him upstairs to the balcony, where they took two seats. 'This is a good film, Tom, I've wanted to see it for some time,' the DS said. They sat there for nearly thirty minutes waiting for the film to start, when the DS said, 'Something's wrong, Tom. I'll go and see, you wait here.'

He was gone for about twenty minutes and returned with two bars of chocolate, which he handed to Tom. 'Enjoy the film, I'm going to operate the projector, the projectionist has walked out after a row. See you later,' he said.

The film started a short time later, and Tom sat back to enjoy it, thinking, *What a decent man the DS is.* When they got back to the nick, the DS told him to doctor his diary to show that they had both been on observations for burglars.

Every CID officer had to keep a diary of their movements each day, showing what exactly they did, where, and at what time they did it. These were examined each week by the detective inspector and provided a complete record of the officers' movements. It was also a back-up in case of any complaints made against an officer, who could identify exactly where they were and who they were with at any given time.

One thing Tom didn't like about the CID was the fact that you had to work many hours overtime each month before you could start to claim any payment; how unfair was that?

One morning, Tom went out with the DS for a run around the metal dealers to check their books. At the first yard, DS Mason said, 'Wait here, I have some business to discuss.' After a few minutes the police radio went off; it was an urgent message for the DS.

Tom went looking for his boss, and walked into the office just as the metal dealer was handing him some cash. They both looked at him, surprised, and the DS hurriedly putting the notes into his pocket.

Tom spoke first. 'There's a message for you on the radio, sarge.' He immediately recognised the metal dealer. It was the big man with the Jaguar, who had slipped the money into his pocket on that cold wet night months before.

The DS asked to use the telephone in the office, and so the big man and Tom walked outside.

'You don't remember me, do you?' Tom asked.

'I don't forget a face, young man,' he said, holding out his hand. 'I'm Jimmy Walker, welcome to the team,' he said, smiling.

Tom introduced himself and the man pushed a five-pound note into his hand. From that day on the DS took him round most of the metal yards and introduced him. He got five pounds, and the DS got ten every time they made a visit.

'We must trust each other, Tom, must stick together, that's the most important thing. Get your friends around you, know what I mean,' the DS said, as he winked at him.

Tom thought, *So that's the name of the game with the metal dealers; we don't look too hard at what they're up to, and they keep us sweet. No harm in that.*

He now also had some black on the DS, but imagined if his assessment of the man was right he would not have to use it. Tom decided to check out Jimmy Walker, as he liked to know exactly who he was dealing with.

He discovered that Jimmy Walker had been a hard man in his young days, and had been born in Dublin, although he had no trace of an Irish accent now. He had come across to Liverpool as a young boy, and had previous convictions for armed robbery. His last conviction was some twenty years ago, when he served five years in prison.

Since then he had been going straight; at least, he hadn't yet been caught in any wrongdoing. Walker reminded Tom very much of Kirk Douglas – he had the same rugged good looks – and was not a character you would wish to cross.

Continuing his research into Jimmy Walker, Tom soon discovered that he was one of the key organisers of crime in the Midlands, and had good connections. He was probably into most everything that went on, but made sure he never took an active part. If anyone got caught, Walker would help them out by whatever means he could. He had a lot of influence and a lot of black on a lot of people, including police officers, of course.

He always stayed on the right side of the law by putting in the odd decent job. Tom wanted to get as close to him as possible, and went out of his way to cultivate a relationship with him.

He also discovered that Jimmy Walker had a very useful vehicle at his disposal. Walker owned an old back taxi cab which he used for special occasions. It was never really noticed by anyone, including the police, and was never ever pulled over. It was a great asset to any setup. *That would come in handy for observations,* Tom thought.

Chapter 18

It was now 1974, and more changes were made to the force through amalgamation when the Birmingham City Police, and parts of the Staffordshire, West Midlands, and Warwickshire forces became the West Midlands Police. The changes made very little difference to Tom's role as a detective and life continued as normal.

It was summer and the weather was beautiful. Tom decided to invite his mother over for a short holiday and sent her the money for the airfare. He had taken a weeks' leave so that he could look after her and show her around. He met her at the airport and after hugs and kisses he took her to his flat.

'Tom, this is a beautiful place you have, and so well furnished. It must have cost you a fortune,' she said.

'You know me, Ma, work hard and live life to the full,' he said.

He took his mother to see Warwick Castle, for a boat trip on the river at Stratford-upon-Avon, and to the place she liked most, Cannon Hill Park, where all the flowers were in bloom. She loved flowers, and Tom bought her a bunch every single day while she was in the flat. He also took her to some of the best restaurants in town, but having simple tastes she ate only the simple dishes. She enjoyed shopping in the large stores without the threat of a bomb going off.

One night, sitting chatting, Tom decided to tell his mother of his relationship with Nina back in Ireland, and all that had gone on. He explained to her that she might very well be a grandmother. At first, she seemed annoyed with him but then her mood changed to one of sadness. He thought, *Typical of Ma.*

'Have you never heard from her since she left Ireland?' she asked.

'No, not a word, but I want to try and find her one day, Ma. I want to know if she had the child and if it was a boy or a girl. I want to know if they're well.'

'How will you ever find out?' she asked.

'When the time's right I'll try and find her, and when I do I'll let you know, Ma,' he replied.

At the end of a week he took her back to the airport and made sure she was checked-in properly. She hung on to him as he kissed her goodbye and tears flowed down her cheeks.

'Goodbye, Ma, I'll come and see you soon, I promise,' he said, and pushed a large envelope containing a sum of money into her hand.

He told her to open it when she was safely airborne, and waved to her as she climbed the steps to the plane. Tears were running down his face now, and he was burdened by that lonely feeling again.

***

The CID staff used the pub over the road from the nick and met there at about nine o'clock several evenings a week. Tom was taking his turn as the night duty detective starting at ten o'clock, but as everything was quiet on the sub-division he went to meet the gang. They stopped in after closing, and at about midnight Tom volunteered to run the two bar-staff home.

He dropped little Jack off first, and then took Maureen home. They had both had quite a bit to drink and, as they sat there chatting in the front of Tom's old Austin 1100, it wasn't long before they ended up in each other's arms.

Her tights and pants hung around one ankle and she had one shoe still on as they made love on the front passenger seat, she with her feet on the dashboard and he on his knees between her legs. It was what Tom would describe as a 'drunken shag', a quick on and off, no real thrills or passion involved.

Next night, Tom got a call from his opposite number on the adjoining sub-division who was also working nights. 'Hi, Tom, do you fancy a bit of rabbit hunting tomorrow night if it's quiet?' he said.

'Yes, where?' Tom said. His colleague told him that he had a rifle, and, if all was quiet, that they should meet at about four in the morning on the wasteground next to the Castle Vale estate. The next night, they met as arranged and were having a fine time shooting at the rabbits when Tom's radio went off.

Responding to it, he was informed that a burglary had just occurred on the Kingsbury Road, close to where they were. The intruder was described as a white teenager, wearing a light blue jacket and a baseball cap. Both men immediately jumped into the other officer's car, throwing the rifle on the rear seat.

Luck was on their side, because as they approached the address, there, running along the road towards them was the burglar carrying a sack. Tom jumped out of the car, ran after him, and caught him. He was quite sure he had nabbed the burglar.

'You're nicked, my friend,' Tom said, and placed him in the rear of the car, climbing in to sit beside him.

'Okay, okay!' the man panted, backing into the corner of the rear seat. 'I'll have the bloody burglary, but I'm not having the fucking firearm,' the burglar said, as he saw the rifle.

Well that was the quickest cough I've ever had, thought Tom.

***

Terrorism in the city, like everywhere else in the country, had become a big threat and security at the police station was being taken very seriously. The uniformed staff took it in turns to stand guard at the front and check everyone in and out.

One of the worst experiences of Tom's life was the bombing of two pubs in the city centre by the IRA, where twenty-one people were killed and many were badly injured. On the night of the bombings he was assigned with other officers to search numerous houses of suspects and IRA sympathisers in the West Midlands. Everyone worked twenty-four hours non-stop, and when Tom eventually got to bed he was completely shattered.

In the local supermarket two days later he got some very angry looks and comments from some of the customers when he spoke to the assistant. At first he couldn't understand what was happening, but then realised that it was his Irish accent and that they were associating him with the atrocity. He thought, *If only they knew what*

I'd been doing all that night, but he could understand their feelings.

One evening a few weeks later Tom was sitting in the office with Danny.

'I want you both here at six o'clock tomorrow morning,' DS Mason said. 'Big job with the Special Branch.' Tom assembled in the office next morning with DS Mason, Danny, the firearms team and two officers from the Special Branch.

'I'm DS Reynolds from Special Branch,' said one of the new faces. 'Following a tip-off we've been watching a house in Park Street. An Irish couple live there, and several men have been seen coming and going there over the past few days.' He continued, 'We intend to raid the house this morning, arrest the occupants and search the premises for any type of firearms, explosives or literature. Understood?'

They went to the house and took up positions, front and rear. The door was kicked in and an old lady in her nightdress appeared on the landing, screaming.

'Police! We have a search warrant, we're coming up,' the DS said, rushing up the stairs towards her.

The result wasn't quite what they expected and Tom felt very embarrassed, as did the rest of the team, when the old lady explained that she had just buried her husband the day before, and the men seen coming and going were attending his wake. The Special Branch had gone down in Tom's estimation. *How unprofessional,* he thought.

Work returned to normal and several weeks later Tom was

informed that he had been recommended for promotion to sergeant and had to attend headquarters to go before a board. An assistant chief constable and two chief superintendents interviewed him.

He thought he had done reasonably well, answering all their questions with some conviction. Experience meant a great deal in gaining promotion to the next rank, as did a good recommendation from your chief superintendent, both of which Tom had. He would now have to wait on the result.

While working in the CID, Danny Black and Tom became very close friends, socialising together in all the pubs and clubs used by the low life, and gaining a deep knowledge of what went on in the criminal circles.

DS Mason left them to their own devices and went about his business in his own way. The DS informed them that he was going for promotion to inspector and didn't want to get involved in any of the dealings any more, just in case it jeopardised his chances.

Tom knew that Danny was a very heavy drinker, and smoked about a hundred cigarettes a day. Tom liked a good drink himself, but he did worry about Danny's health. He got out of breath very easily and was putting on quite a bit of weight. Tom decided that he would have to have a serious talk with him at some point.

To be a good detective, Tom knew he had to have a wide knowledge of the criminals on his patch: where they hung out, their associates, friends, habits, their every move. It was necessary to put himself in their shoes and think like they did, and Tom's own past experiences helped him there.

Danny and Tom soon became accepted into the villains' company and never had to buy drinks in the various establishments they frequented. They were able to put the intelligence they collated to very good use, and as a result arrested several serious robbers and burglars.

Using the information gained, they were also able to recover a lot of stolen goods by arresting the handlers who were receiving it from the thieves. In this position, they could have their pick of the recovered property that could not be identified or returned to anyone.

They would keep some of this for their own use, such as jewellery, electrical goods and, of course, some of the cash recovered. Tom never felt bad about this. *The property will only go to the central store and be auctioned off if we don't take it,* he rationalised. The prisoners never complained; it wasn't their property after all, and they didn't really know what went on anyway.

Plus, it also saved a lot of time not having to book all the items of stolen property into the detained property store, which was a right pain and a waste of time when they could be out catching more criminals instead.

Tom knew he had to be very careful, and so he oversaw all the operations, with he and Danny always covering each other's backs. Remembering the chief superintendent's advice on the three Ps, everything was checked and double-checked so that there were no mistakes. No other officers were involved, just the two of them: no one else was trusted.

Five o'clock one morning, and Tom was woken up by the phone ringing.

Believing it was the office, he thought, *Shit, what do they want at this unearthly hour?* Putting the receiver to his ear he was surprised to hear Pauline McClurg's sobbing voice calling from Manchester. Her old man had been at it again, and had given her a real good hiding. He was now in bed asleep, but she sounded terrified.

'Tom, I need help, I don't know what to do. Is it possible to see you somehow?' she pleaded.

'I need time to think. Ring me back tonight and I'll arrange something,' he said.

'Please don't forget me, Tom,' she sobbed.

He assured her he wouldn't.

Chapter 19

Tom was sitting at his desk next morning and thinking what to do about Pauline when the phone rang. He was informed by the control room that a nasty burglary had taken place in Erdington, and the uniform had requested CID attendance immediately.

He went along to the scene, to be met by the duty inspector who told him that an eighty-year-old woman had been attacked in her home. The woman had been taken to hospital suffering from head wounds and was badly shaken up.

It seemed the intruder had climbed onto the flat kitchen roof at the rear of the house, broken the bathroom window, and climbed in. The old lady had disturbed him, and he had hit her. The burglary had been reported by the lady living next door when she had gone round to do her daily visit, found her injured neighbour, and called the emergency services.

The house was examined by the scenes of crime officers for fingerprints, and they also took samples of the broken glass from the bathroom window for comparison purposes should anyone be arrested.

The old lady was a tough old bird and, after treatment, was able to talk to Tom and Danny about what had happened.

The man responsible was white, about five feet six inches tall, of slim build, and spoke with an Irish accent, but it was doubtful that she would recognise him again. He had ripped her wedding ring from her finger and made her tell him where she had her money hidden. When she refused, he had punched her about the head and eventually she had given in to him. He had got away with about eight hundred pounds, her life savings, which she had kept in a shoebox in the bottom of her wardrobe.

Tom was determined that he was going to catch this bastard and send him down. Then, thinking of his mother, he said, 'When we catch this cunt I will rip his balls off, Danny.' Tom knew that, contrary to films and fiction books, this type of criminal very seldom outsmarted the law. The majority of them were usually cowards, uneducated, and drugged-up or drunk. When on a high they would leave several clues behind. Many were grassed up by their so-called friends; overall, very few could be classed as professional.

Enquiries to trace the criminal began, with Danny and Tom doing the rounds of the pubs and clubs to ask the necessary questions. The second-hand shops and pawnbrokers were also visited and given the description of the stolen ring.

Meanwhile, that night, Pauline rang Tom back and he arranged to travel up to Manchester on the train on the following Saturday and meet up with her. He didn't know exactly how he could help, but wanted to offer his support in any way he could.

Next day, he got a phone call from Joey Brown, one of his informants, and arranged to meet him in a pub straight away. Joey was a crook himself, but like all informants felt the need to keep in with the CID in case he needed a favour should he ever get locked up.

They met in a quiet corner of the pub. 'What have you got for

155

me, Joey?' Tom asked.

'A white youth called Phil Dooley from Nechells is spending well, and doing a bit of bragging about a good job he pulled,' Joey replied.

'Thanks, Joey. If you hear anything else give me a call,' Tom said, and slipped him a tenner before he left. If the information proved genuine, Tom would claim at least fifty pounds from the informants' budget.

He checked out Phil Dooley and found him to have convictions for burglary and assault. He looked a good candidate for this job, so he informed Danny. Six o'clock next morning Danny, Tom, and two uniform officers went to a flat in Doleman Street, Nechells, and arrested Dooley who was curled up in bed with his girlfriend.

'You're under arrest for burglary. Get dressed, you're coming with us,' Tom said, and cautioned him.

'I've done no burglary, you bastards. If you don't believe me ask her – I've always been with her,' he replied.

At that, Danny dragged him out of bed and threw him towards the door. 'Get dressed now, or you'll come like that,' he said. Dooley got the message and dressed himself.

Danny handed him off to the uniform officers and told them to hold him while they conducted a search. In Dooley's trouser pockets he found forty pounds rolled up. Tom searched the room and found a further three hundred pounds under the mattress. 'Where did all this money come from?' he asked.

'I won it on the dogs,' followed by, 'I want my solicitor,'

Dooley replied.

Back at the station, Dooley was booked-in to the office sergeant and a charge sheet was started. Then they took him to an interview room by the CID office where they would not be disturbed.

'We can now do this the hard way or the easy way, it's up to you.' Tom said.

'I've got nothing to say, I'm going straight now. You bastards are trying to fit me up,' Dooley replied.

'You haven't even asked us where the job was done yet, but I suppose you already know,' said Tom.

'I don't know what you're talking about,' Dooley raged back.

Tom struck him around the ear with the back of his hand, knocking him off the chair. He was quite happy being rough with his type, knowing full well he was responsible for doing the old lady. But Dooley still refused to talk so Danny caught him by the hair and lifted him off the floor, giving him a punch in the stomach. Dooley squealed, but still wouldn't admit to doing the job.

'Tell me the truth, you little cunt, or I'll rip your head off your shoulders,' Danny said.

'Go fuck yourself,' Dooley spat.

At that, Danny hit him a second time, knocking him off the chair again. But Dooley still refused to talk. Tom ordered him to take his clothes off and gave him a blanket to wrap up in. *There are two ways of skinning a cat,* he thought.

Tom had been back to the old lady's house and removed some of the remaining broken glass from the window ledge. He later rubbed some of this glass into the legs of Dooley's trousers before wrapping them up to be sent to the forensic science laboratory for analysis. He did this just in case Dooley had got rid of the trousers he was wearing at the time of the burglary – he was not going to let him get away with this.

Dooley still denied the burglary, but was later charged and kept in custody to appear before the magistrates' court the next morning. Tom went to court and queued up with the other detectives outside court number two to wait his turn.

The place stank of urine and vomit, as all the drunks and hard-cases from the night before waited to go before the magistrates. Tom objected to Dooley's bail on the grounds of the seriousness of the case, the possibility that he might interfere with witnesses, and that he might abscond: Dooley was remanded in custody for seven days.

That afternoon, Danny and Tom visited Dooley's girlfriend and his alibi was soon destroyed. She even gave them a clue as to where they might find the old lady's ring, but added she would not give evidence against him at his trial. They later recovered the ring from an old lag in Dooley's local pub, where he had sold it for a score.

It had been a busy week, but Tom kept his promise to meet Pauline on the Saturday in Manchester as arranged. They took a taxi to a pub on the outskirts of the city where she thought they would be safe. She looked ill, and had lost the sparkle he remembered from her days in Birmingham.

'Tom, he's been very good to me since he brought me back from Birmingham, but recently he's started to beat me up again. I'm terrified of him,' Pauline said.

'Pauline, he is a sick nutcase and will end up killing you one of these days. You'll have to leave him for good eventually,' he said.

'I know, Tom, that's why I've got to get away as soon as possible. But this time he mustn't find me.'

'Any idea where you could go?'

'No, I don't, but I've been watching him very closely now and I've got the combination to his hidden safe. When he was out, I opened it and found pornographic photographs and, worse still, child pornography. He's a bastard, Tom, he really is,' she said, crying.

'He isn't a very nice person Pauline, so we have to be careful where you go,' he said, gently.

'There's also lots and lots of paperwork in the safe which I don't completely understand, but I think it's all to do with his illegal dealings. And there's about twenty thousand pounds in cash,' she said.

'When you do get away you'll have to take what you can from the safe with you,' Tom said, thinking about evidence against McClurg.

Pauline told him that she had saved about three thousand pounds of her own money and was ready to leave as soon as possible. She realised that she would have to go into hiding where McClurg couldn't find her, and had thought about the continent as a possible destination. But her husband had connections all over, and identifying a safe place was proving difficult. She knew she would also need a forged passport so that he could not trace her.

'To get myself settled in to wherever I end up I intend to take his money from the safe with me,' she said.

Tom assured her that he would make swift enquiries with his contacts about a passport, and come up with some ideas of where she might be able to go. He then left her in the pub and caught a taxi back to the station. Troubled, he couldn't get the thought of his mother's similar experience out of his mind again. He would have to sort something out for her as soon as he possibly could.

Back in Birmingham, he went immediately to see Jimmy Walker; if anyone had contacts it would most likely be him and, anyway, he owed Tom a few favours. Tom was not disappointed. Jimmy had a place on the east coast of Spain, in a small village outside Calpe. It was still a quiet place and he was adamant that no one would find her there. She could have his place until she found a place of her own.

Jimmy would make all the arrangements in Spain; all Pauline had to do was fly to Alicante and make her way to the apartment. He also had a contact for forged passports, and told Tom it would cost about twelve hundred pounds to obtain one. Tom contacted Pauline and arranged for her to send him a passport photograph so he could get her the passport made up. She was so grateful, and very excited but nervous.

When the passport was ready, and all the arrangements had been made in Spain, Pauline made her escape from Manchester, and arrived in Tom's flat in Birmingham. Tom explained to her where she had to go and what arrangements had been made for her in

Spain.

Using the false passport and the air tickets he had booked for her, she left Birmingham Airport for her new life. Tom hoped everything would go well for her, and made a mental note to keep his wits about him in case McClurg sent a search party his way.

***

Back at work, and Tom was pleased to see the forensic results had come back on the old lady's burglary. Surprise, surprise they had found small particles of glass on Dooley's trousers, which proved a positive match for the broken window.

Later, at his trial at Birmingham Crown Court, Phillip Dooley was found guilty by the jury and sentenced to two years in prison. Being dragged from the dock by the prison staff, he shouted at Tom, 'You bastard, Sharkey, you set me up! I'll get you for this.' The judge was not impressed with his behaviour and told him so. Dooley was really trying to show face to his mates sitting in the public gallery.

The old lady recovered fully, and got her ring and most of her money back, plus compensation from the criminal injuries board.

Tom was very pleased with the result, as was his superintendent, although they were not so impressed with Dooley only getting two years, which meant he would be out again in less than twelve months. They felt the judge was too lenient in his sentencing.

In his position as a detective, Tom got involved with many solicitors and became aware of their various modes of behaviour. On the one hand, there were those who only wanted the money and didn't care what really became of their clients, always advising them to make no comment and keep the legal aid system going as long as possible. On the other hand, there were what Tom called 'the friendly ones', and it was these who usually got the call from the officer in charge of a case saying that the prisoner wanted to be represented. These helpful solicitors would advise the client to plead guilty and that they would get a good deal for them. This was usually the truth; they would make some deal with the officer in charge of the case which would be to the benefit of them all. And the officer would usually get a bottle of spirits for introducing the client to the solicitor in the first place.

Tom was saving a lot of money now, and decided to buy himself a good sporty car. He went to see the owner of a garage he had got to know on the patch. He was a straight enough guy and only ever called on Tom to check out the odd car on the Police National Computer (PNC), just in case it was stolen. As a result of the visit Tom ended up buying an eighteen-month-old Ford Capri 3000 in tiptop condition. This purchase was visibly beyond his reach with his regular pay, and he realised that he would have to be more careful now and not show off too much in case it raised suspicions.

Life continued as normal until late one Friday afternoon when the detective inspector told Tom to go to the chief superintendent's office.

'Congratulations, Sharkey, you've been promoted to uniform sergeant as from Monday week.

You're to go and see the chief constable on Tuesday morning,' said the chief super, shaking his hand.

'Any idea where I'm going, sir?' asked Tom.

He was informed that he would be told on Tuesday morning by the chief constable.

Tom had mixed feelings now; he wanted promotion more than anything, but he also enjoyed doing what he was doing in the CID in partnership with Danny Black. He went on the pop that night with the rest of the office, carrying on until the early hours of the morning and ending up in a curry house in Ladypool Road for a chicken madras.

On the Tuesday morning, Tom paraded before the chief constable with several other officers to be informed of their promotions. He had been transferred to the central division as from the following Monday. He then went to the uniform stores in Duke Street to be fitted out with his new sergeant's uniform.

Next day, he received a phone call from Pauline, letting him know that she had settled in well at the apartment in Spain and was enjoying being away from her old man. She was using the new name she had been given, had already met many British people living over there, and was very happy. He told her of his promotion to sergeant and asked her to keep in touch, but told her to be very careful not to let her true identity slip. Tom was relieved to hear from her. *That's one less thing to worry about,* he thought.

Chapter 20

Back in uniform, Sergeant Tom Sharkey reported at nine o'clock on the Monday morning at the central police station to see the sub-divisional commander, Superintendent George Brown. He stood over six feet tall, with greying hair and a large military-style moustache, and looked very fit for a man in his fifties. He spoke with a Scottish accent as he welcomed Tom to the Division, informing him that he would be posted to work on C Unit.

The super also told him that he had spent most of his own service in the CID, loved being a detective, and at times regretted having opted for the higher ranks in uniform. Tom had mixed feeling about leaving the CID, but hoped he could return as a detective in a higher rank.

Tom was shown around the old Victorian station by the administration sergeant, and introduced to his unit commander, Inspector Paul Haden, who happened to be on duty at the time. Inspector Haden was a scruffy man in his early forties, quite plump, round-faced with red cheeks, and wearing thick spectacles. Tom imagined he was a man who was fond of his booze.

Tom enjoyed the power of being a sergeant in uniform, being able to instil fear into the landlords on the patch, or anyone else he needed to lean on. One of the other perks of the job was for the sergeants to take it in turns to go off duty early at four o'clock in the morning when working nights, just like his old sergeants used to do. They called it 'Plan B'.

While Tom was on night shift one evening at eleven o'clock, Inspector Haden said, 'Tom, I'm going to introduce you to some of the locals, get the supervision car.' They began a pub crawl, and Tom was introduced to several landlords, both male and female. This ritual continued a few nights, and soon he realised that the inspector did indeed have a big drink problem.

One night, Tom was left managing the front office while the inspector went out on his own. At about four o'clock in the morning, the inspector returned to the station having been given a lift back; he was drunk, and Tom had to half-carry him to his office.

An hour later, Tom went back to the office to take him a cup of coffee but the inspector was no longer there. Searching the whole station, Tom eventually found him lying in straw in the rear yard where the stray dogs were kept. He had been sick all over his uniform and his glasses were missing.

Tom got him cleaned up and had one of the senior constables take him home, one he could trust to keep his mouth shut. Tom thought, *That might just stop him for a while.*

Next night on duty Tom was met by Inspector Haden, who called him into his office and apologised for his behaviour the previous night. 'Did I embarrass anyone else last night, Tom?' he asked. Tom assured him that he had not, although added that he had made a prat of himself. Then they both went off to search the rear yard for his lost spectacles, finding them smashed where he had fallen the night before.

Despite his over-indulgence the inspector didn't give up the drink. That night they went out again, and ended up in a pub on the outskirts of the division where Tom was surprised to find his old barmaid friend, Maureen, was now working.

After closing time, while the inspector talked to the landlord and his wife in the lounge, Tom went into the bar to where Maureen was clearing up. She told him that she was now married and her husband worked away from home, only returning at weekends.

Tom realised that she was still interested and flirted with her before taking her in his arms. They began to kiss and, in full uniform, he laid her across one of the bar tables and removed her pants. He undid the front of his trousers, spread her legs and entered her while still standing up. He found it incredibly exciting; maybe it was the thought of possibly getting caught, or it might have been his radio blaring out messages in his ear. Either way, he thoroughly enjoyed himself.

While working at this nick he soon became friendly with the local CID, and spent a lot of time in their office. He met again Detective Sergeant Ken Payne, the man responsible for him joining the police in the first place.

'How's your sister Ann?' Tom enquired.

'Oh, she's a policewoman at Bourneville Lane now, loves it. Why don't you give her a shout,' he replied.

Tom thought he might just have to do that one of these days, she was a nice girl and he hadn't seen her for many years. Later, Ken introduced him to a few of the local club owners. It was always useful to have a personal introduction to some of the heavy men around town. Tom was itching to get back into the CID again, and was missing the freedom of being out of uniform.

Many nights the station got phone calls from the nursing staff at the General Hospital emergency department over the road, asking for assistance with drunks causing trouble. The nursing staff had to take a lot of abuse from these people, who were admitted after being injured in fights, and wished to carry on fighting with them. Tom and the team took great delight in locking them up.

Back on days, and enjoying a large brandy sitting at home one night at about ten o'clock, Tom had a call from Avril, the friend Pauline McClurg had stayed with while in Birmingham. She sounded terrified.

'Tom, it's Avril. I had a visit earlier tonight from those two very nasty men again, asking if I knew where Pauline was. When they realised that I was on my own they pushed me into the flat and threatened me,' she said.

'Did they hurt you?' he asked.

She sobbed. 'No, they only threatened me then searched the place. I eventually convinced them that I didn't know where she was. Then they asked for your address but of course I only have your phone number. I'm sorry, Tom, but I had to give it to them, I was terrified.' she said.

'Don't worry about that. If they come back let me know, but I honestly don't think you'll hear from them again,' he said. *Unlike me,* he thought. With McClurg's contacts it would not take them long to trace his address from his phone number.

Tom's shift pattern threw him back on nights again soon enough, and one night he was out enjoying the buzz of the city with Andy, one of the senior constables, in his panda car. 'Would you like me to show you around my patch and introduce you to a few people, sarge?' Andy asked.

Tom thought, *Why not?* and off they went.

After driving around for about an hour, Andy asked him if he fancied a beer and if he would like to meet a good friend of the police. When Tom agreed, they stopped at a telephone box and Andy made a phone call, then said, 'Follow me, sarge.' Tom followed him up the fire escape of a large bingo hall to where a young man stood at an open fire door, and introduced himself.

'I'm Steve, the manager. Nice to meet you, sergeant, please come in,' he said. The system was that you made a call, let it ring twice, hang up, and the fire door was opened for you. Tom was introduced to a few people and he and Andy enjoyed some free beer.

During that night Andy also told Tom that he had arranged a boat trip on the River Severn in a few weeks' time, and asked him to come along. He explained that it was a joint trip with their opposite numbers on one of the outer divisions. Tom agreed, and on the day of the trip they all met at the other station and went off by coach to catch the boat.

The booze on the boat flowed freely, and everyone was having a good knees-up to the disco. Tom was approached by Janet, one of the policewomen from the other division, and asked to dance. She was quite intoxicated and wouldn't leave him alone.

Her boyfriend, a civilian, didn't like what was going on between them, and spent the evening throwing nasty looks in their direction. Tom ignored him. On the coach home, Janet sat in the seat opposite Tom, and began to chat to him. Tom could see that she was mad for it, but with her boyfriend sitting next to her he couldn't do much about it. She leaned over and whispered in his ear. 'I'll see you in the rear car park of the nick, wait for me there.'

Tom got into his car at the back of the station and saw her come running towards him. She jumped in beside him, and shouted, 'Drive as fast as you can!'

'Where's your boyfriend?' Tom asked.

He discovered that she had left her boyfriend in the station while she went to the toilet, and had climbed out through the rear window into the car park. She knew her way around, and directed him to a quiet spot under the motorway. She definitely was mad for it, and they had a satisfying two-hour session in the front reclining seat of his car before he dropped her off at her parents' home in Chelmsley Wood.

Next day back on duty Tom behaved like nothing had happened, but one of the other constables who was a friend of Janet's boyfriend was not impressed by what she had done, although he didn't know whom she had gone off with.

***

The months passed by in a blur of arrests, late night beers and banter with the shift until one afternoon the inspector and Tom were called into the superintendent's office for a conference. It transpired that information had been received about a gang of female shoplifters from Liverpool operating in the city centre, and the superintendent wanted to set up a plain-clothes unit to combat them.

With his CID experience Tom had been selected to run the small unit of five constables. They were given an office and a car and told to get on with it. Tom immediately arranged a meeting with all the store detectives from the major shops in the city. The meeting proved beneficial, because several of the stores were losing massive quantities of clothing to shoplifting, much more than the normal amount, and were therefore keen to help. With the assistance of these stores, observations were carried out to identify the people responsible.

The plan was not to arrest anyone at that stage, but to follow them to where they were taking the stolen goods. The third day of the observations gave them the lead they were looking for. As he was coming down an escalator with one of the constables, Tom spotted two women stealing a large quantity of children's clothing and so they followed them from the store. The trail led them to New Street railway station, where the women placed the stolen gear in a luggage locker, secured it, and returned to shop for more.

Tom immediately assembled the squad at the railway station to wait on the arrival of the women again. Later that evening, the team arrested a total of six women when they gathered to collect their stolen property from ten lockers that had been crammed full of gear. All the women were from Liverpool as the original information had suggested.

Their plan was to catch the train from Liverpool to Birmingham, shoplift all day, store their loot at the station, and in the evening pack it all up and travel back to Liverpool. Not this time they wouldn't.

For supervising the operation Tom was awarded with a chief superintendent's commendation, which could only benefit him in the future. He knew, of course, that this was just the tip of the iceberg; many of the items would have been stolen to order, and behind the shoplifters were people placing those orders, and other individuals directing the gangs of shoplifters to deliver on them.

These people were real cheeky bastards. They would just walk into one of the top stores wearing white coats, and walk out carrying the most expensive items they could find. If approached carrying a TV, they would just tell the staff they had to take it away because it was supposed to be faulty and it would be back in an hour. This sort of theft was going on every day in a lot of the stores. Unfortunately, the unit was eventually abandoned and Tom had to return to uniform.

Reading the local paper, Tom learned that his favourite country-and-western singer, Hank Locklin, was appearing at the town hall, and decided one evening while on duty to go along and see him. At the town hall he got star treatment when he told the staff he was a big fan, and was taken to a good seat.

When the show ended he was asked by the manager if he would like to go to the star's dressing room and be introduced. Tom jumped at the opportunity, and went to meet his hero.

'Hi, captain, glad to make your acquaintance,' Hank said, holding out his hand. They had a good chat, during which time Hank handed him a large glass of whiskey. Tom was overjoyed. Unfortunately, he had overlooked the time and was late getting back to the station. He was met by the anxious faces of his colleagues, who thought something bad had befallen him. He had turned off his radio for the show.

Tom was settling in well and getting to know his way around the city, but his reign in uniform was only to last for twelve months. Superintendent Brown informed him that he was being transferred back to his old division as a detective sergeant. The look on the superintendent's face told Tom that he had pulled a few strokes to get him back on the CID so soon.

Tom's old detective superintendent must also have had a good say in the matter, otherwise he would not have been able to return so quickly. He was over the moon; back to his old stomping ground and the possible partnership again with Danny Black.

It's not what you know, but who you know, he thought.

Chapter 21

His old detective inspector, Tommy Burns, greeted Tom back to the division. 'Welcome back, Tom. Ray Mason has been promoted but nothing else has really changed. Danny Black, Joe Mooney and the attached man will be on your crew.' Tom didn't know Joe Mooney and thought that sorting him out would have to be his first task.

Know your people and be able to trust them. Now that he had an office, which he only shared with another DS, it was a bit more private and he could use the phone without too many interruptions.

He called Danny into his office and shut the door. 'Can we trust Mooney? You know what I mean,' he said.

'He's sound, a hundred percent. He fell in nicely after you left; he came from the squad and knows the score,' Danny replied, with a big smile.

Tom later sent for Mooney. 'Joe, you've been well recommended by Danny, welcome to my team. You stay with me, keep your nose clean and I'll look after you, know what I mean?' he said.

'I know the score, sarge, I won't let you down,' Mooney replied.

Tom arranged a meeting in the local pub that evening with Danny and Joe to discuss what direction he wanted them to go. He informed them that he wanted to step up pressure on the metal dealers, club owners, landlords and all the well-known handlers on the patch. 'We want to keep the gaffers happy with our arrests and clearances, and at the same time make a few quid, understood?' he said. The other two knew perfectly well what he meant.

Tom continued. 'We must be extremely careful, otherwise the rubber heel squad will be after us and we might end up getting our own collars felt, and we certainly don't want that, do we?' Trust was the vital ingredient, and Tom was confident they had that between them. The new team headed off to a nightclub for a good night out.

One day, Joe came and told Tom he was a bit concerned about Danny, who had been having pains in his chest. When Tom got Danny alone, he asked him outright. 'Have you been to the doc to have a check-up lately?'

'Yes, he sent me to see a specialist last week,' Danny replied, laughing.

'What did he say?'

'*She* sat me down and asked me how much I ate, did I smoke and did I drink much. When I said about ten pints, she said that that was a little excessive for a week. You should have seen the look on her face when I told her that was what I drank in a night,' he replied.

Danny continued to find the whole thing funny, so Tom decided to leave it at that for the moment, but remained concerned about him.

When Tom got back to his flat that night he discovered that it had been broken into, and someone had turned the place upside down. They had not stolen anything, and he suspected that whoever had done it was likely looking for some correspondence from Pauline.

The entry had been made very professionally, but if the intruders were after information on Pauline they would not have found

174

anything. The phone number he had for her in Spain was memorised and not written down, just in case anyone should visit him.

The next morning, he had the scenes of crime officers go over the flat searching for any fingerprints, even though he knew they wouldn't find any. And he was right. This confirmed his suspicions about who the intruders were – anyone working for a man like Harry McClurg wouldn't be stupid enough to leave easy evidence lying around. Tom felt it was maybe time to start sorting McClurg out.

His superintendent asked him about the burglary, having read about it on the twenty-four-hour crime summary, and whether he had any leads. Tom lied, and told him it was probably an opportunist working in the area. He knew if he was going to sort out McClurg he would need to do it in his own way, and not by the book.

Saturday night, just as he booked off duty and was off to the pub, the duty inspector grabbed him as he was going out the door. 'Tom, we've just had a nasty incident on the Tyburn Road, could you have a look at it,' he said.

'What's it about?' Tom asked.

The inspector related the story. A chap had been taking his girlfriend home in his car when they'd had a big row. She had jumped out of the car and headed home on foot. The man had lost his temper, and driven the car at her, knocking her down. He had then continued driving, dragging her along the road before deciding to stop after a few hundred yards.

Realising what he had done, he had called an ambulance, and the police also arrived. They found the man sitting on the kerb, crying.

When the officers assessed the situation, he had been arrested. Tom had a quick interview with him and locked him up for the night. Next morning, he went to Good Hope Hospital where the post-mortem was being carried out.

The body was in a terrible state. One side was void of any skin where it had been dragged along the rough road surface. The other side was also void of skin where the body had had to be peeled from the silencer and exhaust of the car. You could still smell the burning flesh. Tom had never seen such a mess. The man admitted everything, and was charged later that morning.

That afternoon, Tom had a telephone call from Jimmy Walker. 'Tom, can you call round, I may have a good job for you,' he said. Tom understood that this was likely to be one of the very few jobs he was going to get from him, and went round to his yard straight away.

He was informed by Jimmy that a cockney wearing a trilby hat had come to his yard that morning offering to sell him twenty gold medallions. Jimmy had taken a sample medallion and told the man to return in a few days' time, and that he would see what he could do for him. The medallion was still in a rough state, but it had been hallmarked.

Tom and Danny took the medallion to the Assay Office in Hockley, where it was identified as coming from a jeweller's shop on another division in the jewellery quarter of the city. They went along to the shop to have it identified, and were delighted when they were informed by the owner that his premises had been broken into a week earlier. Twenty such medallions had been stolen in the raid.

Bingo, Tom thought.

Jimmy Walker had a phone call from the thief two days later asking if he was interested in buying the gear, and so he arranged for the man to bring it to his yard the next afternoon. Tom and his team staked-out the yard and waited for the man in the trilby hat.

After about half an hour the man arrived, carrying his holdall, and they allowed him to do his business with Jimmy. The thief then left the yard and caught a bus. He was followed onto the bus by Joe, and Tom and Danny followed on in their cars to where the man got off in Aston.

They let him enter his house, and waited for about half an hour before they went in and arrested him for burglary. The man turned out to be an old lag called Pat Laird, from London, who had just been released from Winson Green prison a few weeks earlier. He wanted to know how the police had found him, and Tom told him that he had been seen breaking into the premises. Jimmy Walker had to be protected.

During interview, Laird put forward several bits of information in order to save his own skin. One nugget of information was of particular interest to Tom, as it concerned a series of thefts from churches where priceless pieces of silver had been stolen. These thefts had received a great deal of publicity in the press, both locally and nationally. The police were under a lot of pressure to catch whoever was responsible. *An arrest on that case wouldn't do me any harm with the brass,* Tom thought.

He told Laird that he would look after him if he supplied the details of the person responsible for the thefts, and Laird agreed to do what he could; he really had no other option. Tom took a chance and bailed him from the police station. 'You let me down and I will hunt you out and put you away for a long time,' he warned Laird.

'I won't let you down, Mr Sharkey, on my mother's grave,' the thief replied.

'Make a note to follow up on that, Danny. He's too scared to mess us about, but might need reminding where his priorities lie,' said Tom, as Laird disappeared down the road outside the station.

The medallions were collected from Jimmy Walker and returned to the jeweller, who was most satisfied. That week, Tom received a surprise phone call from Pauline, who told him that she was moving to live in Menorca.

She had met a nice Spanish couple who had a restaurant on the island, and they wanted her to go and live there and manage the business for them. She had agreed, and was moving in a few days' time.

'Be very careful, Pauline, your old man is trying hard to find you,' Tom told her.

'I think I'll be all right in Menorca, I'm going to a quiet spot. I'll ring you when I settle in,' Pauline said.

He didn't tell her what McClurg had been up to, just in case he frightened her too much.

Tom told Jimmy Walker that she was moving to Menorca, and that he could now have his apartment in Spain back. Walker was also concerned; Menorca was only a small island, but busy, and someone could recognise her.

***

Working the late turn one evening, Tom and Danny went to a local pub to meet a couple of metal dealers who had a problem they needed sorting.

It turned out that they had been offered a large lorry load of brass fittings and simply wanted to have it checked out before they bought it. Danny soon sorted it out on the phone and they were promised a cut of the profits when it was sold on. The business over, they all got down to some serious drinking.

One of the dealers, an Irishman called Jerry, had two women with him but they were taking more notice of Danny and Tom than they were of him. They weren't particularly attractive but the one called Maude, a metal dealer's wife from Walsall, had a very fit body and as the night went on Tom began to take an interest in her. She was in her late forties and a bit plain and drawn looking.

They were all drinking brandies and very soon got very drunk. Someone gave Danny and Tom a large bag of sausages each, and at some point a sausage fight began, resulting in sausages being thrown all over the bar. Jerry was so drunk he had staggered off before the sausage fight, and his mate had long since disappeared into the night before him.

The two women wanted to go to a club and they, Danny and Tom ended up in a strip bar in Handsworth. Next morning Tom woke up in a strange bed with Maude beside him. He had a terrible hangover, but she managed to arouse him and they made love for most of the morning. He was not on duty until the afternoon.

She had a very athletic body with small, hard breasts not much bigger than his own, but she was a beautiful mover. The only thing that annoyed him was that she kept calling him 'son'.

He heard Danny's voice coming from another room, and discovered they were in the other woman's house in Lozells. They washed, had coffee and both left for work. The inside of the police car was covered in squashed sausages, on the floor and on the seat where they had sat on them the previous night. 'Christ, she was ugly wasn't she,' Danny said.

'Danny, there is no such thing as an ugly woman – they're all beautiful. Some are just more beautiful than others, and besides, she probably thinks the same about you, you ugly bastard,' Tom said, laughing. Danny whacked him over the head with a sausage.

Another night, he and Danny went out on the booze in the police car with Danny driving, and he hit a lamp post and badly damaged the front wing and bonnet. Having had too much to drink they didn't dare stop, so drove the car to Tom's lock-up and left it there for the night.

Next morning, Tom drove the car to a friend's garage where he donned old clothes and the two of them repaired the damage and resprayed it. The colour wasn't a perfect match but a man on a flying horse wouldn't notice it.

It was several months later, while Tom was walking across the nick car park and about to take the detective superintendent to a meeting, that his boss remarked, 'You would swear that that car was sprayed two different shades of blue.'

'I think it's the way the sun's shining on it, sir,' Tom said. The super made no further comment.

Friday afternoons were a great time for meeting up with the metal dealers at Pat the Hat's place, one of the local pubs. Tom was always playing silly pranks on Pat, such as the time Pat had bought a new, legitimate, sheepskin jacket from someone in the pub and one of the dealers had told Tom about it.

He thought about winding him up, and said, 'Pat, I'm making enquiries about a load of stolen sheepskin coats which are being offered for sale. If you should see or hear anything let me know.'

'Sure I will, Mr Sharkey,' Pat said, nervously.

About ten minutes later, Tom went to the toilet in the rear yard to find that Pat had lit a bonfire and was about to throw his new sheepskin coat onto it. He had to rush over and stop him, and explain that it was only a joke.

Pat was a gentle and humorous man who got his nickname from always wearing a trilby hat everywhere he went. One Sunday morning, Pat went out to get a newspaper wearing his bedroom slippers, and didn't come back. He phoned his wife six hours later from Dublin. He had met a few pals on his way back from the newsagent's and had gone off with them for a few days' unplanned break.

Pat's pub was a great meeting place for all types of businessmen who had problems and needed assistance: for a fee, of course. There were two local councillors who frequented the bar. They offered various services, from arranging planning permissions to many other matters relating to council work. Another regular was a magistrate, who was also worth his weight in gold.

Chapter 22

One afternoon, a sergeant and a young policewoman put their heads round Tom's door, 'Can we have a word with you, Tom,' the sergeant said.

'Yes, come in. How can I assist,' he replied.

'We've just been to a meeting at the Heartlands Hospital regarding one of their infant patients. The staff there are very concerned about the situation and are seeking our help,' he said.

The officers went on to explain that a young child was being treated for attacks of breathing difficulties, but the staff could not understand why this was happening because the child appeared extremely well in every other way. On the latest occasion, the child had again been admitted with breathing problems, and had again recovered fully within hours under the hospital's care.

The hospital had kept the child in and under observations, but all medical indicators were completely normal. They could find nothing wrong, but the child continued to suffer apparently random and severe attacks, on each occasion almost suffocating.

The doctor following the child's case had noticed that these attacks only occurred while the child was with the mother. When the mother was not visiting, the child was perfectly normal. The doctor was now convinced that the mother was doing something to the child, and he suspected foul play.

Tom took an immediate interest. 'I've read about such stories and discussed this type of situation while on a CID course. The mother does something to the child to attract attention to herself,' Tom explained. 'The situation is known as Munchausen Syndrome by Proxy. We must go straight away and see the doctor at the hospital,' he said.

At the hospital, they met the doctor and the nursing staff involved with the child. Tom and his colleagues learned that the mother had insisted on staying with the child whenever possible. Studying all the evidence, they came to the conclusion that all the attacks had occurred while the mother was alone with the child.

A conference was arranged straightaway with the nursing staff, the police and social services to discuss the case. It was agreed by all that covert video surveillance would be set up to monitor the situation.

Tom arranged everything, and twenty-four-hour surveillance was established with two policewomen monitoring the situation from a nearby room on the ward. It was only a few hours later that the mother was observed putting a pillow over the child's face, causing great distress and near suffocation.

The mother was arrested immediately, and readily admitted what she had been doing. It transpired that she had been molested by her father when she was a child and her actions were to attract attention to herself. The child was taken into care and in court the mother was placed on two years' probation. The whole affair was extremely distressing for the officers who had been monitoring the situation and had witnessed the mother's actions.

Tom found the whole situation very emotional. It made him

wonder just how his Nina would be coping with a child, wherever she was, and how he would like to have been able to care for and support her.

***

Back in his office one gloomy April morning, and there was a knock on Tom's door.

A uniform constable poked his head in. 'Sarge, we've just arrested a man acting suspiciously on the canal towpath, and there's something not right about his story. Could your lads have a word with him, please?' he said.

'Sure, I'll pop down and have a word in a few minutes,' Tom replied.

Danny and Tom interviewed the man, and ran a few checks on him. It turned out that he was wanted in South Wales for burglary. 'Danny, get in touch with Wales and see if they'll send someone up to collect him,' Tom said. Danny came back later and informed him that their Welsh colleagues were sending someone up to escort the man back.

Late that afternoon, a detective constable and an attached man arrived to take the man back to Wales. They had a quick interview with him and informed Tom that they were going to stop the night and escort him back next morning on the train.

Later that evening, Danny and Tom took their visiting colleagues out for something to eat, and then took them round a local club. When they eventually got the two of them to bed in one of the

185

local hostels they were quite under the influence.

Tom found it quite comical putting all three of them on the early train next morning from New Street station. As the train pulled out, the prisoner waved to them while the two officers sitting on either side of him were almost asleep.

Two days later, Tom got a phone call from the detective constable in South Wales; 'Sarge, it's Brian Smith. You'll not believe this, but that man we brought back from Birmingham is on the run again. The magistrates granted him bail after a soft story from his brief, so you might come across him again up there.'

'Wasn't he wanted for a few burglaries down there?' Tom asked. *What a joke,* he thought, and wondered who the law was really designed to protect.

It sometimes seemed the law did everything for the benefit of the offender. Such as granting bail when it should be looking at the welfare and safety of the victim. Or prosecuting a burglary victim who had injured the burglar by merely seeking to protect his own property, instead of offering support. Or allowing an offender to get away with their actions in circumstances where the caution was not put to them properly on arrest, even when they had admitted the offence – a full confession to an offence, if not made under caution, was inadmissible in court.

The Police and Criminal Evidence Act, passed in 1984, further curtailed the way suspects could be questioned; the tape recording of interviews and the provision of legal representation became legal requirements, severely hampering the traditional way in which many enquiries were conducted. Also new under the Act was the right of silence in interview, which did very little to assist the police, and the courts didn't seem to pay enough attention to the 'No comment' interviews when raised by the prosecution at trial. Tom concluded that the law was definitely on the side of the offender, and thought of something J. Edgar Hoover once said: 'Justice is incidental to law and order.'

The theft of silver from churches continued on a large scale.

'That prat Laird has not been in touch about the silver thefts, we'll have to chase him up,' Tom said to Danny.

'I'll see where he's hiding out,' Danny sighed. 'Leave it with me.'

Tom, Danny and Joe were invited to a party at a local Greek restaurant that was to start at midnight one Saturday night. The tables were laid out in a long row and Jimmy Walker sat at the head of the table. The party was attended by local businessmen, metal dealers, licensees, club owners, an Irish bank manager and the two local councillors.

The tables were laden with bottles of whiskey, large jugs of beer and abundant quantities of King Edward cigars. Large T-bone steaks were served, cooked to perfection.

Jimmy Walker rose. 'Let's drink a toast, folks, to the Small Heath mafia. Let us relax and have a good night. There is nothing that we can't sort out between ourselves,' he said.

As the musicians played soft music, Tom thought, *He's absolutely right, we can sort anything out*. He knew then just how powerful he had become; his word was respected and people looked to him when they wanted advice or direction.

Tom had a brief word with Jimmy Walker about McClurg in Manchester, and what assistance he might need from Jimmy to sort the bastard out. They agreed to meet at a later date to discuss it. At seven thirty next morning they all left the restaurant, having had a very enlightening and enjoyable night.

A few days later Tom met up with the bank manager, who agreed to open a bank account for Tom in Southern Ireland. He now planned to transfer most of his money over there. He kept topping up this new account, leaving only what he needed to survive on in his Birmingham account. After all, he was making a lot of money now and there was no need to let everyone know about it.

At his meeting with Jimmy Walker, he wanted to find out just what was known about McClurg and his set-up in Manchester. Jimmy told Tom that, just like him, he knew the name but did not know much about the man's business.

They agreed that Jimmy would make contact with a friend in Manchester and then they would discuss the matter further. A few days later, Jimmy phoned Tom and asked for a meet. They met at the metal yard in the evening, after Jimmy had shut up the business for the day.

In the office, Jimmy got out a bottle of scotch and poured them both a very large measure. 'My man up north has been in touch, Tom. He's got knowledge of your Mr McClurg and wants to meet us for a bit of a chat. Shall I organise it?' Walker asked. Tom agreed, and told him to make the necessary arrangements.

Next morning, Tom and Joe were interviewing a prisoner who had been arrested by the uniform staff for being in possession of drugs. Joe asked him for his address and he gave it as number fifteen, Single Policewomen's Quarters.

'Stop messing us around. You can't live there, you prat, now where do you live?' Joe raged.

'Honestly, I do, I live with a policewoman. Believe me, it gets a bit dodgy at times because one of your inspectors is giving her one, too,' he said.

'What are you talking about?' Tom asked.

'Well, some nights he comes to the room and I have to hide under the bed while he does the business. She puts up with him for the easy time he gives her on duty,' he replied.

Tom told him to move out of the single quarters immediately and said he would sort out his bail for him, but instructed him not to tell anyone else about the matter. Tom realised that he had to do something about the situation and later had a quiet word with Inspector Beard, the officer involved, who was quite embarrassed and worried by the whole incident.

Beard was a married man with two children and was frightened of what Tom might say or do, but Tom assured him it would go no further and Beard got the message. Now he owed Tom one. He would call in the favour when and if he needed it.

Tom didn't have to wait too long, because one night a few weeks later he got a call from an informant's wife saying her old man had been arrested for driving under the influence. Lucky for him and Tom, the duty inspector was Beard and the charge was sorted out, no questions asked.

Several days later, Tom travelled up the M6 with Jimmy Walker in the dealer's new Jaguar, to meet Jimmy's Manchester contact in a motorway service area. In the restaurant, Tom was introduced to a man in his early forties who stood about six feet tall, had a broken nose and several features that suggested he had been a boxer in his time. He was dressed immaculately, in a cream suit.

'Tom, meet Mick Moore. Mick, this is Tom Sharkey, my mate from Brum,' Walker said. Mick Moore gave Tom's hand a firm shake.

They sat down at a quiet table, and Jimmy said, 'Go ahead, Tom, you ask what you want to know about our friend.'

'Mick, I'll tell you my interest in McClurg,' Tom said.

He then related the whole story to him about Pauline, and the burglary at his flat. About forty minutes later they parted company with Mick, and made their way back to Birmingham.

Tom now knew that Harry McClurg was an evil man who ran a gang of terror in Manchester. He was heavily involved in drugs and serious crime, although most of his business was related to drugs and pornography.

He was a very wealthy man who got anything he wanted. The fact that Pauline had left him had dented his pride. It was known that if McClurg could get his hands on her he would likely kill her, and was prepared to pay big money to discover her whereabouts.

McClurg would not do it himself; he would have someone else do his dirty work. He was very clever, and not been convicted of any crime since his release from prison years earlier. He always had an alibi when the law called on him. Tom knew he would have to change that situation, but just didn't yet know how.

Joe came into his office. 'Sarge, Pat Laird has been trying to contact you,' he said. 'Says he wants to meet you in the Swanpool tonight. That he has some information on the church thefts.'

'About time. We'll go down there at about seven thirty,' Tom replied.

They went along to the pub and met Pat Laird in the smoke room. The pub was quiet, so they were able to talk. Laird told them that he had found out an address in Halifax, in Yorkshire, where a man called George Hunter lived. He was supposedly involved in the theft of the silver from the churches. He could add no more.

Chapter 23

Back at the nick, a check of the Electoral Roll confirmed that a George and Margaret Hunter did live at the address in Halifax that Laird had provided. Two days later Danny, Joe and Tom travelled up to Yorkshire in the CID car to check out Laird's information.

Arriving in Halifax, they called at the local police station, which was manned by an elderly police constable. The officer had been stationed there many years and knew practically everything about the area. He didn't know the man George Hunter, but was aware of a Margaret Hunter from that address who worked in the local pub as a cook. He gave them directions to the address where she lived. Tom went to the address with the lads, but they got no reply at the door so decided to wait in the car until someone showed up.

Some thirty minutes later a woman arrived and let herself into the house. She was a mature, plump woman, who looked to be in her late fifties. They knocked on the door, which was eventually answered by the woman. Tom identified himself and asked her if he and his colleagues could come in, and waited until they were inside the house before explaining why they were there.

'We have reason to believe that you have stolen goods in the house and we are going to search it,' he said, knowing that he had no warrant if she refused to let them. It was obvious the woman had no idea what was going on.

'Carry on, sir, I've nothing to hide, I've never been in trouble with the police in my life,' she replied.

All three of them searched the house, but found no stolen silver.

'Where is your husband, George?' Tom asked.

'My husband died seven years ago, and his name was Robert.'

'Who's George, then?' Danny asked.

'That's my son, but he's not at home at the moment.'

'When will he be home again?' asked Danny.

'He's in Birmingham on business, and won't be home for a few days,' she said.

Tom thought, *Bloody hell, we've travelled all the way up here to Yorkshire and he's in Birmingham.* 'Do you know where he's staying in Birmingham?' he asked.

'He's stopping in the George Hotel on the Hagley Road, he rang me from there last night,' she replied.

Tom sent Danny to the local police station to contact the CID in Birmingham and ask them to go to the George Hotel and detain Hunter, and take possession of any property he had with him. They were then to lodge him at the station, and Tom's team would be back to interview him in a few hours' time. Once it was confirmed that Hunter was in custody, Tom apologised to Mrs Hunter and they headed back to Birmingham.

Tom and Danny interviewed George Hunter, who was in his mid thirties and a sales representative who travelled the country for his work. It transpired that Hunter, on his movements around the country, would just walk into random churches during the times that they were open, steal the silver, put it in a sack and walk out. It also turned out that he had never been in trouble with the police before in

193

his life. He saw the thefts as an easy way to make some money. When he had collected enough silver, he would travel to Birmingham where he would sell it to a local man called Kevin Smith, who ran a second-hand shop in Saltley.

Hunter, while he was staying in a hotel in Birmingham, had met Smith who was having a drink there, and they had become friends. Tom went with the team to the second-hand shop and searched it for the stolen silver. They soon found a quantity of what they were looking for in the cellar, and so they arrested the owner, Smith.

There was a large sum of money now due to Pat Laird for his information, because without it the thefts could have gone on for a very long time.

Tom and his team got a great deal of publicity for the arrests, and were awarded a chief constable's commendation for their excellent work. This called for a celebration to beat all celebrations in the local club, where Tom was treated as a celebrity after all his press and television interviews.

With all the excellent results the team were producing, Tom was now promoted straight to detective inspector, and transferred to another busy division. The detective superintendent on his new division was the old detective chief inspector under whom he had first served as a DC, and who gave him a warm welcome to the division. Tom had no doubt that he had pulled a few strings to get him on his divisional team.

After settling into his new office, Tom went along to introduce himself to the uniform sub-divisional superintendent and got the surprise of his life. There was David Hamilton, the pompous prat from the training school, now a superintendent. Tom couldn't forget the little episode at the training school, but it was obvious that Hamilton had not remembered the young recruit.

'Welcome to the division, Inspector Sharkey,' he said, and shook Tom's hand. 'We need a good DI here to sort things out. Our figures are a shambles. I will not stand for sloppy work, or for the CID pissing around, I want one hundred percent commitment.' Tom sat down, and Hamilton continued. 'I will also want action plans, the targeting of active criminals, and more proactive policing from all your staff. I'm sure you can understand.' Tom could see that he had all the platitudes off pat, such as, 'Will take that on board, I'm mindful of that, I'll flag that up' – phrases all used by the so-called high flyers.

He was still a pompous prat.

Tom got the impression that he was anti-CID, and realised that he could have problems working with him. The only good thing was that the CID were directly answerable to the detective superintendent and the DCI, but of course, working on the sub-division meant that you also had to work with the uniform superintendent and keep him happy, too.

Tom's staff of three detective sergeants and nine detective constables were all experienced officers, but Tom wanted a few of his old and trusted staff to work with him. As soon as he had settled he made it his first task, with the agreement of the DCI, to reorganise the staff.

Within months he had got Danny transferred over to the division, and they were back in business again. Unfortunately, this arrangement didn't particularly please the detective sergeant with whom Danny was partnered. Being so close to Tom, Danny always bypassed the DS and came straight to him. Tom didn't fully trust or really like the DS, and so went about having him replaced with one he did trust.

Very soon his old friend DS Ken Payne arrived, and so Tom felt his team was complete. Tom became aware that Ken's sister, Ann, was also now serving on the same division, and he arranged to take her out for a drink one night.

They went back to the club where he had first taken her years earlier, and enjoyed a night of free drinking with the club owner. While there, they were joined by Ken and Danny, who were out for a night on the town. Tom sat at the bar, thinking, *Here I am, at last, with a faithful team round me; what else do I need?*

He and Ann went back to his flat, shared a nightcap and went to bed. She was a beautiful woman who enjoyed her sex, and he felt very comfortable being with her.

'Why have you left it so long, Tom, you know I enjoyed being with you,' she said. He felt unable to explain. The truth was that he had spent all his time getting his act together, fulfilling his ambitions, and had had very little time or inclination to take any woman seriously. He also knew in his heart that he still loved Nina and, while he suspected Ann would understand that part, he liked her and felt it would be too insensitive to voice it.

Tom received a telephone call one morning from the area manager of a local brewery, enquiring if he knew Mr Ted Burke, an ex-licensee. Tom informed him that he knew Ted from when held the licence for the Old Talbot. The manager told Tom that they were going to offer Ted the position of manager at one of their pubs, and that he had given Tom as one of his references. Tom told him that he was an excellent landlord and recommended him highly. He did not mention his wife Sandra. The area manager thanked Tom for his assistance, and told him that Ted would be running the Red Bull in Hockley.

On leaving his flat one morning to go to work, Tom noticed a silver Ford Granada parked in a spot he had never seen a car parked before, which made it quite noticeable. The car followed him for a distance as he drove to work. Two days later, he saw the same car following him and realised that it must either be the rubber heel squad or something more sinister, like McClurg.

He pulled over sharply to the side of the road so that the car had to pass. He noted the registration number and on his return to the station checked it on the Police National Computer. The car was registered to a woman in Bolton, which convinced him it had something to do with McClurg. He contacted the traffic department and arranged for a car to patrol in the area of his flat on the lookout for the Granada. He told them he thought it might be involved in robberies in the area, and instructed them to do a routine check on the occupants and pass the details to him.

Three days later, a traffic constable came to see him in his office, and informed him that the car was being driven by a man called Edward Bonnar, from Manchester. The passenger was a Mark Dunn, also from Manchester. They had claimed they were working for a roofing company from Manchester and were in the Midlands on business. They had been unable to produce any driving documents, so the constable had issued them with a production slip. Since the vehicle was clean and the occupants were not currently wanted, he had let them go. Tom thanked him.

The vehicle was still registered to a Mrs Gray in Bolton, so Tom contacted the police there and asked them to go and see her, and check if she still owned the car. He told them it was urgent and to reply to him as soon as possible. Within an hour he got a message back, stating the woman had sold the car to a man called Dunn several weeks earlier, but that she had no address for him. Tom now knew that McClurg was involved.

Later, Tom had a call from Jimmy Walker, asking to meet with him urgently. They met in a local pub.

'Tom, I have a bit of information, I think, on your friend McClurg,' Walker said.

'What have you got, Jimmy?' Tom asked.

'A man called Dunn called at my yard this morning, asking questions about you and how well I knew you. He was giving the impression that he knew you, and wanted to know if you were sound. He said he was thinking of doing a bit of business in Birmingham and he might need some help from the law.'

'Did he say what type of business he was into?' Tom asked.

'He only said he worked for a big man in Manchester, and they were thinking of expanding the business to Birmingham,' Walker replied. 'He didn't say what type of business he was in, but I'm sure he came from McClurg. I've phoned Mick Moore in Manchester to find out what he knows about Dunn and he's promised to ring me back.'

'Thanks for the info, Jimmy. Keep me posted,' Tom said, and they parted company.

That night, Tom had a call from Jimmy Walker, who informed him that Dunn was definitely one of McClurg's heavy men, who did all his dirty work for him. McClurg was either moving into Birmingham or, more likely, he was still trying to trace Pauline. Tom would have to wait and see.

Superintendent Hamilton would often praise Tom for all the results he was getting; arrests levels were high and departmental crime clearances were way above the force average, but he still kept pushing Tom for more.

Tom thought he was a two-faced liar who said one thing to your face but another behind your back, and underneath it all he saw him as a megalomaniac. He looked over the desk at Hamilton during one meeting, and thought *I've got the full measure of you now.*

Hamilton wasn't a cop any more, if he ever was, that is. He was a bureaucrat. He was nothing. He only saw crime, the spilling of blood, the sufferings of humans, as statistical entries in a log. At the end of the year the log told him how well he had done. It was the kind of personal arrogance that poisoned many of the senior officers.

And it isolated them.

Hamilton spent a lot of his time switching off lights around the station to save electricity, and sticking labels on the telephones that stated: 'Not to be used for private calls'.

Hamilton called Tom into his office one morning. 'Tom, I've been asked to investigate a death in police custody and I want you to assist me,' he said. 'I have to attend the post-mortem this afternoon and want you to come along.'

'Okay, sir,' Tom replied. He could see that Hamilton was reluctant to go to the PM. Tom was not worried. He had trained his mind and practised the psychology of objectification when dealing with dead bodies. Dead bodies weren't people, they were objects. He had long ago realised that, for him at least, adopting this view was the only way to deal with it and get the job done. It was the easiest way to survive. At the PM, it pleased Tom to see Hamilton look at the body. Like many senior officers, his climb up the ladder had not taken in much of this type of work and it was great to see Hamilton get a dose of what real cops had to deal with. After the PM Hamilton looked very pale, and Tom had to smile to himself.

***

Tom had made a lot of good acquaintances now, and was able to put some of them to good use. One such acquaintance was a wealthy building contractor he had met one night in a club. Andrew Long was born in Longford in Southern Ireland, but had moved to live in England in his early twenties. He had now built up quite a large empire in the Midlands. Among his many interests was breeding racing horses, which interested Tom very much. *There's a chance of making money here,* he thought.

Over the course of several meetings Tom learned from Andrew that he had bred a great horse which he believed would make big money one day. 'I'll give you the tip-off, Tom, when he's ready to run. You won't get many chances before the price drops so get ready to put your shirt on it,' Andrew said.

'You're very confident,' Tom said.

'Trust me, Tom. You'll only get one good chance. Be ready for my call.' That chance came one morning when Tom was in a bank interviewing the manager there over an incident, and his pager went off.

He was going to ignore it, but then decided to ring the force control room to see what they wanted. 'May I use your telephone?' he asked the manager. The control room informed him that an Andrew Long wished to speak to him. He again used the phone, this time to call Andrew.

'Tom, it's running at Newmarket at 2.30 pm, get in quick,' Andrew said.

Tom apologised to the manager and left the bank, promising to return later. He was only able to raise £1,500 at such short notice, and found a bookmakers' shop and placed the bet at odds of twenty-to-one. The horse came in first in the race.

Tom telephoned Andrew to thank him. 'Andrew, that was a great tip. I just managed to make it in time. I'm extremely grateful.'

'Just thinking, Tom, how would you fancy going to a charity lunch next Thursday?' Andrew asked.

'Where's it at?'

'Edgbaston cricket ground, at one o'clock,' said Andrew.

'That would be great, I'll see you there,' Tom replied.

Tom met up with Andrew as arranged and got a real surprise when he discovered that George Best was also a guest. He was now retired, but still a footballing legend in Tom's book. There were several other sporting people present, but Tom was keen on meeting George. After the lavish lunch had finished, Tom went along to where George was seated and introduced himself. They had a long chat and Tom was thrilled that he had been able to fulfil one of his dreams. 'Thanks again, Andrew, that was a fantastic day,' said Tom, before leaving.

Another morning, while sitting in his office looking out of the window and admiring the greenery in the neighbour's garden over the road, a constable knocked on Tom's door and came in. 'Guv, there's a man downstairs in the front office wanting to speak to you. Says he's a friend, a mister Parkhill, shall I bring him up?' he asked.

Tom thought, *I can't believe it, Dave Parkhill.*

'Yes, please bring him up,' he said.

When Dave Parkhill walked into his office they embraced each other like reunited lost brothers.

'It's great to see you, Dave, what the hell brings you to these parts?' Tom asked.

'Would you believe I'm playing with a showband in the

Shamrock Club in town on a permanent basis? It's taken me weeks to track you down, Tom,' he said.

Tom ordered two teas from the canteen. 'Sit down, Dave, we have a lot of catching up to do,' he said. They spent the rest of the morning reminiscing about all the old times back in Derry.

'Tom, you being a policeman after all that went on back home, I couldn't get my head round it at first. Then I thought you must have some scam going for you otherwise you have really turned over a new leaf,' Dave said.

'Dave, you know me better than anyone and you're right, I do have a few little things going on,' Tom replied, knowing he could possibly use his old friend's help.

He went on to tell Dave about some of his little perks, and how Dave could help him again, if he wanted to. Tom then explained to him that he would need to keep him away from his colleagues in the force, and that when they got together it would need to be in secret. Dave fully understood the situation, and said, 'Tom Sharkey, you are as devious as the devil.' Tom took him to one of the local pubs for lunch and a few drinks.

Tom ordered two pints and Dave turned to him, and said, 'It's as flat as—'

'—a witch's tit,' finished Tom, and they both laughed.

Tom asked him how their three old mates Roy, Jack and Victor from back home were doing. Dave told him that Jack had joined the army and was stationed somewhere abroad. Roy and Victor were both now living in Glasgow. *How things have changed,* Tom thought. But this was a man he could completely trust and depend on. After a good drink, Dave went back with Tom to his flat and stopped the night.

Back at work, Tom and his team would regularly visit convicts in prison with a view to getting them to admit other offences they may (or may not) have committed prior to being sentenced.

Under Home Office regulations, if an offender was prepared to admit to other offences while incarcerated, the crimes would be written off to them and no further action would be taken against them. This was a legitimate way of clearing offences to make the crime figures look healthier, and the prisoners concerned were guaranteed a clean sheet when they were eventually released.

In exchange for cigarettes, Tom's team would get the prisoners to sign several blank sheets, and when they returned to the station they would fill in the blank pages with all the uncleared offences they could find. This could amount to hundreds of clearances. Most detectives knew the score, but Tom thought, *If only Hamilton knew the truth, he would have a fit.*

Tom decided one lunchtime to go along and see his old friend Ted at the Red Bull, and took Ken along to meet him. He was anxious to see how Ted was settling into his new pub. The Red Bull was an upmarket establishment and full of office workers enjoying a lunchtime tipple. After introductions, Tom and Ted had a quick chat about old times back at the Old Talbot. 'Tom, I've got to nip over the road. I'll only be a few seconds, can you keep an eye,' Ted said.

He had just left when two well-dressed businesslike men came to the bar to order a drink. Just then, out of nowhere, came Sandra. 'What can I get you?' she asked. They ordered two whiskeys. 'Where are the fucking scotch glasses,' she mumbled, looking round the bar. The men were obviously shocked by her actions, but Tom realised she was drunk. Before he could do or say anything she grabbed two pint glasses and poured two whiskeys. Thankfully, Ted returned and ushered her upstairs away from the bar.

Tom explained to Ted what had taken place, and the look on Ted's face said it all. Sandra was back on the booze. Tom realised that this kind of behaviour could not be tolerated in such an establishment, and felt extremely sorry for Ted. When they eventually left the pub, Tom wondered just how long Ted would survive. A few weeks later Tom got a telephone call from Ted saying that he was leaving the pub and going back to live in Ireland again. *What a great shame,* Tom thought.

***

George Bird, the chief superintendent of the division, was a bully and a nasty man, especially when he got drunk, which was quite often. He usually ended up in some pub after-hours, and when he'd had enough to drink he would call the controller and demand someone take him home. It was usually a young bobby in a panda car who got lumbered and had to stand the abuse from the bastard without being able to say anything.

He was a much-hated man by all the staff, but there were a few who were so afraid of him that they would bow and scrape to him.

This little group could be seen drinking with him and licking up to him, just to stay on his good side, but beneath their smiling faces lay a deep-seated hatred for the man. Several times the chief had asked Tom out for a drink, but he always made some excuse not to go. The chief didn't like being brushed-off by Tom, and this made their relationship rocky.

Many afternoons, after the chief had been on the booze at lunchtime, he would send for Tom and, with his deputy, would give him a hard time over various policing matters. The chief was an obnoxious bastard and Tom had to bite his tongue to stop himself saying something damning. He often thought, as he left the office, *My day will come, believe you me, you evil bastard.*

And it did come, one Sunday morning when the chief came into the office and informed Tom that he was borrowing one of the CID cars. He took the keys and off he went; Tom never thought anything of it. Nearly a week later, Ken came to him enquiring if he knew where the car had gone because it was needed badly by the staff.

It then dawned on Tom who might just still have it. His enquiries revealed that the chief had gone with his wife on holiday to Cornwall, and had taken the CID car with him. Tom explained to Ken what had happened to the car and they decided to report it stolen from the police station. This would surely cause a rumpus, especially as Tom let the news slip to his friendly reporter at the local newspaper.

Tom had no hesitation in making an official complaint to Superintendent Hamilton that the car had been stolen, but Hamilton, who obviously knew exactly where the car was, tried to play it down. Tom waited a few days, and then revealed to Hamilton that he had just discovered that the chief superintendent might have taken it on a family holiday.

Hamilton then tried even harder to play it down – even he was scared of the chief. But Tom had already leaked news of the theft to the press, and insisted he wanted to complain; Hamilton pleaded with him to think of his future. Tom informed Hamilton that he had forwarded a copy of his report to the chief constable and left Hamilton to make up his mind how he handled the matter. Tom knew he would have no choice – he would have to report it, or drop himself in the shit.

Of course, the only consequence for the chief was a move sideways to a desk job in headquarters, and Tom's report was never even acknowledged. This was no doubt to avoid any bad publicity and, frustrating as it was, it at least got rid of the bastard from the division. Tom had no doubt that the chief would bear a grudge against him when he found out that it was he who had shopped him. Tom didn't really care, and Hamilton never mentioned the incident again to him.

***

Tom's early night in bed was disrupted at 1.30 am by his phone ringing. *Can I ever get any peace?* he thought, as he answered. 'Yes,' he said, curtly.

'Boss, it's Ken. Sorry to disturb you but I'm at the Black Horse on the high street and we have a very nasty wounding.'

'Give me twenty minutes and I'll be there,' Tom said.

He was met by Ken at the scene, who explained to him that four Asian men had been playing cards in the pub. The stakes were high, but one was found to be cheating and an argument had started. They had all ended up in the street, where one of the men had grabbed the back of a 'Keep Left' sign and hit the cheater on the head with it. This had resulted in him having the top of his head practically chopped off.

The man had been taken to hospital by ambulance and the uniform staff had arrested the three men involved.

The three were locked up for the night, but in interview refused to admit which one of them was responsible. Tom and Ken went along to the hospital to ascertain the condition of the man. The surgeon who had operated on him informed Tom that a section of the man's brain had been badly damaged, and that his skull was now padded out with cotton wool. It was highly unlikely that he would survive.

The three men continually refused to answer any questions, and so all of them were charged with grievous bodily harm and kept in custody to appear at the magistrates' court. At their subsequent trial at the Crown court all three pleaded not guilty, but on hearing the evidence, were found guilty by the jury. They were sentenced to terms of imprisonment.

The injured man survived but was left like a cabbage. His wife and children had to care for him twenty-fours a day and were struggling financially due to the loss of his earnings. Tom felt very sorry for the family, which prompted him to do everything in his power to ensure that the man was awarded compensation by the Criminal Injuries Compensation Board. The money would help his family survive and deal with his future care.

Tom realised that Ken had done an excellent job on the case, and he sat him down in his office to congratulate him and to discuss his future career in the force. Ken was a happily married man with two teenage sons, and did not play around with other women. 'Why don't you take the inspector's exam, Ken, and go for promotion?' Tom said. He continued. 'You'd make an excellent inspector and could do the job standing on your head.'

'I'm not really interested, boss. I'm happy doing what I'm doing, and don't want the hassle,' he replied.

'You know, I'd do everything possible to get you promoted, Ken,' Tom said.

'I know you would, but I'm honestly very happy the way things are. If you look round the office, who's as happy as me? Look at Danny, he's not really happy.' Tom knew this was true.

He had learned that Danny had once left his wife and kids and gone off with another women, but after a few months when it did not work out his wife had taken him back. Tom could see Ken's point, and the matter was left at that. When Tom thought about the offices he had worked in, he realised there was a high percentage of divorcees in each.

He reflected that there were probably more divorces in the police force than in Hollywood. And that was going some.

Chapter 24

Several months went by, and nothing really changed. Tom and his team were still fighting crime on their patch and life was busy for Tom, but steady. That was until Hamilton came to Tom's office one lunchtime, looking flustered and carrying his travel bag and briefcase. He said, 'Tom, I believe you know about cars?'

'Yes, sir, a little,' he replied.

'I've got a bit of a problem. I'm just off to Bramshill on a course and my wife has phoned to say that her car has broken down and she's stranded in the library car park. Could you possibly have a look at it for her? It's a black Ford XR3i,' he said.

'Yes, sir. You carry on and I'll go and see what I can do,' Tom said, reluctantly.

The library was within walking distance, and so he strolled down there to look for Mrs Hamilton and her car. As he entered the car park he saw the car, with its bonnet up and two men looking at the engine. He approached the woman sitting in the driver's seat and introduced himself. She was an Asian lady in her mid thirties, quite attractive with beautiful brown eyes and long black hair.

As she got out of the car she said, 'Thank goodness. David said he was sending someone round,' and shook Tom's hand. She was about five feet two inches tall, with a slim figure, and dressed in a miniskirt and white boots.

Tom thought, *What is a beauty like you doing with that prat?* He had a quick look at the car and decided it was the fuel injection system that had packed up.

'It'll have to be taken to a Ford dealer. I'll arrange that for you. Now, how are you getting home, can I give you a lift?' he said.

'Please, I'd be very grateful if you could,' she replied.

They walked back to the station and he let her into his car while he went off to phone the garage. Then he drove her to her large detached home in Knowle, where she asked him if he would like a coffee.

He couldn't – and didn't want to – refuse, so he accompanied her inside and was soon settled on the sofa, drinking a very nice cup of coffee. 'So, you work with David,' she said. 'I bet you see more of him than I do, Tom.'

'He works long, hard hours,' Tom said, trying to cheer her up, as she seemed quite down.

Tears came into her eyes and she was on the verge of crying, as she blurted, 'I'm fed up with the whole damned situation. I'm in this house on my own day and night while he pursues his precious career.'

'Have you got any children, Mrs Hamilton?' Tom asked, trying to calm the situation.

'No, David doesn't like kids,' she replied. 'And please, call me Jiti.'

It was obvious to Tom that she was a lonely woman, who was feeling deserted by Hamilton while he pursued his career. Tom knew he was doing the wrong thing by putting his arm around her shoulder to console her, but she seemed so sad and vulnerable.

She wept softly, and slowly spilled out all her troubles to him. He pulled her close, trying to comfort her, and as he kissed her cheek he could taste her tears.

'I'm so lonely, and just feel like life is passing me by. David seems to have very little time for me these days. Don't get me wrong, he provides well for me and gives me plenty of money, but he offers me very little affection,' she said.

Tom held her tight. She raised her face to meet his and they kissed, the tears still running down her face.

'You're a beautiful woman, Jiti, please don't cry,' he said.

They sat talking for ages, and she told him how she and David had met in India while he was in the army. She explained that life had been great before he joined the police, but after that things had seemed to go downhill rapidly.

She went to make another coffee and returned looking a bit more relaxed. 'I'm sorry, Tom, for lumbering you with my troubles,' she said.

'Don't be silly, I don't mind. I don't like to see anyone unhappy,' he said.

They put their arms around each other and kissed again. She seemed to melt into him as he kissed her face all over.

'Would you like to go out for a relaxing drink one night with me while David is away at the college?' he asked. He knew he was doing the wrong thing, but he couldn't help himself.

'I'd love to, but wouldn't it be risky with you working with David,' she said.

'Let me worry about that. Would you like to come out?'

'Yes, but where and when can we meet?' She then told him that David had gone away for five days and that she could meet him the following night, provided she had her car back. Tom kissed her goodbye, promising to phone the next day.

On the way back to the station, he thought, *What the hell are you doing you idiot? Your brains are between your legs again.*

Despite knowing how risky it was for them both, Tom phoned Jiti and they arranged to meet that night in Studley, miles from where they both lived. She parked up and got into his car, and he gave her a hug and a kiss.

'I'm very nervous Tom, I've never done anything like this before. I'm on the pill and I don't play around, believe me,' she said. He kissed her and they drove into the country where he found a little pub. She was dressed in a navy-blue two-piece suit with the mini skirt showing off her lovely thighs. She drank Bacardi and Coke, and he sipped a pint of bitter.

They sat chatting in the corner of the lounge for ages, discussing their pasts, their likes and dislikes, and he thought how easily he could really fall for her. She reminded him very much of Nina: same height, build, eyes, hair and lovely skin.

They left the pub and returned to Tom's car. He put his arms around her and kissed her passionately as he slid his hand up under her jacket and felt her braless breasts through her silk blouse. She began to take off her boots and stripped completely naked as he reclined the seat.

He was taken aback at her boldness, but soon removed his trousers and climbed over into the passenger seat beside her. He kissed her small firm breasts and sucked her nipples, which seemed to drive her mad with passion. She was caressing his hardness, which was now throbbing and ready to explode. He felt the parting between her legs as she gave out a little groan.

'Take me, Tom, take me,' she whispered. He was between her legs and inside her, thrusting in and out as she wrapped her legs tightly around him.

'I love your prick, Tom, it's so big, it fills me up,' she groaned.

Then she screamed, 'I'm coming, I'm coming, fill me up, I love it, fill me up!' Tom came with throbbing bursts as their bodies tensed together.

Breathless, he said, 'That was fantastic, you are something else,' and he kissed her tenderly.

They lay together, caressing and kissing each other before he eventually returned her to her car. They arranged to speak to each other next day.

Tom's relationship with Jiti developed into something special, and for the first time since Nina he felt he might be in love. His pangs of guilt at this realisation led him to wonder if he was subconsciously using Jiti as a substitute for Nina, and then he felt bad about that too. He decided he was content to follow his feelings for Jiti and see where they led him.

At every opportunity, they met and made love: in his flat, in one of their cars, and even in her house. One lunchtime, while David was out of town on a one-day seminar, Tom went to her house and she made him steak sandwiches. He had parked his car a few streets away and walked the remainder so as not to be seen.

After he had eaten they went to bed and were making love when the phone rang. He lifted the receiver, as it was on his side of the bed, and passed it over to her to answer.

'Hello, David. Yes, I'm just doing a little housework. How are you getting on?' she lied, as Tom gently made love to her. As she talked on the phone he caressed her breasts and she had great trouble controlling herself. When she had finished talking she handed him the phone to place back on the receiver. *Sitting in office meetings listening to Hamilton ramble on will never be the same again,* Tom thought.

Jiti turned out to be a very sexy woman, and as they sat in a pub one night she caught his hand under the table and placed it on her thigh, pushing it up under her miniskirt. To his delight, he discovered that she was wearing no pants, and as they sat in a room full of people he ran his fingers along her moist lips. From that day on she very rarely wore any pants, and it used to drive him mad.

Tom had started to watch Hamilton very closely to try and get some more black on him in case the wheels should come off his affair with Jiti. He suspected that Hamilton must be getting his thrills someplace else, because he was not bothering with his wife at all.

He had discovered that at about noon most days Hamilton would go off in his car and come back an hour or so later. One day he decided to get Ken and Danny to follow him and spy on his movements. They reported back that Hamilton had gone to an address in Lichfield where he had been let in to the house by a young woman. He had stayed for about an hour.

Further enquiries revealed that the house was owned by another superintendent and his wife, who was a dentist, and continued observations confirmed that Hamilton was having an affair with this woman even though her husband was a close friend of his. *Got you now, superintendent, should the need arise to sort you out in the future,* Tom thought, but never told Jiti of his findings.

Weeks later, Tom was sent on a CID course to Wakefield, and Jiti went along to spend a night with him after telling Hamilton she was visiting relatives in Bradford. They booked into a small bed and breakfast, as it was actually the first time that they had spent the whole night together. They shared a lovely bath before going to bed.

Tom told Jiti that he was in love with her, and in turn she revealed to him that she felt the same way. She also told him that she wanted to have a baby by him, and was prepared to leave Hamilton and move in with him. Tom was taken aback by the impact of her words, and told her that they would have to discuss such a serious matter a great deal more. In the morning, she left to drive back to the Midlands.

Tom loved her, but he was still very ambitious. He wanted to progress further in the police force, and wondered how settling down with Jiti might affect his chances. It was a selfish attitude, he knew, but he had to be honest with such life-changing decisions to be made. And there was still Nina on his mind.

On the course, he met Detective Chief Inspector Ron Bannister from the Manchester force. They were very much alike and hit it off immediately. They talked the same language and were able to relate to one another.

At the end of the week Tom decided to discuss the situation with McClurg and Pauline with him. Ron knew McClurg and all about what he was doing, and was trying to build a case against him.

He confided that it was very difficult because of the way McClurg operated. He also told Tom that he was concerned about Pauline's disappearance from the scene in Manchester, and had begun to think that McClurg had somehow got rid of her.

He further explained that Dunn was McClurg's deputy, and an evil man who was capable of anything, including murder. Dunn had already served ten years for stabbing to death a taxi driver in Bolton. Now that they were on the same wavelength and Tom knew he could trust him, he told Ron the whole story of Pauline, and of McClurg's antics in Birmingham. They agreed to keep each other informed when they returned to their respective forces.

Over the weeks that followed, Jiti came off the pill and Tom felt himself being drawn into something he was not a hundred percent sure about. He didn't know if he could handle a family, and if he could really settle down. It was at this stage that Jiti discovered the photo of Nina in his wallet one night, and asked him who she was. He explained the whole story to her, including how he had felt about Nina. She accepted his explanation and never mentioned it again.

The inevitable happened: she became pregnant. The time had

come to do some serious talking. Tom eventually accepted the idea of becoming a father but wondered how Hamilton would react to it all. And what would become of his career now.

Hamilton made the decision easy for them. His own affair had blossomed and, before they could confront him with their own news, Hamilton told Jiti that he was leaving her and going to live with his friend's wife. The story hit the headlines: 'Senior police officer runs off with another senior officer's wife'.

Jiti was very surprised, but at the same time relieved by his decision. Hamilton was not even aware that Jiti was pregnant, but Tom knew he had no loyalties to anyone other than himself, and doubted that knowing the truth would have made any difference to his decision to leave.

Jiti moved into Tom's flat a few weeks later, and started to prepare for the birth of the baby. Tom woke up one night to hear her crying in the bathroom. He rushed in to see what was the matter and found her haemorrhaging. He called an ambulance immediately and she was rushed to Good Hope Hospital.

The doctor attending her pulled Tom to one side, and said to him, gently, 'I'm afraid I have some very bad news. Your wife has lost the baby, I am so very sorry.' The worst was still to come, because when they had carried out further tests on Jiti, they discovered that she had cancer.

Tom was devastated, by the loss of the baby, and by the news of the cancer. The depth of his pain surprised him. He visited Jiti every day while she was in hospital. He realised how much he loved her, and missed her so much that he would sometimes in the middle of the night go into the hospital grounds, tap at the window nearest her bed, and whisper to her into the small hours. Eventually they allowed her home.

Jiti appeared to be holding her own now, but several months later her condition deteriorated and she was rushed back to hospital for more treatment. Tom would visit her at every possible moment, but as he sat there holding her hand he knew he was losing her.

She was so thin and listless lying there and he felt so useless being unable to help her. After visiting her he would sit in his car, crying. Then one morning he got an urgent call asking him to attend the hospital; he felt the worst. He was met by the doctor who informed him that Jiti had had a very bad night and, that he didn't think she would last much longer.

She looked like a rag doll as Tom held her in his arms and whispered to her, but he wasn't sure she understood what he was saying. Then, she opened her eyes, pulled him tight to her and whispered, 'Thomas, I love you.' She then passed away in his arms.

He cried for days; he really did love her so much and for a long while he didn't believe he could live without her.

Tom found it very difficult to handle his grief, and agonised over how such a tragic thing could happen to such a lovable and beautiful woman as Jiti. He found comfort in the bottle, and began to hit it hard.

He now buried himself in his work and money-making schemes as a way of hiding from and coping with the situation. He was feeling terribly lonely, and was doing all he could to mask his feelings from his friends and staff. It was only with the help of his two friends Ken and Danny that he eventually began to pull himself together.

When he *was* able to get Jiti out of his mind, all his energies were directed to the police force or, more pertinently, to how he could make very serious money. He had to fight his sadness, and move on.

Chapter 25

The telephone rang in Tom's office one day, months later; it was an old detective chief inspector friend of his. 'I need to have a serious discussion with you, Tom, as a matter of urgency. Where can we meet?' he said.

Tom was intrigued. 'What's it about?'

'We can't talk on the phone, meet me in half an hour in the Cross Keys, Erdington,' the DCI replied.

They met as arranged and his friend got the drinks in before ushering Tom to a quiet table in the corner.

'One of your lads has arrested an acquaintance of mine, Gerry Green, for the theft of some heavy machinery,' the DCI explained.

'Yes, I know about the case,' Tom replied.

'If we can find some way of dropping the charges I'm sure we'll be well taken care of,' the DCI said.

'How much are we talking about?' Tom asked.

'Seven grand between us, if it can be done,' the DCI replied. Tom assured him that he would do everything he could, and they parted company. *For three and a half grand, It'll be sorted,* he thought.

Back in his office, Tom called for all the case papers and examined them very carefully to find any way he could have the case dropped. It turned out to be quite simple, because all the evidence against Green was documentary. This type of evidence could disappear, and the CPS (the Crown Prosecution Service) would not be informed it was missing until the day of the trial. In those circumstances, the CPS would have no alternative but to offer no evidence, and withdraw the case against Green.

And that was exactly what happened on the day of the trial. The CPS were not very happy, and sent a report to the division stating their disgust. The report eventually landed on Tom's desk to be dealt with but, like many other matters, it disappeared under mountains of paperwork, never to be seen again.

A large brown envelope was eventually deposited with Danny, and brought to Tom. Ken and Danny received a decent share of the payment.

A lot of money was now coming in, but Tom realised that it was also becoming increasingly difficult to hide. *The time has come to call on Dave Parkhill,* he thought.

Tom was now being pushed by his superiors to take the promotion board for chief inspector; little did they know what was really going on behind the scenes. He didn't want to lose his earnings on the side, but he also thought that maybe as a chief he could do even better.

One night, lying in bed, he decided that he would have a try for the promotion; it was the old ambition thing raising its head again, rather than the money. Next day he applied for the board.

It had been a while now since Jiti died, and Tom felt like he was starting to find himself again. He realised that he was craving the company of a woman, any woman, and so one Wednesday night he went with a few of the lads to the grab-a-granny do at the local ballroom.

Sure enough, he pulled, and got off with a married woman called Joan from Brownhills. They ended up making love in the front seat of his car somewhere in the country about a mile from her home. She kept telling him that her husband didn't understand or appreciate her and that she had a need to be loved Tom knew he would enjoy having sex with her, but doubted very much if he would ever love her. She was just a convenience.

The first stage in his bid for promotion was an extended assessment, for which Tom attended Tally Ho for a day, and was put through five tests. He studied the other inspectors who were going through the system and realised that he was head-and-shoulders above them in terms of experience and ability. *This should be a doddle,* he thought.

One of the tests was producing an operational order on an imaginary event, and briefing the superintendent and the two chief inspectors on the assessment team of the action he would propose to take. He found the whole situation quite boring, having carried out the real thing on numerous occasions.

Another part of the assessment was being interviewed on television by a news presenter regarding an incident requiring publicity. He had carried out many appeals and been interviewed on television several times, and here again he found little to challenge him.

His biggest problem was having to act out a contrived incident, where he was assessed on how good an actor he was, rather than as a police officer. Tom found this whole scenario very hard to handle. He could deal with the real thing, but found it very difficult acting out a role.

He failed the assessment, and was disappointed because he knew he could buy and sell the other contenders, most of whom got through and were eventually promoted. His superintendent informed him that he would have to adapt to the situation if he wanted to succeed in the higher ranks of the force. 'You're a real enigma, Tom. At times I can't make you out, but I know you can do it if you try,' the super said. It was a game Tom would have to learn to play.

It was at this stage that Tom began to recognise what was happening to some of the senior officers in the force. They were clones of each other, several Hamiltons organising and running the show. Which was a good thing, Tom realised. He was relatively safe doing what he was doing in his current role because there were just a few of the senior officers who had the ability to catch him out.

His detective superintendent, a real cop, would not let the promotion thing rest there because he knew just how good a copper Tom was and how much ability he had. He pushed and pushed him to have another go.

Tom eventually resat the tests two years later, and was amazed to find that the two chief inspectors on his panel were two of the inspectors who had been through the assessment on his previous attempt. *Again,* he thought, *all bloody clones of each other.*

This time he had made up his mind, if he wanted to get promoted he had to act the part for the duration of the day, and

225

model himself on these robots. He lied about his feelings and his views, agreed with all their opinions, and just like that he got through.

The interview was the easy part, where he easily convinced the board that he was the cat's whiskers and they recommended him for promotion. Tom continued his duties as detective inspector, locking up villains and managing his extra income until a suitable vacancy for a chief inspector came along.

It was a Sunday morning, and Tom was down at the transport cafe for breakfast with a gang from the office. The police canteen didn't open at weekends because the budget holders didn't think police officers ate at weekends. He was settling down to his full English when the control room called him on his radio. A young girl of about eight years old had been walking her cat on some waste ground at the rear of her garden, close to a main road. She had come across what looked like a dead body or a dummy half hidden in the undergrowth. Terrified, she had run home and told her father who, on investigation, realised that it was in fact a dead body and had called the police.

Tom abandoned his breakfast to attend the scene, and saw that it was the remains of a woman's body, which had been quite well preserved due to the protection afforded by the shrubbery. He immediately called the scenes of crime officers and the police pathologist. Following red tape, a police surgeon also attended to certify the death – he looked at the body, and certified that it was dead. *What a waste of money,* Tom thought. After the necessary examinations and photographs the body was removed to the central mortuary so that a post-mortem could be carried out.

The PM revealed that the woman had been five feet four inches tall, and from the sizes of her blouse, skirt, pants and bra she was estimated to have been of slim build. She'd had long dark hair, and her age was estimated to have been in the early twenties. Found in the breast pocket of her blouse was a set of darts, and the cause of death was deemed to be a blow to the head that had fractured her skull.

With all this information to hand, Tom called a conference of the CID staff. The first task was to try and identify who this young woman was. From the missing persons bureau records it was established that there were two immediate possibilities, and one of the missing girls on record proved to be a positive match. The body was that of a twenty-year-old local girl by the name of Jean Hall, who had disappeared a month earlier. This was a lucky break, which saved many hours of searching various regional and national records. Her file was examined, and it transpired that she had gone missing one evening after leaving a pub with her boyfriend, Darren Grey, where they had been playing darts. The file revealed no suspicious findings at the time, and it was presumed that she had just run away from home.

Grey had no previous convictions recorded against him. He was arrested on suspicion of murder and interviewed at length by Ken and Danny, who gave him a very hard time. After several interviews he eventually admitted killing Jean, and the officers were able to piece together what had happened. On leaving the pub on the night in question, Jean and Grey had had an enormous row, during which she had told him that she wanted to finish with him. He had lost his temper completely, dragged her from his car, found a concrete slab and hit her over the head with it. Then, realising he had killed her, he had called his brother, Norman, who had helped him move the body and try to hide it.

Grey's brother was arrested, too, and they both were charged. Tom was delighted with the outcome of the case, as was his superintendent.

Again, good luck was to shine on Tom, because a vacancy opened up around the same time, and he got promoted to chief inspector with the added bonus that he was able to remain in the CID on the same division.

It meant he had the same staff in the CID department, with the exception of the new DI who would take his place in the office. He knew that this could cause problems if the new DI didn't fit in, but he had no great say in who was to fill the vacancy.

The new DI turned out to be one of the clones who only wanted to get into the CID to further his career. Fortunately, he had never been in the CID and was very green to what actually went on in the department. This made it easy to keep him in the dark.

Newly transferred Detective Inspector Fred Black only had about seven years' service, which had all been spent in uniform and most of it in departments at divisional headquarters. He was a graduate from Oxford, well-spoken and quite intelligent, but he lacked experience or intuitive policing ability.

As Danny would say, he couldn't track an elephant in the snow. None of this seemed to matter to the brass, just as long as he possessed the so-called managerial skills they looked for in their high-ranking clones.

Tom called a meeting with Ken and Danny in one of the local clubs that catered for a more diverse clientele than their usual haunts, to be sure they were undisturbed by wandering colleagues. It was agreed that they would all have to be extremely careful now.

Tom instructed Ken and Danny that they would have to keep a safe distance from him so as not to raise any suspicions from the DI. The two of them would continue to carry out their 'extra' duties and meet up alone to discuss their private business. At the same time, they would show every respect to the new DI and act the part of his loyal officers.

Business over, they ordered a delicious goat curry and rice, cooked to perfection. It was the only food on the menu. They then noticed one of the few other white men in the club, who was well dressed in a suit, shirt and collar, and sitting at one of the tables looking uncomfortable. The man had obviously ordered a meal and was poking around at it with his fork. He looked around anxiously and, spotting Tom and the crew, he rose and came over. 'Have you ever eaten here?' he asked.

'Yes, often,' Danny said.

'I just ordered a chicken curry, but there's a very large bone in it. I don't think its chicken,' the man said.

'Oh, don't worry, it's good food. It's Alsatian, you must have got one of the leg bones,' Danny said, joking.

The man immediately started to heave and ran off towards the toilet, but they never saw him again. They all saw the funny side to it because they knew the food was good.

***

Watching television at home one evening, Tom received a telephone call from Superintendent Peter Kirby whom he had not seen since his early days when he was completing his CID attachment.

'Tom, I'm calling you from a phone box. Need to meet you somewhere very private, where do you suggest? Preferably out of town,' he said.

'Must be something very important, Peter,' Tom replied.

'Something you need to know, Tom. Believe you me, I'm putting my head on the block.'

'Let me think,' Tom said, then remembered the old pub he went to while at the training centre. 'Yes, a pub called the Old Bull outside Coventry, you know it?'

'I don't, but I'll find it. When?' Peter asked.

'If it's so important I'll see you tomorrow night at 8.00 pm.'

'Good. See you then, and you never had this call,' Peter said, and hung up.

Next morning, Tom made discreet enquiries as to where Peter Kirby was now stationed and got a bit of a shock when he discovered he worked in the complaints department at police headquarters.

It was a lovely, hot June evening when Tom arrived at the pub, and the children's area and the outside dining area were packed with customers.

He thought, *Maybe this wasn't such a good idea after all. It's far too busy for a secret meeting, but still, I'm here now.* Inside was much quieter, and he found Peter Kirby sitting in a corner of the lounge sipping a pint of beer. He immediately ordered Tom a drink and they sat down together.

'Nice to see you, Peter, and thanks for contacting me,' Tom said.

'Wish it was under better circumstances, Tom, but nice to see you anyway,' Peter replied.

'What's it all about?'

'Tom, I'm taking a big chance here, this is between us and nobody else must know,' Peter explained.

'You have my word on that, Peter,' Tom replied. Peter then went on to tell him that he was working in the complaints department and that an investigation team was looking at Tom and his activities. The investigation was being carried out by Chief Superintendent Bird personally, and was being handled very secretly by a small team. Peter was not working on this team but had learned enough to realise who the investigation related to. Tom realised that it was payback time for the old chief superintendent he had reported for misuse of the CID car.

'I don't know what the plan is, Tom, but they will attempt to catch you red-handed doing something you shouldn't be doing,'

Peter said.

'I understand,' Tom replied.

'They won't rush, Tom. They'll try to set you up and will take as much time as is necessary. From here on in you'll have to be whiter than white.'

'Thank you for the information, Peter, I really appreciate it,' Tom said.

'Be very careful, Tom,' Peter warned, as he left.

Tom got back in his car and slammed the door in frustration, and banged the steering wheel in anger as he drove back to his flat. He was annoyed that all his extra-curricular activities would have to cease for the time being: no more wheeling or dealings. He also felt relieved that he had such good contacts in the force. It would now become a contest of wits between him and the chief superintendent.

As soon as he possibly could he met up with Ken and Danny. 'I've just had an anonymous tip-off from someone, who informed me that the rubber heel squad are looking at me. So, for now and the foreseeable future we'll deal with everything above board.'

'Any idea who it was, boss?' Ken asked.

'No idea, other than it was a man.' Tom replied. He had to protect Peter.

Chapter 26

In one respect, the new DI's lack of experience was of some benefit because he never made any real decision without consulting Tom. He looked to him for guidance and became a sort of lapdog. The downside was that Tom could not really trust him to do anything on his own.

The team were now seeing a big increase in the number of house and shop burglaries in the area, with mainly cash and jewellery being taken. This made it more difficult to identify stolen property. At one of the burglaries, two men had been disturbed by the owner, who had been asleep upstairs when they had broken in.

Tom sent Danny to interview the victim and obtain a comprehensive statement of what the burglars looked like. Ken and Danny came to his office next morning to bring him up to date on their findings.

'The two men who were disturbed were white, and in their early twenties,' Danny said. 'The only thing the owner can remember about them is that one had a tattoo of a swallow on his hand between his thumb and forefinger.' Enquiries at criminal records revealed several men known to the police who had such a tattoo, but all of them were much older than the suspects. Tom knew that this type of tattoo was common among men who had served in the armed forces during the war, especially those who had been in the navy.

'There's something else, boss. They've left fingerprints at several of the jobs which have failed to show up on record, which means they're newcomers to the scene,' Ken said.

'They've been very lucky up to now, because they don't even bother to hide their faces,' Danny added. Tom told them to continue with their enquiries, and keep him informed.

Several days later, Ken reported to him that there had been a cashier's till snatched from one of the local supermarkets; two young white men were involved.

'And guess what, boss? One of the offenders had a tattoo of a swallow on his right hand,' said Ken. Tom realised that the bastards were expanding their empire; they would have to nail them.

'Have we been round all the local tattooists yet, Ken?' he asked.

'Yes, and none of them has any first-hand knowledge of anyone having such a tattoo,' he replied.

'I've had a thought, Danny. Remember that old chap called Albert Brooks from the Shareholders Arms we used to drink with? He used to be a tattoo artist; he might know of someone with ink like that, or he might know someone in the same game who could help us,' Tom said.

'I'll track him down and get him on the case,' Danny replied.

Several days later they got a good result. Albert Brooks had a mate who knew of two young brothers who both had the same tattoo on their right hands.

The brothers were Steve and Paul Duffy, who lived in Winson Green. One was twenty years old, and the other was twenty-two. Early next morning, armed with a search warrant, Tom went with Ken, Danny and six uniform officers to the brothers' home in Heath

Street and arrested them. They both sported the same tattoo, but denied any knowledge of any wrongdoings. Upon searching their house, the team found numerous item of jewellery, and two thousand pounds in cash. Their excuse was that they were running a jewellery stall in the market and had bought a lot of stock from various people over recent weeks.

Tom organised an ID parade, which took place at Bridge Street West police station under the supervision of a uniform inspector. Everything was done above board, just in case the rubber heel squad were around, and to Tom's satisfaction the brothers were picked out by several witnesses. Their fingerprints also matched the ones lifted at several of the crime scenes.

The brothers were charged with two robberies and seven burglaries and kept in custody to appear at court the following day. The team decided to go to a local club to celebrate the good result with T-bone steaks and a large quantity of beer.

John, the bouncer at their club of choice was quite a character, and ran a tight ship. He had the biggest neck Tom had ever seen; he wore a twenty-inch collar and was known as the bull. Tom thought, *I wouldn't have your job for any amount of money.*

John, however, loved doing what he was doing. 'Hit them once and make sure they don't get up. It's the only way to survive in this game,' he explained. With the scum he had to contend with he was probably right.

During the course of the evening, Danny commented, 'There doesn't seem to be any movement from the rubber heel squad does there, boss.'

'I wouldn't trust that chief superintendent and his team as far as I could throw them, but you're right, I haven't heard a dicky bird,' Tom said. 'But we'll play it by the book for a little bit longer.'

While having lunch in the George one day on his own, Tom got a call on his personal radio to contact the control room urgently for a message. He finished his lunch quickly, and returned to the office where he got the message to ring a Detective Sergeant Evans in Wales, urgently.

He rang the number and asked to speak to the sergeant. A man came on the line and said, 'Detective Sergeant Evans here, can I help?' in a strong Welsh accent. Tom introduced himself and informed the sergeant that he had received a message to ring him.

'Thanks for ringing sir, we have a very unusual situation here. We've found a dead body in a car boot and just arrested three individuals we think may be involved,' Evans said. 'From what we understand so far, the people we've arrested here – a mother, with her son and daughter – killed the father in your force area yesterday and drove the body up here.'

'Where did they kill him?' Tom asked.

'The address is 22 Water Street, and I believe you cover that, sir.'

'Yes, we cover Water Street. Have they admitted the murder?'

'Yes, they're quite helpful and have told us most of the story,' said Evans.

'I'll go and look at the address and get the forensic team started straight away. I'll contact you later and make the necessary arrangements to bring them back here, okay,' Tom said.

'I will wait to hear from you, sir,' Evans replied.

Tom got hold of the DI and they went together to 22 Water Street, which was a mid-terrace house. It was all locked up and looked quite normal, so they went round to the rear door. The door was locked, so they forced it open and very carefully stepped inside so as not to disturb any evidence that might be there.

Inside, the house was in complete disarray, blood everywhere. There was no doubt that a good struggle had taken place. Tom immediately requested the forensic team and the force photographer to attend the scene.

With the team assembled, he explained the situation to them and returned to his office. Tom telephoned DS Evans in Wales and listened while he related the whole story to him, and then informed him that he had visited the murder scene. He then contacted his detective superintendent and related the whole story to him.

'Do you need any assistance, Tom?' the super asked. Tom informed him that he was going to travel to Wales and take four officers with him, two men and two women, and would stop the night and travel back next day.

'Keep me posted, Tom,' the super said. Tom then briefed his detective inspector, and instructed him to go and take charge of the scene. Ken, Danny, two female officers and Tom then headed off in a minibus to Wales. They were met by DS Evans and his detective superintendent, who took them to the incident room they had set up and briefed them fully.

Tom's team learned that the family were Polish and had lived in England for over thirty years in the same house. They all spoke English fluently. It seemed the father had been quite well off, but spent most of his time drunk. The mother said that he was an incredibly violent man, who had regularly beaten her unconscious. She had been certain that one day he would kill her. The son and daughter had discussed for months what they were going to do about him, and had decided to kill him. Unknown to the father, the son had begun to transfer his father's savings and investments into his own name by forging the father's signature. The son was studying to be a solicitor, and was quite capable of carrying out these transfers.

When all the necessary transfers had been completed the son and the daughter, who was a junior doctor at the local hospital, had planned to kill the father. The mother was eventually brought into the plan and, being in such a frail state, had agreed to it.

The son had hired a car under a false name and address; Tom was quietly impressed at how he had managed to pull this off. He had placed polythene sheeting all round inside the boot. The scene had thus been set for the killing to be carried out two days later, but their plan had quickly unravelled.

Their first mistake had happened almost immediately, because that night the father had come home very drunk and begun to beat the mother up. The so-called plan for a controlled and orderly murder had been forgotten when the son, in order to protect his mother, had hit his father over the head with a steam iron and continued to batter him until he was dead.

The daughter had shaved off the father's beard and hair, completely changing his appearance. They had then both stripped him naked, rolled him up in a blanket and placed his body in the boot of the car.

The next stage of the plan had been to drive the body through Wales to the coast around Harlech, and dispose of it in the sea, hoping that it would never be identified. They had not planned to report the father missing to the police. The mother had made a flask of tea and prepared a box of sandwiches for their journey to dispose of the body.

Their second mistake had happened in the Welsh mountains where the son, not being a very good driver and never having driven in the country, had skidded off the road and crashed the car. The car had been badly damaged and was undriveable.

By this time it was 3.00 am, they were all tired and overwrought and had not been thinking straight. The son had set off on foot, with no real plan of what they were going to do.

On the hillside he had seen a cottage and had gone and knocked on the door. He had explained to the elderly occupier that they had just had an accident in their car and needed to contact a taxi. The old man had got his wife out of bed to make the son a cup of tea, while the son had explained to them that his family were in the car and asked if it was all right to fetch them.

The couple had agreed, and so he had returned to the car to fetch them. While there, he had removed the number plates and the tax disc from the car and hidden them in a nearby field. He had then taken the family back to the cottage. The old man had managed to book them a taxi but, one which would only take them as far as Welshpool even though they had stated they needed to get to Birmingham. The taxi had eventually arrived, and off they had gone.

After they had left, the old man had thought the whole situation was very strange: three people in the middle of nowhere at the dead of night and just abandoning their car. He had dressed and walked to where they had left the car and, upon discovering the car without number plates, he had become even more suspicious. When he had got back home he had discussed it with his wife, and decided to drive to the local police station and report the matter.

Unfortunately, the police station was closed at nights so he had returned home and decided to phone the main station at Welshpool, who had informed him that they would take a look at the car. Things had finally started to happen early next morning when the local bobby had arrived at the scene, and found the car without number plates or a tax disc. The car had also been left open, which had made him very suspicious.

He had searched the inside of the car but had been unable to find anything to identify the owners, or the occupants who had taken off. Not being completely happy with the situation, the officer had made the decision to force open the boot, just to see if it revealed anything. He had quite a shock on discovering the wrapped-up body. He had immediately contacted his control room and a search was begun to trace the local taxi involved.

When the taxi driver had been traced, he told them that he had dropped his three passengers off in Welshpool, where they were attempting to hire another taxi to take them on to Birmingham. Due to the very early hour, and the few taxi companies in Welshpool, enquiries by the police had soon revealed that the three were in a taxi on the M6 on their way back to Birmingham.

The taxi registration details had been passed to the motorway police in the Midlands and the taxi had been stopped on the motorway close to Walsall. The three occupants had been arrested and escorted back to Welshpool.

With all the necessary paperwork completed, all three suspects were escorted back to Birmingham where they again all readily admitted their involvement. They were later charged with murder and eventually went on to plead guilty at the Crown court.

Their plan to get rid of the father had gone completely wrong for them. In a way Tom felt a bit sorry for them, especially the old lady. Having experienced his mother's distress at the hands of a violent bully he could understand the lady's desire to bring an end to the hurt, and the relief she must have felt at being offered a way out by her children. But he also reflected on his part in Oliver's demise back in Derry – that had been a happy accident as far as Tom was concerned, but it was far from premeditated murder. He wondered, *Could I resort to that, if a situation demanded it?* The level of discomfort he felt even thinking about it reassured him. His behaviour may be less than lawful at times, but a killer he most definitely was not.

Chapter 27

Back in the old routine and things went quiet for a few weeks for Tom, until six o'clock one morning when he was woken up by someone ringing the doorbell of his flat. Ken Payne, who had been on night duty, was standing at the door. He said, 'Boss, I have some terrible news: Jimmy Walker is dead.'

'What do you mean, dead?' Tom asked.

In the flat, Ken continued. 'He was killed in a car crash at about one o'clock this morning in North Wales. It seems there were no other vehicles involved; he was drunk and drove off the road.'

'That seems very strange, him being drunk in Wales at that time of night. It's not his scene, is it,' Tom said.

Ken agreed that it was very unusual behaviour by Walker.

'Was there anything suspicious about the accident, or any witnesses?' Tom asked.

'I haven't spoken to anyone down there. It was his wife who phoned, looking for you,' Ken said.

'You get off to bed. I'll contact Wales and will speak to you later,' Tom said.

He was shattered by the news and could not really take it in. *The second accident in Wales in such a short period of time,* he thought.

At nine o'clock in his office he phoned the police in North Wales and spoke to the duty inspector. He relayed his doubts to the inspector and asked him if there were any suspicious circumstances surrounding the accident.

Walker's car, it appeared, had skidded off a mountain road and crashed down into a very deep gorge, falling about a hundred feet before colliding with a rock face. He most likely died immediately.

'Were there any suspicious injuries to his body?' Tom asked.

'Nothing that was noticeable, other than the injuries from the collision. But he did smell strongly of alcohol and most likely lost control on the winding road,' replied the inspector.

'When's the post-mortem? I'd like to attend,' Tom said.

The inspector informed him that it would probably be next morning, but he would let him know.

Tom went immediately to see Irene Walker, Jimmy's wife, at their home. After expressing his sympathies, he said, 'Irene, when did you last see Jimmy?'

Tears ran down her cheeks, and she sobbed, 'Last night when he left about eight o'clock saying he had to meet someone on business.'

'Did he say who he was going to meet, or where he was going?'

'He didn't say, but he did say he wouldn't be very long.'

'Did he mention anything about going to Wales?' Tom said.

'No, but I doubt that Jimmy would go there at that time of night; it was a very strange thing for him to do, I just can't believe it,' she said.

Tom left her, saying that he would call and see her again next day. Tom knew from his own experience how treacherous Welsh mountain roads could be if not respected, but still he had his doubts about this accident.

He attended the PM in Wales with Ken. There were bruises on

Walker's body, head, face, wrists and the backs of his hands. The pathologist could account for all the bruises apart from the ones on his hands and wrists. Tom was convinced that the ones on the hands were caused by Walker defending himself, and believed the ones on the wrists were from where he had been tied up. Walker was a tough man, and the only way an aggressor could have handled him would have been to have tied his arms together. The body contained a small amount of alcohol but it was established that Walker had not been over the drink-drive limit.

The cause of death was noted as a brain haemorrhage resulting from a fractured skull. Tom was convinced that Jimmy Walker had been murdered, and the accident was invented to cover that fact. He was now concerned that if this was the work of McClurg, he might now know the whereabouts of Pauline. That is, if they had been able to make Jimmy Walker talk.

Before leaving Wales, Tom had a long conversation with the local detective sergeant and told him about McClurg. The DS promised to investigate the death thoroughly, but without any witnesses or evidence of foul play it would be hard to prosecute anyone.

Jimmy Walker's funeral was one of the biggest seen in Small Heath for many years. It was attended by many police officers of all ranks from all over the Midlands. There were also several very well-known criminals, businessmen, bankers and politicians in attendance. Walker had been well respected. Tom would certainly miss him.

Tom was not sure whether to contact Pauline and warn her about what had happened, or to sit tight for the moment and try not to worry her. But the decision was made for him when things started to happen very quickly: too quickly for his liking.

He got home from work very late one night not long after Walker's death, and after having a drink with some of the staff from the office. He discovered a message on his answering machine.

It was from Pauline. It said, 'Hi, Tom, thought I'd catch you before you left, I'm really looking forward to seeing you. Bye for now, see you around eight.' The message was timed at ten o'clock that morning.

Tom broke out in a cold sweat; somehow Pauline thought he was on his way over to Menorca to see her, but he had made no such plans. He immediately rang her apartment but got no reply, and so tried the restaurant. They said that she had gone away for a few days' break, but they didn't know where. He was now extremely concerned for her safety; something was very wrong, but he seemed helpless to do anything about it.

Tom rang Birmingham Airport to find out what time the next available flight was to Menorca, and was told it was 10.30 the next morning. He then rang Manchester Airport, and was told that from there he could get a seat on a flight at 6.10 the next morning, which he booked, thinking *Where's my passport, and is it still valid?* He found it and stuffed it into an overnight bag with a few essential clothes for the journey. It was 2.15 am when Tom drove to Ken's house, where his friend was waiting to drive him to Manchester

Airport.

On the way, Tom explained to him what had happened. Ken wanted to fly with him, but Tom told him to go to work and cover for him. If the wheels came off, Ken was to tell the superintendent that Tom's mother was ill, and that he had gone off to Ireland to be with her.

At the airport, Tom had time for a slice of toast and a cup of tea in the restaurant. A news flash on the television made him drop his cup: 'British woman dies in Menorca hotel balcony fall.'

'The bastard,' he muttered. He knew it was her; McClurg had got to her.

He rang Ken at home, hoping he had got back from the airport. When Ken answered, Tom recounted the news story and told Ken to ring Interpol and have someone meet him at Mahon Airport.

'And you'd better tell the superintendent where I'm going but don't tell him the whole story, keep it brief,' he said. Ken understood.

Tom was extremely restless on the plane over to Menorca. He could not get interested in anything, and concern for Pauline filled his mind. He even tried to convince himself that maybe it wasn't her.

Relieved to get off the plane, Tom was met by a man, who said, 'I'm Detective Constable John Glynn seconded from the Met, pleased to meet you, sir, sorry it couldn't be under better circumstances.'

'Thanks for meeting me, John, and would you please call me Tom,' he said.

'I've been making enquiries since speaking to your DS on the phone, and it very much looks like it is the woman you thought it was,' John said. 'I've made some arrangements and will take you to the Policia office in Ciutadella and introduce you. They're dealing with the incident.' They left the airport to drive across the island to Ciutadella.

'Did the incident take place there?' Tom asked.

'No, it all happened in a tourist area just outside, but it's being dealt with by the Policia at Ciutadella,' John replied. He went on to inform Tom that Ciutadella was the biggest town in the area, and had been the old capital of the island until the eighteenth century when the ruling British turned Mahon into the capital instead. The drive took them about forty minutes.

Ciutadella was a typical old Spanish town with narrow cobbled streets, where most of the houses had wooden shutters and doors, all of which were painted green or brown. The numerous street bars and shops were full of local people and holidaymakers enjoying themselves in the glorious sunshine. Tom thought that, under different circumstances, he would like to visit this town.

The Policia office in the town square was much like any police station in England, with police cars and motorcycles lined up outside. After introductions in the Policia office with John acting as interpreter, Tom learned that the hotel room had been booked in his name, for Pauline and him.

He then related his suspicions to the Policia inspector, who explained that the rooms had been booked by a man using a passport in Tom's name and paid for by cash. The hotel staff had been interviewed but never saw the man again after he had booked the rooms. They did add that he insisted on a top floor room.

The body had not yet been identified, and Tom was taken to the morgue at the local hospital to undertake this grim task. He thought morgues in any country smelled the same. He looked at Pauline's lifeless body lying so peacefully, and tears filled his eyes.

'Yes, that's Pauline McClurg,' he said, then muttered under his breath, 'I'll kill that bastard, I promise you, Pauline.' Turning to John, he said, 'Could I see the hotel where she was killed, please?'

He was taken to the hotel in Cala en Blanes, a quiet little resort ten minutes' drive from Ciutadella. The hotel was four stories high, and Pauline had been pushed from a fourth-floor balcony and had landed on concrete below. The rail on the balcony from which she had fallen was well above waist level: she had definitely been pushed. She had been murdered.

The post-mortem, which Tom did not attend, was carried out that afternoon and the cause of Pauline's death was revealed to be a broken neck and fractured skull. There was slight bruising on the arms where Pauline had put up a good fight.

She had been drinking, but it was established that she had not been drunk. McClurg's plan was likely, therefore, to have been to convince the authorities that she had been drunk and had accidentally fallen from the balcony. By using Tom's name, they had lured Pauline to her death, and the Policia were now convinced that she had been murdered.

248

John took Tom to a cafe in Noco Placa in the centre of town, where he had a coffee and a toasted sandwich, and tried to relax in the sun and take in the whole situation. There was only a vague description of the man responsible and security was stepped up at the airport in an effort to detain him.

CCTV cameras later revealed that the man had left Palma airport on the island of Majorca at 7.35 am on the morning after Pauline's death, bound for Manchester, and again using a passport in the name of Thomas Sharkey.

It was believed that he must have caught the ferry from Menorca to Majorca soon after killing Pauline. *McClurg had won again,* Tom thought.

In the evening, he tried to unwind as he sat listening to an Abba tribute band at a Jimmy Hills bar in the square of Cala'n Forcat. He thought, *Maybe one day I might return for a holiday.* It was a lovely place.

Tom returned to Birmingham, leaving the Spanish Police still putting together a case for murder. An investigation would involve enquiries in Manchester with a view to interviewing McClurg regarding his part in the plot, and efforts to identify the man responsible for events in Menorca. It would be an uphill struggle for the Spanish authorities and the Greater Manchester police.

When he was back in England, Tom rang his old pal Detective Chief Inspector Ron Bannister in Manchester, and put him fully in the picture with everything that had happened in Menorca. Ron assured him that he would make contact with the Spanish police and get matters moving. He promised to keep Tom informed, but he could not see any charges being brought against McClurg. *He'll still have to be sorted,* Tom thought.

Chapter 28

Back at work, Tom went along to see the detective superintendent and told him the complete story, from when he had first met Pauline until her murder in Menorca. 'We'd better keep the bit quiet about you helping to get her the false passport, otherwise you'll be in the shit. You agree?' the super said.

'I do appreciate what you're saying, boss, but I wish I could do more to catch that bastard, McClurg.'

'His time will come, Tom, they don't escape forever. Now I suggest you take a few days' leave and maybe go home to Ireland.'

'Yes, I think I will. Thanks again, boss,' Tom said.

Next day, Tom caught a flight to Belfast and the train on to Londonderry. His mother was delighted to see him. 'This is a wonderful surprise, son, why didn't you let us know you were coming?'

He didn't want to upset his mother, so said, 'Just had a few days' leave and thought I'd surprise you, Ma. Anyway, I didn't want too many people to know of my visit.' Things had settled down at home, and Tom spent three days seeing Tilly and his two brothers.

Tilly's husband, Eddy, told Tom that he had become friendly with a Greek family in the town, with whom he did business. Eddy had discovered that this family were related to Nina and that she had tried on several occasions to contact Tom but without any success.

'Is it at all possible to find out, discreetly, where she lives now?' Tom asked.

'I'll try, Tom, but I have to be careful because there is still a bit of hostility towards you,' Eddy said.

Tom went to the local park to locate the revolver he had hidden there years earlier. If he could find it, he was going to travel back to England by ferry and take it back with him. He decided it would be safer travelling with it in his hand luggage on the boat, rather than attempting to get on a plane with it.

He found the box where he had hidden it, and it was untouched. He removed the parcel, took it home and put it in his travel bag. Passing by the Bogside on his way home, he had to smile when he read the large sign that stated: 'You are now entering free Derry'. Tom reflected on the amount of blood that had been spilled on these streets, where rioting had resulted in many deaths and injuries. And for what? Because nothing had really changed.

His next visit was to his young sister's grave where he placed a large bouquet of flowers. As he stood there, tears in his eyes, he reflected on her short life. *Yes*, he thought, *I'm living life to the full, but there's only one sure thing in life and that is that you are going to die. All the money and respect in the world can't change that fact.* He wrapped his jacket around him and shivered, feeling suddenly tired and alone.

When it was time to travel back to Birmingham he hugged his mother and headed for Larne to catch the ferry, promising to go back soon and have a proper holiday.

Seeing his family had made him realise that he was definitely not over Pauline's death, and felt he would have to do something to avenge it or he would never feel at peace. His journey back on the ferry from Larne to Stranraer was uneventful; he was not searched by anyone. He now had a gun in Birmingham for his protection, and for if he decided to take action against McClurg.

Tom gave the gun to Dave Parkhill to look after for him, and even he was a bit surprised at his actions. Tom went on to tell Dave the whole story of McClurg and what he was responsible for. 'I'm going up to Manchester in a few days' time to have a look at that bastard,' Tom said.

'I'll come up with you,' Dave replied.

A week later, having put a plan together, they both travelled to Manchester. Tom had got the addresses of where McClurg lived and worked. At his home in a high-class area McClurg was nowhere to be seen, so they went to have a look at his so-called place of work.

From the information Tom had gained, they soon found McClurg's work premises. Across the road was a Chinese restaurant, where Tom and Dave found a table by the window. About twenty minutes later, a Jaguar pulled up outside and two men got out. From the descriptions Tom had it was obvious that this was McClurg and one of his henchmen. McClurg was about six feet tall, carrying a lot of weight and had long, straggly grey hair. 'So that's the bastard,' Tom said.

'He doesn't look that tough,' Dave commented. 'What are we going to do about him? Are we going to take him?'

'For now, we do nothing, but at least we know what he looks like and where he hangs out,' Tom replied. They then travelled back to Birmingham.

Several weeks later, and standing in a local bar one lunchtime, Tom was approached by a man he did not recognise. 'Mr Sharkey, can I have a word please?' the man said.

'Who are you? I don't think I know you, we haven't met before,' Tom said.

'I'm Roger Noble. And no, we've never met before but a mutual friend of ours has recommended I talk to you about a little problem I've got,' he replied.

'Who is the mutual friend?' Tom asked.

'I'd rather not mention his name in the circumstances, but he said you would help me out,' the man said. Tom's suspicions were aroused, and alarm bells were ringing in his head.

He decided to play along, and asked, 'What's your problem, Mr Noble, and how could I possibly help you.'

'All I will say at this stage, Mr Sharkey, is that I've been arrested for drink driving, and I can't afford to lose my licence because I drive for a living,' the man said.

'When was this?' Tom asked, his mind racing.

'It's a long story, and I just hope you can help me. I'll give you all the details later,' he replied.

Reluctantly, Tom replied, 'I might be able to help you out.'

'Okay, Mr Sharkey, I'll give you all the details later, and as our friend suggested I'll put a few quid in an envelope for your trouble. I'll contact you later and arrange to meet you. I have your private telephone number,' he said.

When Noble had left, Tom sat down and had a large brandy and Coke. He decided the whole situation did not ring true. *And how did he get my number? I'm ex-directory,* thought Tom. He was convinced that the rubber heel squad had something to do with this and were trying to set him up. He needed a plan of action. And fast.

A few days later, Tom received a call from Noble on his private line. *So you did manage to get the number somehow,* Tom thought. *But that wasn't a clever move. You've just given yourself away.* Noble asked if he could meet Tom in the Crown pub in town at 7.00 pm on Friday night, and said he would have a brown envelope for Tom for his trouble. Tom agreed.

He had to decide now whether to go along with this circus, or to forget Mr Noble completely and simply not turn up. He later contacted Dave Parkhill: he had a plan.

On the Friday night, Tom arrived at the Crown pub at about five minutes past seven. He did not recognise anyone outside or inside the pub at first but then, inside, he saw Noble. Tom didn't acknowledge him but got himself a pint of beer and stood at the end of the bar by the toilet doors.

After a few minutes, he nodded at Noble and indicated towards the toilets. Tom went into the toilets and was followed in immediately by Noble, who was very nervous and handed him the envelope.

'All the details are inside, I have to rush. I'll contact you later,' he said, and left.

Tom waited a few seconds and left the toilet where, as he had expected, he was met by two men.

'Mr Sharkey, I am Superintendent Niven, I would like a word with you in private, please follow me,' one of them said, and walked out to the hallway of the pub.

Both men produced their police warrant cards and the superintendent said, 'I'll take possession of the envelope you have in your pocket, please.' When Tom handed over the envelope, he continued, 'I'm arresting you, Mr Sharkey, on suspicion of corruption,' and formally cautioned him.

'We're going to the Central Police Station, just down the road, if you will come along with us,' he said.

'What's this all about?' Tom asked.

At the station he was placed in an interview room and searched. 'What's this all about, sir,' he asked again.

'I think you're perfectly aware, Mr Sharkey,' said the superintendent, and threw the envelope on the desk between them.

'No, I'm not, sir,' Tom replied.

A little irritated now, the superintendent ripped open the envelope to reveal the contents. The horror on his face said it all when two Aston Villa match programmes dropped out. 'What's this?' he muttered.

'A couple of programmes a friend promised me for one of my nephews back home in Ireland,' Tom said.

'You think you're clever, Sharkey, do you,' the superintendent said, and stormed out of the room. Tom thought, *It looks like it's my word against Noble's at the moment.*

He was left in the interview room for about half an hour. No doubt a serious conference was taking place with the chief superintendent as to what had gone wrong. The superintendent came back in. 'You know what's going on here, Sharkey. You've won this time, but we know what you're up to and we will have you,' he threatened.

Tom was released and wondered if what he'd done was really worth the trouble, just to get one over on the chief superintendent. He decided that yes, it was. Next night, out with the team, Tom explained to them what had happened.

'I'd arranged for a very good friend of mine to be sitting in one of the cubicles in the toilet. He'd been sitting there reading a book from about six o'clock,' Tom explained.

'Do we know him, boss? He must be some friend to sit there all that time,' Ken said.

'You don't know him, and yes, he was marvellous. He's a diamond and he'll be well rewarded,' Tom said.

'I figured the skinflints would use police-issue stationery, so I'd taken the programmes with me in a standard envelope and passed Noble's envelope under the door to my friend. He waited a while, and just walked out of the pub when we'd all left.'

'I would love to have seen the superintendent's face when he opened the envelope,' Danny said.

'It was a picture, but I was lucky this time,' Tom replied.

The time had now come to walk the straight and narrow, no more schemes. It had been a good effort by the chief superintendent, and it was only a matter of time before he tried again. He had just underrated Tom this time.

Tom later contacted Dave Parkhill and told him to keep the money but to be very, very careful because the notes were probably painted with dye.

About a month later, Tom had a phone call from Tilly. She told him that Eddy had found out that Nina was supposed to be living somewhere on the Greek island of Zante. It was not known where exactly, but he had been told that she had given birth to a baby boy. Tom was a father to a son; he was completely overjoyed.

Chapter 29

In the summer of that year a whole new world of experience was to develop for Tom.

He was having dinner at the Belfry Hotel just outside Birmingham with Martin Pickering, a retired police officer who he had served with in his early days.

Martin was now employed as an investigator for an insurance company in London, where he now lived. Anytime Martin was in the Midlands, he would make a social call on Tom for a chat and an update on what was happening in the local area. He would entertain Tom on the company expenses.

On this occasion, he was seeking information about a silver robbery which had taken place in Birmingham, and was hoping Tom could get him an introduction to the officer in charge of the case. Tom gave him the officer's name and told him that he would make the necessary arrangements for them to have a meet. The business now over, they settled down to enjoy a meal and a few drinks.

At the next table sat two businessmen having dinner. It was a quiet moment in the restaurant and there were only the four of them present. After dinner, Tom and Martin were enjoying a bottle of brandy, while the two gentlemen at the other table were drinking a bottle of champagne.

After some time, one of the men on the other table spoke to Tom, and invited them both to join them at their table. Tom was surprised but, never one to pass up on an opportunity to make new contacts, he and his friend took their bottle of brandy and joined their fellow diners. It turned out they were strangers to the area and just wanted a little company. They all ended up drinking champagne and brandy.

Tom could not have known it at the time, but one of these men, Costas Christodoulou, was to have a great influence on his future life.

Costas was on holiday from Greece with his wife and members of his family, who were all staying at the hotel. That afternoon he had been playing golf with a few businessmen from the area. Martin had to leave early but Costas, his friend and Tom decided to make a night of it.

As the night progressed Tom learned that Costas was a Greek millionaire who had booked a section of the restaurant for the following night to entertain all his friends and family.

Costas was about fifty years old, had long black hair streaked with grey, and was quite handsome but slightly overweight. He confessed to Tom that he had overheard some of their conservation and realised that he was a policeman. 'I always like to keep in with the law and keep them on my side,' Costas said.

We might be able to use each other here, Tom thought.

He and Tom had hit it off immediately, and spent most of the remainder of the night discussing various topics – their outlook on life was very similar, it seemed to Tom. On parting company, Costas had invited Tom to the party the next night in the restaurant.

By the end of the party, Costas and Tom had exchanged

telephone numbers and Tom had been invited over for a holiday to Greece, with Costas promising to take care of all the arrangements and necessary expenses. Tom was wary of Costas' generosity, but didn't see any reason, yet, to distrust him, so decided to go with the flow.

About three weeks later. Tom received a call from Costas. He was coming back to England and wanted to meet up with him. He told Tom he had a serious matter he wanted to discuss with him. *Here we go,* thought Tom. *You don't get something for nothing in this life. There's no such thing as a free lunch – or holiday.*

A week later, Tom received an envelope containing an air ticket from Birmingham to Heathrow in his name. A note explained that he would be met at Heathrow and taken to the Grosvenor Hotel where a room had been booked for him.

Tom had to make arrangements fast: the flight was in four days' time. A visit to his detective superintendent soon made the necessary alterations to duties, and he was ready to go to London.

When he reached his room in the Grosvenor Hotel he found a note that read: 'Tom, gone shopping. Have booked dinner for 7.30. See you then. Costas.' Tom got another surprise when Costas arrived at the table for dinner.

The lady accompanying him was not his wife, but a young woman in her late thirties, also Greek with long black hair, beautiful brown eyes and a slim figure squeezed into a long black dress. Costas introduced her as Nicki, a very good friend, but Tom had got the message they were more than friends from the way they acted.

She reminded him very much of Nina.

After dinner Nicki excused herself, saying she was tired after a long day, and went off to her room for an early night.

'I arranged that. I need to talk to you at length on our own about a few matters. Anyway, it would only bore the pants off her … that's if she's wearing any,' Costas said, grinning.

'Who is she, anyway, if you don't mind me asking,' Tom said.

'She is the real woman in my life, Tom. I love her dearly, but things being what they are in Greece, it makes life very difficult,' he replied.

Costas went on to explain the elaborate plan he had made to get her over to England with him. She was a married woman, but had confided in her sister and her sister's husband about her relationship with Costas.

In order to get her to England, Costas had also paid for a holiday for her family confidantes, so they could travel with her. The other two were staying in a different hotel in London, and he had given them a thousand pounds of spending money. As far as Costas' wife was concerned, he was elsewhere on business and not with them.

'How much has this little romantic break cost you?' Tom asked.

'About three or four thousand, but it's worth it, Tom, take my word for it,' he said.

'I believe you,' Tom replied.

'Now, down to the real business, Tom,' Costas said, turning serious.

Costas explained that he owned a treasured old Rolls Royce

which he drove around his land in Greece, but that it had no air conditioning fitted. He could, of course, afford to buy several new cars, but he loved this old one. The last time he had been over in England playing golf, he had met a man who told him that he had connections in Coventry who could arrange for air conditioning to be fitted if he could get the car over to England.

Costas had been delighted, and had had the car transported over to Coventry where it was to be upgraded with air conditioning. The body was to be modernised and resprayed at the same time. When the work had been completed, Costas' son had asked if he could travel over to England and collect the car, and use the visit as an opportunity to take in some of the sights of the country. Costas had agreed.

Arriving in Coventry to collect the car, the son had been surprised to see that it had a sunroof, which it had not had before. The men had explained that as his father had spent so much money on the car, they had decided to throw in a new sunroof at no extra cost. His son had thought nothing of this, and paid the bill. He had then headed off to return to Greece with the car.

When the vehicle was examined by Greek customs in Athens, it was discovered that the engine and chassis numbers did not match the original numbers held on file for the car from when it had left the country. Costas' son had been arrested for attempting to smuggle illegal goods into Greece. Costas explained that his son was now in custody awaiting trial, and could face at least two years' imprisonment. Costas was hoping Tom would assist him in clearing his son's name.

'Have you no contacts in the law in Greece?' Tom asked.

Costas explained that he did have contacts, but had fallen out with a senior customs officer some time ago who was now out to make a point by sending his son down. Tom explained that the car must have been stolen in England, and that he would need all the paperwork relating to the car now in Greece.

He would also need to know the details of the man who arranged for the work to be done. Costas produced all the documents relating to the arrest, and handed them to Tom. He also explained that he had tried to make contact with Tony Adams, the man who had arranged to have the work carried out, but without success.

Tom took the name and telephone number for Adams; he would make a start with him. When Tom was leaving the hotel next day, Costas said, 'Tom, whatever it takes or costs to free my son, do it, and I will look after you for life, you have my word.'

'I'll do what I possibly can, Costas, I promise you,' Tom said.

Back at work, Tom called the team into his office and gave them all the details relating to the car and the man involved. The chassis and engine numbers of the car now in Athens related to a Rolls Royce stolen from Walsall several months earlier. Tony Adams proved to be a car dealer from Birmingham who was running a business in Bearwood.

Tom said to Ken and Danny, 'Go and pull Adams in on suspicion of stealing the car, and put some pressure on him. See what he comes up with. I don't think he'll be involved, but he'll know something.' Adams was most upset at getting pulled in, but he soon broke down when threatened with being charged unless he assisted with the identities of the other people involved.

He gave the name of two brothers, Phil and Greg Wheeler, who ran a small car repair business in a back street of Bordesley Green. Both men had very little form but were being watched closely by the force stolen vehicle squad, who had received intelligence that they were ringing cars.

Tom met with Paul Higgins, the detective inspector from the vehicle squad, and told him that he wanted to pull the brothers in on suspicion of stealing the Rolls Royce.

'Listen, Tom, we're keeping observations on them and are setting up an operation to try and catch them at it. Why don't you wait for us?' Higgins said.

'I like that idea, Paul, but I'm being pushed for time, I need a quick result. What timescale are you talking about?' Tom asked.

'If all goes well we could carry out a raid next week; we have a young grass working next door who owes me one and is very eager to clean his sheet,' Higgins replied.

'Okay, let's play it that way,' Tom said. They parted company, planning to speak within a few days.

Just two days later the phone rang in Tom's office. 'DCI Sharkey, can I help?'

'Tom, I think we might be able to go tomorrow morning. Let's have a meet in the Red Bull at one o'clock,' Higgins said.

They met in the pub and discussed tactics. From information

Higgins' team had gathered, it appeared that the brothers were currently working on a stolen BMW on their premises. A raid was set up for 7.00 am next morning. The vehicle squad would carry out the raid, assisted by Ken and Danny.

Next morning, Tom arrived in his office at nine o'clock to be greeted by Ken who informed him that the raid had been a success. They had found the two brothers working on the stolen BMW, which the vehicle examiners had established had also been stolen from Walsall. A quick search of the premises had found evidence relating to dozens of stolen cars which had passed through their hands.

'What about the roller, anything on that?' Tom asked.

'When I left the team they were searching the bins and sifting through rubbish in the rear yard. They'd been burning stuff,' Ken replied.

Ken and Tom went back to the garage. They were met by Danny, who showed them partly burned documentation relating to the stolen Rolls Royce. Tom breathed a sigh of relief. The officers from the vehicle squad carried out the interviews with the two men, which suited Tom because it moved any suspicion of unfair play away from him and his men.

After several interviews, Greg Wheeler confessed to receiving the stolen cars from a third party, but refused to name him. The operation the brothers had set up was that they took orders for cars from innocent buyers – the make, colour, and model required – and they would pass the details on to the thief who would steal to order.

When the old roller had arrived from Greece it had been stripped down and eventually scrapped. The stolen one was fitted with the old registration plates and any other parts which helped to make it look like the genuine car. The finished stolen car was then taken to another lockup in Coventry, from where it was collected and paid for by Costas' son, before being taken back to Greece.

The Wheeler brothers were eventually charged with several offences, including the one involving the Rolls Royce. The brothers had taken a big chance and had not changed the chassis or engine numbers on the Rolls Royce as they would normally have done because the car was going back to Greece. *What fools,* Tom thought.

He telephoned Costas and filled him in on the progress he had made, and promised to contact him in the very near future when everything was sorted. Costas was delighted.

Following Tom's next update a few weeks later, Costas flew to Birmingham and the two arranged to meet for dinner.

Costas greeted Tom warmly. 'Thank you, my friend,' he said, as he threw his arms around Tom. 'For what you have done I will be forever in your debt, I promise you, Tom.'

'There's still work to be done. Let's sit down and discuss the case in detail,' Tom said. They sat down at the dinner table and as the meal was served they discussed what it would take to convince the authorities in Greece that Costas' son was innocent.

When he had finished eating, Tom produced all the paper evidence from his briefcase and they went through everything together.

'Tom, I've discussed the matter with my legal people and they want you to travel to Athens and meet them. I don't think you'll have to go to court because they seem to think it won't get that far now. But they want to meet you, can you come?' Costas asked.

Tom thought for a moment, and then replied. 'I have no problem with that, but it would be better if we made it all above board. Could your people write to my guv'nor and formally request my attendance?'

'That won't be a problem, if that's what it takes,' Costas said.

'In the meantime, I'll discuss it with my boss and make sure there's no issue,' Tom said.

They then retired to the bar for the evening, where Costas introduced Tom to Demetrius, his travelling companion. 'Demetrius goes everywhere with me. He's what you might call my bodyguard,' Costas explained.

'I've not seen him before. Is this his first time in England?' Tom asked.

'He's been with me every time I've been here, you just didn't see him. He remains in the background, just in case he's required. You see, Tom, I'm a very wealthy man and I do have my enemies. His presence is just for security,' Costas said.

Tom discovered that Demetrius was an ex-boxer, and was considered to be a villainous man in Greece. He would never let Costas out of his sight. He was dedicated to the man, and to protecting him at all costs. Tom realised then that there was a lot more to Costas than first met the eye.

A few days later, back in his office, Tom received a call from

DCI Ron Bannister in Manchester who confirmed what Tom had thought would happen.

'The enquiries are now complete regarding Pauline's death, and guess what? McClurg has walked. They've charged one of his henchmen with her murder, but he refuses to implicate McClurg,' Ron said.

'I suppose McClurg has looked after him and his family financially.'

'You know he has, the crafty bastard,' Ron replied.

The detective superintendent sent for Tom to come to his office. 'Tom, everything has been arranged officially. You'll travel to Greece on Tuesday week. The papers requesting your attendance and the money to cover your expenses have been received at the chief's office, and they've given permission for you to travel,' he said.

'That's great, boss, thanks for your help,' Tom said.

The superintendent gave Tom the plane tickets and money to cover his out-of-pocket expenses. Then, he said, 'A nice bottle of Greek brandy would go down well on your way back, Tom,' and gave a wink.

It was only when he got back in his office that Tom discovered the tickets were to travel from Birmingham to Rhodes, and not to Athens as he had expected.

Chapter 30

Tom telephoned Costas at his home and asked him what the change of plan was for.

'Tom, my friend, you're coming to meet me on my yacht in Rhodes. You'll meet my solicitor there, where all the business will be carried out,' he said.

As promised, Tom was met at Rhodes airport and taken to the Belvador Hotel where a room had been booked for him for one night only. He made the most of his stay in the delightful surroundings. He would be picked up by Costas the next day, and taken to his yacht in the harbour.

Tom could not get his breath when he saw the immense size and splendour of the yacht. It even had a speedboat on deck and was manned by a full crew, including a chef and a waiter. He was introduced to Costas' company solicitor, who sat down with him and went through all the paperwork. When the business had been completed, they all sat down to a magnificent feast.

With the meal finished, Costas and Tom moved up onto the deck. 'Tom, my solicitor is very happy with all the documentation you have produced, and is confident he can clear my son's name. As I've said before, I'm forever in your debt,' Costas said.

'I'm very happy I was able to help, my friend.' Tom beamed.

'I want to reward you for your hard work. Please give me details of your bank account,' Costa asked.

'There's no need, Costas, you've looked after me very well and I am having a great time here in Rhodes,' Tom said.

But Costas insisted, and so Tom gave him the details of his bank account in Ireland.

Tom then had a nosy wander round the spacious yacht, and was completely amazed by it all. He found it difficult to take in the sheer opulence before him. He found his cabin, which was as glamorous as the hotel room he had just left. *To think how we used to live in Fawney. I wonder how much this cost,* he thought.

The pair of them sat drinking into the night, and Costas told him of his hard upbringing in Athens and the devious methods he had often used to achieve the wealth and stature he now held. His background in his young life had been very similar to Tom's, and although Tom had now made a lot of money along the way, his personal wealth was far short of that enjoyed by Costas.

Costas owned hotels and property all over Rhodes, Cyprus, several other Greek islands and in mainland Greece. He employed hundreds of people, and asked Tom if he would consider giving up the police and coming to work for him. Tom thanked him for this very generous offer, and said that he would give it serious thought.

Feeling quite tipsy, Tom went on to tell Costas of his brief relationship with Nina back in Derry, and about her family sending her back to Greece.

'Would you really like to know what became of her? If you would like, I could make enquiries for you,' Costas said.

'I believe she is living on Zante and had a baby son, but I wouldn't like to cause her any trouble or embarrassment,' Tom said.

Costas assured him he would be very discreet, and wanted to know as much information about Nina as Tom could provide.

During the course of his stay with Costas, Tom also told him the story of McClurg and the deaths of Jimmy Walker and Pauline. Costas was surprised that Tom had done nothing about McClurg, but understood when Tom explained to him how being a police officer made it impossible to act independently. Costas wanted to learn all about McClurg, where he lived and what he did. Tom told him everything he knew.

After three days of partying, Tom was taken back to the airport. On the flight home he reflected on the lifestyle Costas led and wondered about the amount of wealth he might actually possess. Even his most wild speculations appeared to be confirmed when he discovered that Costas had deposited fifty thousand pounds in his bank account.

With the security of his now healthy bank balance offering a tempting alternative to the pressure of keeping ahead of the rubber heel squad, Tom was seriously considering leaving the police force. The stakes were very high now, and he thought back to his timely escape from the garage in Derry.

He loved his job in the police but thought there might be a new adventure for him out there somewhere, possibly involving Costas. Tom rang Dave Parkhill and arranged to meet him for a pint, in order to discuss his present situation with him. 'What's this all about, Tom?' asked Dave.

'With my income from the job and my other dealings, I've got quite a bit of money stashed away. And now a Greek friend of mine has promised to try and trace Nina for me. With all this going on and trying to avoid getting caught, I'm seriously thinking of leaving the police,' Tom said.

'What would you do, you love your job?' Dave asked.

'I do love my job, but maybe it's time for a change. I've been lucky up to now. What do you think?' Tom asked.

'It's a big decision, Tom, but it's down to you and I'm sure you'll do what's right,' said Dave.

'Let's have a few more pints and forget it for now,' Tom said, and they settled down for the evening.

***

A few weeks later, as he was getting ready to go to work one morning, Tom received a phone call from the duty inspector. Danny had suffered a heart attack and had been taken to the Heartlands Hospital. Tom immediately jumped into his car and headed for the hospital. He was met at the ward entrance by Danny's wife, Jane, and Ken.

Jane was crying. 'Oh, sir, he's dead, he's dead.'

'Oh shit, no. I'm very, very sorry, Jane. What happened?' he asked.

Between sobs Jane told him that Danny had woken up in the night with chest pains and had thought it was indigestion. He had gone downstairs to take some medicine to relieve the pain.

She had heard him moving around in the kitchen and, when he

hadn't come back to bed, she had gone down to see what was happening and had found him collapsed on the floor. She had immediately called an ambulance, and was convinced that he had died on the way to hospital.

Tom excused himself and went to the toilets where he sat and cried in one of the cubicles. Danny had been one of his best friends and he was really going to miss him, both as a great friend and as a colleague. He knew he could never replace him; they had too much trust and so many secrets between them.

Danny's funeral procession was led by two police motorcyclists, and his body was carried in a horse-drawn carriage. There were so many people at the service that many of them never got into the little church. The music was 'My Way', by Frank Sinatra. Tom thought, *Yes, you really did, pal.*

After Danny's death, Tom and Ken felt quite lost. Ken started talking about retiring from the force as he had completed enough years to go on a full pension. Tom decided that if Ken did retire, he would consider resigning and moving on. He thought often of the offer Costas had made to him and he was considering it very seriously.

He could also see the way the police force was going and he didn't like it; the government had introduced many new laws that seemed, to Tom, to offer a ridiculous amount of protection to the villains.

The new laws ranged from the now obligatory tape recording of all interviews under caution, to offering the crooks the right of silence; all to protect their human rights and never mind the rights of the innocent victims. Another stupid thing was also happening: all informants had to be handled by a special team. Anybody with any sense knew that most informants would only talk to people they knew and trusted; Tom could see a lot of their information not being forthcoming in the future. Most good informants were suspicious and would not accept the new system.

In the meantime, Costas called Tom and told him he would be travelling to Birmingham on business and would like to meet up. Tom was looking forward to discussing his offer of work in more detail.

Next day on returning to his office he found a scribbled note on his desk from Ken, which said: 'A man rang looking for you, could you please ring the following number. Didn't leave a name.' Realising it was a Manchester number, Tom wondered if it had anything to do with McClurg. He was about to ring the number when his phone rang.

'Tom, my friend, did you get my message? I'm on my way to Birmingham.

I'll contact you again when I get there,' Costas said. He continued, 'I've found Nina, she is living on the island of Zakynthos, better known to you as Zante. She lives with her son, just like you thought. I'll tell you the whole story when we meet.' Tom realised that Costas had telephoned him from Manchester, and wondered what he was doing there.

They met up in Birmingham. 'The son has a strange name,

Tom,' Costas said. 'He is called "Tas". It's not a Greek name I have ever heard before.' Tom had to smile to himself: she had called the boy after him.

Costas also told him that Nina was working as a receptionist in a holiday hotel, and Tas was the manager of a good restaurant and bar. It appeared he had worked hard and studied well at school, and was now doing well for himself. Costas gave Tom the details of the restaurant in the holiday resort of Argassi on Zante island, and told him that he would make the necessary arrangements if he wanted to make the trip over.

Tom thanked him for finding them but said he would have to book some leave and inform his gaffer before taking off, and would contact him later. This information could change his future. He had spent so much of his life thinking about Nina, but a part of him was scared: if he went to see her, would she reject him? After all, it had been many years since they had last seen each other.

Before parting company with Costas, Tom asked, 'Did you fly to Manchester this time?' He was curious.

'Yes, I had a little business to complete there,' Costas said, but added nothing more. Tom wondered.

Tom had a lot on his mind now, and felt like he was on autopilot. He just couldn't think straight, but knew he still had to try and concentrate on his work. There had been a significant rise in the number of house burglaries in high-class properties in their area. The figures showed that they were being committed during daytime hours when the residents were out at work. Residents were getting very concerned about leaving their houses unoccupied, and were putting pressure on the police to do something.

As a result, the areas concerned were being patrolled by the CID and local uniform officers as often as possible. Tom called an office conference to discuss the situation, but no useful information came to light.

A few days later, a uniform beat officer came to Tom saying that he might have a lead. 'What have you got?' Tom asked.

'Well, it may be nothing, sir, but there is a very large travellers camp on my patch. I've noticed a lot of activity on the site during the day, a lot of comings and goings by the younger members. Just this afternoon I saw electrical items being moved about,' he said.

'What type of items are we talking about?' Tom enquired.

'Televisions and kitchen goods. And something else, sir. Some of them are driving around in brand new Ford Escort XR3is.' Tom thanked him for his information and asked him to continue monitoring the situation, saying he would look into it further.

It transpired that the travellers' camp was located on a disused factory site, and there were thirty caravans parked there. Further enquiries by Tom's team revealed that the group had recently purchased five new cars from Bristol Street motors: for cash.

Tom, the detective superintendent and the sub-divisional superintendent had a meeting to discuss how they would handle the situation, and it was decided to make an early morning raid on the site in a few days' time.

The plan was that they would arrest all the men on the site on suspicion of burglary. Each person detained would be given a number, with which he would be photographed and fingerprinted. Because individual travellers were sometimes known to use a variety of names, this method would be used to establish their true identities.

Once the photographs and fingerprints had been taken, the details were to be ferried immediately by motorcycle to the Midland Criminal Record Office for identification.

On the morning of the raid, the superintendent briefed the CID officers, sixty uniform officers, which included local officers and members of the special patrol group, and two dog handlers. The raid went off without any great problems, apart from the womenfolk shouting abuse. A lot of stolen property was recovered and logged, to be identified later by the victims.

The fingerprint identification process revealed a number of positive results. The majority of the prisoners were found to have previous convictions, and many were wanted for offences by other force areas around the country. Most of the recovered property was identified by the various householders as having been stolen in the recent burglaries and, after lengthy interviews, a total of eight of the prisoners were charged with burglary.

Tom reflected on a very successful operation, and believed that it could be his last.

A week later he caught a flight from Birmingham to Zante, where Costas had made arrangements for someone to pick him up from the airport and take him to a hotel in the town of Argassi.

The driver informed him that the restaurant he was looking for was only a few minutes' walk from the hotel. Tom booked into the hotel, had a shower and then, in a mingled state of excitement and trepidation made his way to the restaurant where Tas worked, which he found was only about two hundred yards away. *How very considerate of Costas,* he thought.

As Tom walked to the restaurant he was concerned about how he might appear to Tas. Had Nina ever told him who his father was? Had she explained to him what had happened in Derry? He stopped short of the restaurant and tried to get his mind focused. He felt edgy and frightened about what lay ahead. He decided he had to find out the truth, and entered the restaurant.

Inside, the premises were clean and inviting, but he couldn't see anyone who might resemble the manager. He was shown to a table by a waiter and he ordered a meal. The food and the service were excellent. After eating, he ordered a brandy and sat a little more relaxed. *Got to make a move,* he thought.

'Who is the manager, and is he about, please?' he asked the waiter.

'I hope everything was to your satisfaction. Sir, if you—'

Tom interrupted him. 'No, everything was great, thank you, I just wish to speak to him.'

The waiter looked relieved. 'He will be back later, in about fifteen minutes' time,' he said.

A short time later Tom got the shock of his life when a slim young man about six feet tall came into the restaurant and disappeared behind the bar. It was just like looking at a younger version of himself. It was quite uncanny, and he chased down the lump in his throat with a large gulp of brandy. Tom didn't really know what to do, whether to run out or to speak to him. He wondered how Tas would react if he approached him. After all, he didn't know Tom from Adam.

He suddenly realised that he had not really thought this whole situation through at all. But curiosity got the better of him, and he went to sit at the bar.

'What can I get you, sir?' Tas asked. When Tom replied he could see the young man's eyes begin to fill up. He knew. 'You must be Thomas?' he asked.

'Yes, I am. And you must be Tas?' Tom said, as he held out his hand, not knowing how it would be received.

Tas took it, and shook it firmly. 'Yes, I'm known as Tas.'

Tom knew, but asked anyway. 'Why Tas?'

'Short for Thomas Anthony Sharkey,' he said. 'After my father.'

Tears filled Tom's eyes, as they embraced across the bar.

When Tom managed to pull himself together, he asked, 'How's your mother?'

'She always said you would come here one day, and she was right,' Tas replied. 'My mother explained to me what happened in Ireland, and how she was sent back home to Greece. She did write to you many times, but couldn't understand why you didn't reply.'

'I never received any of her letters,' Tom explained.

'But I have some very bad news; my mother is in hospital. She was knocked down by a bike a few days ago and is lying in hospital unconscious,' Tas said.

'Oh god, no. When did this happen?' Tom asked, his heart thumping in his chest. He thought, *Surely this is not happening; I can't lose her again.*

Tas went on to explain that his mother had been knocked down by two tourists driving a hired quad bike. The local police were investigating what had happened. 'Just how bad is she? Could I go and see her, please? I would really love to see her, I've always thought of her and what had happened to her,' Tom spluttered.

'I'll take you to see her. She's in Zante General Hospital, about twenty minutes away,' he said.

Tas explained to the waiter what was happening, and then they set off. Tom's heart was pounding. How was this happening again?

At the hospital Tom was ushered into a tiny room where Nina was lying in bed surrounded by beeping equipment and glowing monitors. She looked just as though she was fast asleep. Tom sat down at the side of the bed and gently took her hand.

She was a little older – *Aren't we all,* he thought – but as beautiful as ever. He knew he still loved her. She had received severe damage to her head in the accident and her right arm was in plaster where it had obviously been broken.

Tom and Tas spoke to the doctor who informed them that a scan and tests had shown no extreme injuries to the brain. 'How long could she remain in a coma?' Tom asked.

'It's hard to tell,' said the doctor. 'Some patients remain in a coma for a few days while others can be comatose for years, but the length of time does not affect the success of recovery. Some patients return to normal very quickly with their lives unaltered. Others suffer severe physical or psychological difficulties and never recover,' he explained. 'Nina is a very sick woman, and only time will tell if or when she will recover.' Tom was extremely upset. He felt so helpless just watching her lying there and being unable to do anything about it.

Tas had to return to the restaurant and Tom told him that he intended to stop with Nina, if that was okay. Tas was happy to know that his mother would not be alone. Tom continued to hold her hand and talk to her about their days together back in Derry. He stayed by her bed during the night, and continued talking softly to her.

Next morning, Nina's brother arrived at the hospital and Tom felt quite awkward being in his company. The last time they had met was one night in a dark alley in Derry, but Tom realised that this was neither the time nor place to mention it. In all fairness to her brother, he put his hand out, and said, 'I'm very sorry for what happened back then, Tom, it was a stupid thing to do. I'm glad you're here for Nina.' They shook hands, and the past was laid to rest. The real worry now was Nina.

Two days later there was no change in Nina's condition, and all the doctor could say was to be patient and wait and see.

It was about 10.00 am on the fourth morning, almost dozing off by her bedside, that Tom thought he felt her hand move. Or was he just dreaming? He continued to rub her hand and talk, and this time he was positive she had moved. He immediately called the doctor, who calmed his excitement, and gently explained that such movements were not uncommon in unconscious patients, and that he should not get carried away.

On the fifth day, Nina stirred and opened her eyes a little and looked at him with a flicker of recognition. After some time, she said, 'Thomas, is that you?'

'Yes, it is,' he replied, and bent over and kissed her on the forehead. She was confused, and having a real problem trying to figure out just where she was.

Eventually, she said, 'Where am I, how did you get here?' with tears running down her cheeks. Tas had joined them now and was overjoyed to see his mother awake. After talking to her for a while, Tas discreetly left them alone together, mumbling something about having work to do.

Tom learned that Nina had never got married; there had never been anyone else in her life, only her son. Or, as she pointed out, their son.

Tom knew that he had never stopped loving her. Their lives were about to begin again together at last. Well, that's what he hoped for. There was a lot to do to make up for all the time they had lost. Over the hours that followed, Nina drifted in and out of sleep, in between trying to understand what had happened to her.

'How did you get here, and what have you been doing? Tell me how you found me?' she said.

'It's a very long story, but basically I met a Greek man called Costas in Birmingham, where I work now, and he tracked you down for me,' Tom explained.

'Now I know why a man has been asking questions about me around town. He must have been trying to trace me and I never realised,' she said.

Tom went on to explain how Costas had offered him a job in Greece if he was interested, but that he was waiting to see how things turned out between them before making any decisions. 'There's no rush,' he said. 'We have time now and the important thing is to get you better first.' Nina, Tas and Tom spent the next week together at the hospital, when visiting hours allowed. When Nina was eventually discharged, she and Tom went to her little house in Argassi where they spent another few days together getting to know each other again.

The years rolled away as they realised that the spark that had brought them together in the first place was still there. Soon, they both realised that they each had a great deal to offer the other.

Tom didn't want to waste any more time and, although he knew it was a risk, he took the bull by the horns and asked Nina to marry him, a proposal she accepted immediately with tears in her eyes. She explained that it was all she had ever wanted. Tom now accepted that he was ready to talk to Costas and discuss his future life in Greece. He knew this was a life-changing scenario, but it was what he wanted.

Decision made, Tom telephoned Costas and told him that he would like to take him up on his offer, but that he would need to sort out several things first back in Birmingham. Costas said that he was travelling to England to play golf in a few days, and suggested they meet up to discuss everything then.

Tas and Nina gave Tom a lift to the airport, with the happy understanding that he would be returning again when all the necessary arrangements had been made. Tom hated parting company with her, but knew he would be returning soon, this time to stay.

Chapter 31

A few days later, Tom met up with Costas at the Belfry Hotel where he was staying and where it had all begun between them. Dave Parkhill had gone along with Tom, who introduced him to Costas and Demetrius. After the introductions, Dave and Demetrius went off to the bar and left Costas and Tom to discuss their business.

Costas offered Tom the position of overlooking several aspects of security at his Hotels in mainland Greece, Cyprus and Rhodes. He told Tom that if he accepted the job he would be based in Zante, and could live in a villa that he owned on the outskirts of the capital.

Tom accepted his generous offer, and explained that he intended to resign from the police, but would have to give twenty-eight days' notice. Costas took Tom at his word, and agreed to make all the necessary arrangements. When Tom told him of his plans to get married, Costas was overjoyed and asked if he could take care of all the wedding arrangements. Tom thanked him for the kind offer, and said he was sure Nina would be delighted, but that he would let Costas know once they had talked about it.

Tom also had a meeting with Ken, and discussed his impending life changes with him. Ken agreed that he should grab this great opportunity with both hands, and went on to say that he, too, had decided to retire from the force.

For Tom, knowing he was in such a secure financial position and could leave whenever he wished was liberating and very reassuring. He wrote out his resignation report and took it along to his superintendent who was most surprised that he had decided to leave.

'You're losing a great deal of your pension, Tom, by going early,' the super explained.

'I realise that, sir, but I've thought it over and my mind's made up,' he replied.

'What are you going to do with yourself?' the super asked.

'For now, I'm going to take a very long holiday in Greece,' he replied. Tom had no intention of telling him the whole story at that stage. He knew he would lose a bit of his pension, but he was quite a wealthy man now with all the money he had accumulated over the years. He also had the flat to sell, which had gone up quite a lot in value since he bought it.

He knew he was in a strong position to survive, even without Costas' offer but there was no way he was going to refuse it. The fact that he could if he wanted to gave him the confidence to make the change that he felt ready for in his life. He was truly independent now.

Tom and Ken had a joint leaving party, where all the staff and their friends were invited to a good booze up and all the food they could eat at one of the local clubs. Tom did admit to having mixed feelings; he enjoyed the police but recognised he would never have an opportunity like this again. Let alone one that would also give him the chance to fulfil his dream of a life with Nina and their son. He had to take it.

He booked a flight to Belfast so he could see his mother and explain everything to her: about his decisions to leave the police, and to go and live in Greece, but most of all about Nina and her new grandson. She was delighted to hear about Nina and Tas, but was sad about Tom moving so far away.

He explained to her that she could come and stay with him for as long as she liked, and that he would arrange and pay for everything. This pleased her greatly; she very much wanted to meet Nina and her grandson.

Tom returned to Zante a few weeks later, having said goodbye to all his friends and colleagues. He had plans to make with Nina.

With Nina's blessing, Costas had organised the wedding ceremony, the reception and the travel arrangements for all the family and guests. Tom had given him all the details of the people he wanted invited. Nina was a little concerned about her family, but Costas assured her that all would be well, he would take care of everything.

Costas sprang another surprise when he informed them that he had bought the restaurant Tas worked in as a wedding gift for the family. Tas could continue managing it. The three of them didn't know what to say, but after overcoming the shock eventually thanked him. Tas and Nina were dumbfounded.

Two days before the wedding, Tom's mother, his brother Paul, sister Tilly and her husband Eddy all arrived in Zante where they were met by Tom and Nina in a joyful reunion. His brother Peter was unable to attend, as his wife was due to give birth at any moment. Their mother was quite old and frail now, but was very excited at meeting Nina and Tas and made a great fuss of them. She loved what she saw of the island but had trouble getting used to the heat: it was her first visit abroad.

Tom reflected on how good Tilly looked; she reminded him of the lovely actress Maureen O'Hara. Next day Ken, his wife and Dave Parkhill arrived from England. Tom's Uncle Harry and Aunt Bet unfortunately couldn't make the wedding, but sent a present and their blessings.

The day of the wedding came, and Nina's brother arrived with his family. Her other brother was still living in Ireland and sent his apologies as he couldn't make it. Many of Nina's other relatives, friends and neighbours also made the journey to Zante to celebrate the couple's delightful day. Costas' yacht was moored off Zante Town, and he and Demetrius were making all the final arrangements for Tom and Nina's special day.

The service was quiet and beautiful. Tas gave Nina away and Dave Parkhill was the best man. Tom, a very happy man, glowed with pride as he kissed his bride. After the ceremony everyone retired to Tas and Nina's restaurant where the reception was being held. The food and drinks were plentiful, and the music was played by a Greek quartet. It was a typical Greek wedding, plates were smashed and everyone pinned money on the happy couple. Then Dave, accompanied by the quartet, managed to sing 'Danny Boy' with Tom and his mother attempting to join in.

Tom sat for a quiet moment on his own and thought about the deaths of his father, his baby sister Kathleen, Danny Black, Pauline McClurg, Jimmy Walker and Jiti, and wished that they all could have still been alive. How lucky he was to have survived everything that had happened over the years. He remembered the now tattered photograph of Nina in his wallet and resolved to show it to her, but having found her he realised he didn't need it any more.

He then reflected on his past, his schemes, the police, and his women. *Was it all worth it? Would I do it all again? Of course I would.* He smiled.

Next morning, having returned to the restaurant to sort the mess out from the previous night, Tom, Costas, Dave and Demetrius all sat round a table having a chat over a cup of coffee.

Eddy had gone off to the local supermarket looking for an English newspaper to get the sports results. He returned some time later and dropped a copy of *The Sun* newspaper on the table in front of them all, asking if they wanted a read.

The front headline stood out in bold, black letters: 'Manchester Gang Leader Assassinated.' The body of Harry McClurg had been found at his home early that morning. Everyone just sat very quietly; no one spoke. Eddy looked round the table at the blank faces, and said, 'What?' Still no one spoke.

Printed in Great Britain
by Amazon

36085699R00165